DATE DUE

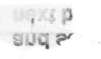

ALSO BY
WILLIAM SHATNER

TEKLAB

TEKLORDS

TEKWAR

TEK VENGEANCE

TEK SECRET

TEK POWER

TEK MONEY

TEK KILL

TEK NET

MAN O'WAR

THE LAW OF WAR

WILLIAM SHATNER

AN ACE/PUTNAM BOOK
PUBLISHED BY
G. P. PUTNAM'S SONS
A MEMBER OF PENGUIN PUTNAM INC.
NEW YORK

An Ace/Putnam Book
Published by G. P. Putnam's Sons
Publishers Since 1838
a member of
Penguin Putnam Inc.
200 Madison Avenue
New York, NY 10016

Library of Congress Cataloging-in-Publication Data

Shatner, William.
The law of war / by William Shatner.
p.   cm.
"An Ace/Putnam book."
ISBN 0-399-14360-2 (alk. paper)
I. Title.
PS3569.H347L38   1998   97-39451 CIP
813'.54 — dc21

Printed in the United States of America

1   3   5   7   9   10   8   6   4   2

This book is printed on acid-free paper. ∞

Book design by Julie Duquet

I dedicated a previous book to a wondrous creature who came into my life. I said then that she pounded and pummeled her way into my heart—and now, at my age, to have found romance and lust, love and enlightenment, is astounding. What I have learned about her—and, as important, about myself—has drifted into my books. Giving and sacrifice have merged with my being; to listen to my soul, to hear the whisper of adoration, has led me to untrammeled paths. I dedicate this book and myself to my bride:

Nerine.

To Carmen LaVia, who talks money and has ideas.

To Susan Allison, who talks ideas and has money.

To Chris Henderson, the fountainhead, who has many ideas and no money . . . which we're valiantly trying to change.

PROLOGUE

THE DARKENED CORRIDOR was not unusual. Shipwide operations had been scaled back to a minimum to conserve—as general order #832B had strained to make clear—"absolutely everything possible." The two massive battlewagons orbiting Mars were both being manned by skeleton crews for a simple reason—the fewer marines aboard, the fewer burning lights needed, fewer oxygen pumps in service, toilet flushes, requests for heat, et cetera.

" 'Absolutely everything possible,' " quoted one of the figures moving through the hall. He whispered the words softly, amused by the hint of silver they formed in the freezing air. "Never really thought I'd come to see any personal advantage in living this way."

The woman moving beside the man did not answer aloud. She flashed a wry grin, however, not wanting him to think she did not see the humor in his remark. Dark and dry as his comment had been, she understood. But she also understood that if anyone discovered the treacherous mission they had taken upon themselves, they would both be dead. Without trials. Without a doubt.

The pair were only two of the thousands of marines sent against the Martian colony almost a year earlier by the Earth League. Their mission had seemed uncomplicated then—Ambassador Benton Hawkes had gone rogue, betraying the confederation of corpor/nationals and nation states that had invested in him the power to negotiate with the colony. The simple, practically minor, differences between the labor and management of Red Planet, Inc., had been blown out of proportion by the scheming diplomat, turned into an ugly civil war which could not be allowed to disrupt the vital commerce between Mars and Earth. Hawkes had to be stopped, not merely out of a need for justice, but for the good of mankind.

At least, that was what the troops had been told. The truth—as is so often the case—turned out to be somewhat different.

Hawkes had radioed the battlewagons, arranging for meetings between their captains and Red Planet representatives, offering to surrender without incident if the captains could not be swayed to break off their attack. All those selected to hear him knew with whom they were dealing.

This was no ordinary grating political appointee—this was Benton Hawkes, the highly decorated military hero who had entered the foreign service at age twenty-two, the negotiator who had scored more diplomatic coups by the time he reached thirty than most statesmen imagined accomplishing in a lifetime. Sent from one violent field post to another, he had crafted carefully deliberated judgments between warring factions time and time again, carving out a name for himself as a trustworthy man of high morals.

Hawkes's reputation was spotless. And yet, the commanders and crews of the U.S.S. *Roosevelt* and *Die Berlin* had been asked to believe that this time—*this time*—he had turned on all that was honorable and decent. This time it was he who was the villain and not to be trusted. Despite all the billions of lives he had touched for the better, this time he was acting in a self-interest he had somehow never before shown, and thus deserved no quarter and no mercy.

The League's lies had not worked. Those not overwhelmed by Hawkes's reputation alone were won over by his words. He had pleaded the Martian case so clearly and flawlessly that the grand majority of the marine contingent could not bring themselves to be the instrument of even his incarceration, let alone his death. And since not following their orders meant their own court-martials and executions if they were to return home, the same grand majority decided to abandon the Earth League, pledging their allegiance to the new nation of Mars. Those not comfortable with following that decision had been allowed to return home, their numbers amounting to little more than a handful. The only problem was, not everyone with objections to the mutiny actually left Mars.

"Movement."

The man heeded his partner's sotto voce warning. The two split apart from each other, cramming themselves into accessways along the corridor walls. Pressed up against the near-frozen metal, they felt the cold pouring through them, etching into their spines, chilling every contact point. Frigid as it was inside their suits, however, both marines found themselves sweating.

Don't stare, thought the woman. Shutting her eyes, pulling in on herself, she forced her conscious mind away from the corridor. Don't anticipate. Don't care. Forget they're coming—*forget*.

Both marines redirected their attention, fighting to ignore the approaching footsteps. Each knew how easily a bored sentry could feel the heat of hostile eyes. Both had stood their share of watches, had felt the unexplainable fire of desperate fear boring into their backs as someone watched them go by—someone who was not supposed to be where they were. Finally a figure turned the corner, arc lights mounted on their security plate, rapid-response needlers on both wrists—their gait slow, manner casual.

Not looking for us, the man realized, turning his eyes from the sentry. Working to ignore the figure moving through the darkness, the marine turned his attention toward the cold instead. Clamping his teeth tight together, he willed himself elsewhere, picturing mountaintops in his head, fields of snow, forest cabins filled with women waiting to warm him. Memories flooded his brain, each taking center stage for its individual split second—sled riding, snowball fights, making snowmen . . .

The sentry moved by, noticing nothing. On the sides of the corridor, both marines risked moving just enough to break contact with the bitter walls. By the time the heavily armed guard had continued on another dozen yards, the pair had quietly disappeared out of the range of the sentry's gauges.

"We snagged luck that time, Leah," whispered the man.

"Why we picked a cold out-route, Darren," the woman answered. "Might take longer, but you know as well as I do how many dog-barks turn off their sensors to keep more power for their heaters."

"Comfort." Darren grinned. "It'll ruin the service yet."

Leah stopped moving, punching up the ship's schematics on her gauntlet screen once more. Tabbing her helmet's magnifier lens into place, she focused on the tiny clear square, checking their best route. Her partner directed his attention to their surroundings. Not every camera was listed in the blueprints to which they had access. Nor every motion sensor, nor those searching for body heat, or noise, brain waves, displaced weight . . .

Gotta keep lookin', thought Darren. Keep our eyes open and our wits about us, and we maybe might live through this.

Leah tapped her partner's shoulder, then motioned in standard directional sign language, outlining the rest of their journey. A smile broke Darren's lips. He had not realized they were so close to the lifeboat. Noting his grin, Leah raised one eyebrow and moved her head, signaling she shared his relief. Neither spoke, though. Having gotten so close to their goal, the two marines understood it was no time to suddenly get careless.

The pair moved ahead with the same caution they had utilized throughout their journey. At first they had hoped to simply send a message using ship's communications. That idea had been thwarted by a massive solar flare-up which had silenced everything throughout the system from radio waves to beacon channels. When the storm showed no signs of abating, a new plan had been needed. After no little deliberation they had settled on the Rumrunner.

Lifeboat 96, dubbed "the Rumrunner" by those who knew of its special features, was not connected to the bridge's monitors. Jury-rigged years earlier by a pair of old sergeants not above a touch of larceny, it had been used for everything from illegal parties to working the off-world black markets. Invisible to ship's sensors as well as being berthed below the operations bridge's line of sight, it could be released and returned to the ship unseen by command. Stealing the Rumrunner was not a foolproof scheme, however. More than a few things could go wrong.

"We could just do nothing," Darren had reminded Leah when they first discussed their plan. The woman had considered her partner's words seriously. What they proposed doing was not only risky but practically suicidal. Playing dumb, she realized—going along with the status quo—meant safety and a greatly improved chance of growing old. But as that thought crossed her mind, she remembered her career-soldier father's words. When she graduated from the academy, proud as he was, he had given her only one piece of advice.

"Always be brave, always march straight into battle, because, little girl," he had joked darkly, "there's nothing uglier than an old soldier."

Thus emboldened, she had refused the path of self-interest, choosing an all too clear duty instead. Weeks earlier, she and Darren had discovered a cache of documents while editing ship's files. Only a trace fragment of a much larger transmission deleted earlier, it was enough to spell out that some of the officers on their ship were still working with the Earth League.

The fragment's details implied many things—that the League was gathering information on Martian defenses, that they still planned to use force to regain Mars, and that their captain had proposed general order #832B to get as many as possible of the marines who were not loyal to him off the ship. Thus Darren and Leah knew they could trust no one except each other—and that if they were going to do anything, they would have to do it alone.

It had taken the two marines a good while to decide how to proceed. They quickly discovered they could not gain access to ship-to-planet communications. Neither could they reach Mars in person. The next personnel rotation was not scheduled for seven months, and if they had extrapolated from the fragment correctly, they did not have that much time to wait. Finally they had decided on the Rumrunner. If they could just get to it . . .

Yeah, *if,* thought Leah. Too damn many ifs. *If* we can get to the 96, *if* we can get to Hawkes, *if* he believes us . . .

Suddenly cold fear gripped the woman—a terrible dread that she and Darren could not make it, that they had not planned carefully enough, that their luck had run out. She had no facts, no evidence, just a horrible feeling stabbing through her that they had failed somehow and the end was rushing toward them. Leah fought the boiling panic, pushing it out of her head with exact marine precision.

Another dozen meters, she told herself, and it's all over. Just keep moving. One foot after the other. One after the other.

The pair moved down the last corridor leading to the lifeboat. The escape vessels were full runabouts in their own right, capable of carrying hundreds of people or tons of supplies. Each of the battlewagon's one hundred and twenty lifeboats needed its own launch facility. Turning the corner that brought the pair in sight of Bay 96, both marines let go a sighing breath of relief.

"We made it," whispered Darren, barely believing his own words. "I really didn't think we had a chance."

"Neither did I," answered Leah. Forcing her escalating heart rate downward, she confided, "In the last couple of minutes, I got the overwhelming feeling we'd made some kind of mistake. I hate to say it, but I almost panicked out on you."

If Darren had an answer for his partner, he was not given the time to make it.

"Drop your weapons. Do not resist. Drop your weapons."

Ignoring the voice booming through the overhead speaker, Darren launched himself at the access panel that would open Bay 96. Instantly Leah grabbed her sidearm, cocking it while moving to cover her partner. The man had already indexed the first two of the door's three access codes before the vacuum entrances around them began to open.

"Keep on it!" shouted Leah, bringing her weapon to bear on the farthest door. Grimly she computed their chances in her head—lines of approach, exit time needed, open fire paths, available cover . . .

We're not making it, she realized. Her survival instincts flooded her consciousness with thoughts of lifesaving surrender. As the vacuum doors continued to slide upward, she growled, "No ugly soldiers in our family, Daddy." And then it started.

Squinting, she released a short burst against the far door, then wheeled around in the opposite direction. Behind her Darren had entered the third access code. As the bay hatch began to slide upward, he had just enough time to cock his weapon before the firefight began in earnest.

Hands appeared in each doorway, firing unaimed weapons, filling the access dock with ricocheting needles. The two marines tried their best to resist the onslaught, but they had no chance. Without cover, without extra ammunition, they were easy targets for those firing upon them from the safety of their positions behind the heavy bulkhead walls. Both went down easily, neither able to even empty their weapon before they were knocked down by enemy fire.

Leah, hit in both the chest and head, died instantly. Darren hung on, however, having only had his legs blown out from under him. Feeling his life bleed out over the plate flooring, the marine eyed the approaching figures, noting that the captain was with them. A part of his brain longed for some kind of explosives, remembering scores of vid entertainments where the hero sacrificed himself at the end by making sure his foe died with him. But real life did not work that way. He and Leah were soldiers in an actual military, the kind that kept weapons secure and accounted for. It had taken everything they had to acquire the pair of sidearms which had proved inefficient and too little in the end.

"So, Mr. Schulty," said the captain. Using his foot to flip over Leah's body, he added, "And Mr. Rohmsberg. I didn't go against the general feeling of rebellion when all of you raced to betray our home planet, because I know how to bide my time. It really is a trait every good soldier needs."

"Should I get 'im boxed for the meds, sir?" asked a lieutenant. The captain's eyes narrowed, anger overshadowed by impatience filling the space remaining. Raising his weapon, the captain aimed it at Darren's head and then tabbed the trigger, sending a burst of needles stabbing through the marine's face. The man's skull imploded as the needles' electric charge shattered everything around them.

"The dead don't need doctors, Mr. Bradley," explained the captain. Heading for the exit, the warship's chief officer ordered, "Now clean this mess up before anyone else unsympathetic to our views decides he wants to be a hero."

The officers dropped to their task immediately. In less than an hour all traces of Leah Rohmsberg and Darren Schulty, both physical and those electrically recorded, would be purged from the ship. The captain and his coconspirators could rest easy. All their loose ends had finally been taken care of—there would be no more mistakes. In less than six months, the colony would learn its lesson, its leaders would be imprisoned, its people put back to work once more for the comfort of Earth.

And Benton Hawkes . . . He would be executed, of course. And then Mars' little flirtation with freedom would definitely be over.

STANDING BEFORE THE mirror in his Manhattan hotel room, Benton Hawkes stared at his reflection. All the bits and pieces he had grown accustomed to over the decades—the strong, solidly chiseled face, the etched lines, the thick-boned shoulders, the hair just beginning to gray—were still in place. The one thing he did not recognize, however, was the smile.

"Now," he asked his reflection with mock curiosity, "where could *that* possibly have come from?" The prime minister of Mars spent only a moment searching his slate-blue eyes for an answer, then turned his attention to his attire. The official floater assigned to him for that evening's function would arrive soon.

"Have to look our best," he muttered with a sarcastic tone. Picking a piece of lint off his tuxedo sleeve, he returned his eyes to the mirror, or more specifically, to the smile reflected within it. "I'd still like to know where I could have picked you up, though."

Hawkes had a right to wonder. Nearly a year earlier, his life had gone to hell. A man who detested outer space, he had been forced to abandon his beloved mountain home for life in the cramped and lifeless tunnels of Mars. A hater of war, he had lived through several skirmishes that had nearly turned into full-fledged revolutions. Then, after war had been narrowly avoided, he had spent the last ten months of his life traveling back and forth between Mars and Earth, working out the details of what he hoped would be a lasting peace for both planets. In short, the last year of his life had left him with little to smile about.

"Well," he told his reflection, "that's about to end. A few more weeks and the treaty will be finished, and that will be that." The prime minister reached for a water glass resting on the sink, when suddenly the hotel adviser's voice center was triggered.

"Pardon our interruption, Ambassador, but your transport will arrive in the front traffic circle in no more than ten minutes."

Hawkes swallowed the last of his water, then set down his glass and headed for the door. Turning at the last second, however, he stared at the mirror from across the room, checking to see if he was still smiling. Only days from retiring, from putting the solar system's cares behind him, he could not remember the last time he felt so good. If he had known how soon his smile was going to disappear—and for how long—he might have committed it more firmly to his memory.

● ● ● SITTING FORWARD IN his chair, Senate majority leader Michael Carri thought to himself, This is your fault, Hawkes. All of it. Rising, the large-framed man moved around to the front of his desk, half his mind racing over the points of the speech he was about to give, the rest focused angrily on the Martian prime minister.

All you had to do was go up there and shut up a few loudmouths. But no, you couldn't do that. That didn't sit well with your personal little code of honor. No, you had to lead a goddamned revolution and turn everything upside down. Well, pat yourself on the back while you can, you self-righteous bastard. You're going to pay for that, Bennie boy. And I'm going to start adding up your bill right now.

"Gentlemen, ladies, ambassadors, fellow League members . . . we all know why we're here. We have . . . a problem. And its name is Benton Hawkes."

Carri let his eyes skim the room as he said the prime minister's name. Carefully he watched as many sets of eyes as possible, working to gauge his audience's reactions as he continued. "Single-handed, the man destroyed the Earth's relationship with her first far-planet colony. Sixty years ago the Earth League was formed. Corporations and nations working together for the good of the planet. As our first great undertaking we built the Skyhook elevator. Once it was in place, establishing a lunar colony was child's play. Then, with the immediate neighborhood firmly under our control, we set our sights higher."

Carri paused for a breath. He did not need one—he was too experienced an orator for that—but he did need a moment to size up how much agreement he could count upon. From the looks on the faces before him, Michael Carri knew he had nothing to worry about. When he was finished, he had no doubt that those he had gathered would give him everything he wanted.

"Forty years ago the first colony ships set sail for Mars. Hundreds of trillions were spent turning that hellish wasteland into a place where people could live. We broke the World Bank to extend our grasp farther than any have ever dared dream possible. We made Mars into a midpoint for bending the entire solar system to our wishes. Already fledgling bases have been established on the moons of the outer giants. The limitless resources of the Asteroid Belt, of Jupiter and Saturn, not to mention Mars itself, are ours—*ours* to do with as we please. We paid for them a hundred times over. And this bastard Hawkes thinks it's his place to deny the League and her peoples the bounty of their toil."

Dark muttering wound its way to Carri's ears from every corner of the room. Someone less sure of himself might fear the grumbling was aimed at the fanciful exaggerations he had made as to the extent of mankind's control of the solar system, but the majority leader knew it was all directed at Hawkes. Although the League-built lunar and Martian facilities were substantial, nothing beyond them amounted to much more than the occasional grim survival dome. Still, the distortions served to make Hawkes's betrayal of the Earth League appear all the greater and so the majority leader heaped them on, only his iron control keeping his lips from curling into the smile he so deeply wished to wear.

Later, he told himself smugly. Soon. Right now you have an audience to win. Talk to them.

He did.

"Our good ambassador did his work well. His old commander, Val Hensen, helped him and the other rebels buy a majority interest of Red Planet, Inc., the governing corporate entity through which Mars is ruled. Let's not mince words over this. Some of you people panicked. No one wanted to get stuck with a bad investment, so when the revolution started you dumped your shares. Just what Hawkes wanted. Now, legally, the Martians own their contracts. Legally, we no longer have a say in how things are run up there."

As Carri anticipated, a score of voices spoke out, half accusing others in the room, those others defending their actions. With practiced ease he let the two sides tear at each other for a moment, then raised his hands and called for peace, forcing the room to turn to him for calm leadership. Demanding an end to the recriminations, he declared that the League had to stick together—now more than ever. Then, having regained everyone's attention, he explained why.

"We sent two battle cruisers up there. Instead of restoring order and giving us our colony back, their mutinous crews signed on as the damn Martian navy."

"All of them?" asked the ambassador from Deutscher Chocolate, the vast corpor/national that owned New Zealand.

"No. Those who didn't were sent back to Earth with a shipment of raw materials. Still, the vast majority of them went over. But that's not what you're referring to, is it?" When the questioner agreed, Carri explained to the others, "Mr. McCay has come to tell us that Mars doesn't have quite as loyal a navy as they think. Why don't you explain, Dan?"

The corpor/national ambassador explained that one of the two warships sent to Mars was a Deutscher Chocolate fleet ship. Its captain had no desire to surrender to Mars. But due to the overwhelming numbers of his crew that had done so, he had decided it best to appear to go along with the mutineers.

"He has several loyal officers who will help him take control of his ship at the right time. They have been able to get several messages to us, but this has been difficult to orchestrate, of course, what with the terrible communications blackout." Several assembly members chuckled when the ambassador made reference to the solar storm. A glance from Carri silenced them, though, allowing the Deutscher Chocolate ambassador to continue.

"Their orders are to maintain their pose until they can either eliminate their sister ship and rejoin the fleet, or at the worst, destroy their vessel. One way or the other, Benton Hawkes does not have nearly the power to confront us he thinks he has."

Polite applause rose around the chamber. Knowing it was then safe to do so, Carri finally released the smile he had been holding back. Also, knowing better than to step into silence, he started talking again while McCay retook his seat, before the clapping sub-sided completely.

"Now, Mars might not have a navy, but it does have a govern-ment. Sam Waters, who was once our general manager up there, is now Mars' president. And our good friend Benton is her prime min-ister. To this new government he has donated his ranch in Wyoming's Absaroka mountain range, to serve as the Martian em-bassy. This he feels will protect it. So far it has."

"Are you saying that could stop?" The question was put forth by the delegate from France, a tall man with a bristly gray crew cut. There was dark anger in his voice, a grating harshness that put off even a veteran plotter like Carri. Not letting his distaste for the Frenchman show, the majority leader answered him politely.

"Ten months ago Hawkes and his Martians, feeling they held all the cards, proposed a treaty—a pact of mutual cooperation."

"And you're saying they don't?" the Brazilian ambassador snapped angrily. "Mars grows three quarters of our food. They cut off shipments, we starve. Billions die. Billions! And that means food riots, plague, cannibalism!" The Brazilian paused to catch his breath, forcing himself to take a deep lungful before his voice cracked. Focusing his gaze on Carri, he added, "You say they *feel* they're holding all the cards? They have the power to topple the foundations of civilization as we know it!"

Others began shouting, each screaming louder than the next in their attempt to be heard. Normally sober, temperate individuals, the assembled League members felt the dread of an unknown future crushing in on them, and they reacted with panic. Standing in front of his desk, Michael Carri was actually somewhat shocked.

The people in the room with him were the primary representatives of the planet's major concerns. Not a one of them could be described as weak. Weak individuals did not survive in the Earth League. The thought was laughable, if for no other reason than the fact that politicians like Carri had destroyed their gentler counterparts so far back in the past no one could now remember their names.

The League had replaced the United Nations six decades earlier. Earth had changed since the UN was formed—so radically that the old alliance could no longer serve its members in any reasonable form. Many countries had already been purchased—acre by acre— by large multinational companies, turned into corporations instead of nations, housing employees rather than citizens. The strongest of them formed the League under the guise of facilitating world trade between the new corpor/nationals. Once the League was established, the guise was quickly dropped.

Over the following decades, the new organization tightened its stranglehold, bit by bit forcing the rest of the world to play by its rules—through whatever means necessary. They started scores of wars, authorized the use of chemical, biological, and nuclear weapons, condoned the rape of nonmember nations, and shared in the profits from the enslavement of entire countries. They were not weak individuals, nor was there anything of pity or compassion in their complaints about how Mars had been handled.

Knowing what was motivating those before him, the majority leader bellowed, "Listen to yourselves. *Just listen!* You're so filled with fear that you might lose your grip on your piece of the pie, you can't see that there is no pie anymore." As the assembly quieted, Carri locked eyes with the Brazilian ambassador. If he was going to intimidate the crowd, he knew, best to start with the most vocal of them. Letting his anger flow from his eyes alone, the master politician shifted his voice to its command level.

"You think Mars is holding all the cards in this game, Julius, you think this treaty puts us out in the cold, then you haven't been paying attention." As soon as he got the chuckle from the gathering he expected, the Senate majority leader of the United States added, "But since I'm your friend, allow me to explain why I don't think we have anything much to worry about."

Carri did not have to talk for long before most everyone assembled was agreeing with him.

BENTON HAWKES STARED at the ornately framed vidscreen before him, somewhat desperate to formulate any kind of opinion about its image. His eyes tried with little success to focus on it or even find some central point to it. Splashing indigo and chartreuse were shattered by random crimson bursting through vibrating apricot and chrome lines that blurred into bronze wheels spinning inward from the edges, then folding back outward toward the frame to begin the process again. The woman next to the Martian prime minster had asked his opinion of the piece, leaving him at a loss to answer with anything more insightful than, "Very colorful, isn't it?"

"Oh," responded the matron, "now I see why they say you're such a good diplomat."

Hawkes shrugged good-naturedly, wishing the woman would leave. Not leave the gathering necessarily, just leave him alone. She was, in the parlance of the ambassadorial corps, a galasucker, one of the legion of moneyed do-nothings whose lives revolved around being seen with the right personalities at the proper functions.

You don't have the slightest idea why people are here, do you? he thought, smiling to accept her compliment as well as to mask his anger. To you, this is just another reason to drag your jewels out of storage and parade before the cameras. Two worlds go to war. Hundreds die—hundreds who gave their lives to keep the toll from climbing into the millions. And you wouldn't have heard a thing about it, unless of course *Savoir-Faire* ran a spread on Martian Chic, or maybe Rebel Fashions for Spring.

"So, tell me, Mr. Ambassador," asked the woman, arranging her face in her closest approximation of a serious expression. "How is this treaty of yours progressing?"

Hawkes turned his head slightly, just enough to spot the cluster
of people the woman was trying to impress. He had attended
enough similar functions throughout his career to understand what
was happening when an empty-headed fool abruptly tried to appear
intelligent. Either the cameras had turned in their direction or
someone of a higher social order was closing in. This time it was
both, Arthur Cowan, the city's leading art critic—headed in their
direction with two photographers following in his wake.

"The treaty . . ." he mused aloud absently, as if actually having
to think about his answer. "Oh, I suppose it's pretty much wrapped
up now. But then, after ten months, one would certainly hope so."

The woman began asking another question, but Hawkes cut her
off gently. Feigning surprise at Cowan's arrival, he kept his place
politely for the requisite number of pictures, then deftly manipulated the woman and the critic into a conversation with each other
while excusing himself.

For once, Hawkes was finding no satisfaction in playing the
game. He was tired—too tired. Since the revolution he had not had
more than a dozen good nights' sleep. Traveling back and forth from
Mars to Earth, sitting through never-ending rounds of meetings and
conferences, getting this side to agree to that compromise, then
selling it all to the other side, constantly revising and fine-tuning
the treaty everyone said they wanted but no one within the Earth
League seemed actually interested in completing was taking its
toll.

I need a vacation, he thought, moving to another of the exhibits.
Hell, I need eight vacations.

Hawkes smiled wryly at his joke. At times during the negotiations the only thing that had kept him going was dreaming about his
coming retirement. In an era when people had started living rou-

tinely to a hundred and fifty and even beyond, to shut himself away from the world at the age of fifty-seven might appear slothful to some, but he did not care. Hawkes had endured enough of the world before he set foot on Mars the first time.

At that time he had only hated Mars and all it represented to him. Now, he hated everything—Mars, the League, politics, people in general. All of it had left him feeling tired, used up, finished.

I've got property and money, he told himself. Enough to keep me comfortable even if I make it to two hundred. And, he added as he looked about the room, getting out of this business and away from people like these will most likely greatly improve my chances of that.

Continuing on into the next cubicle, the prime minister pretended to study the painting on the first wall he encountered, while actually planning the first weeks of his retirement in his head. Of course, he was realist enough to know that people like Mick Carri would not make it easy for him—that because of his defense of Mars he dare not turn his back on the League. What he did not know was how many Martians were rooting for the League instead of him.

● ● ● THE FIGURES MOVING through the crumbling Deep Below tunnels maintained strict silence—as always. It was not illegal for them to be there. They were not fugitives. No one was hunting for them. But it was the way things had been done before the revolution started. And since, as far as the current membership of the Resolute was concerned, the revolution was not only not over but just beginning, it was the way things would continue to be done.

The old corridor was in bad shape—roof cracked, walls unstable, floor pitted, thick with dust, some stretches ankle-high. It was the initial Deep Dig the Originals had carved four decades earlier. They were the first to come to Mars, the ex-soldiers, the landless farmers, the disenfranchised and the ruined who had been told Mars was their second chance. They were the Gran'olds—the iron eaters who poured their blood into Mars' rusty brown soil, forsaking lives of their own for the future of their children.

My life in chains that my children's souls might never know shackles—the slogan that attracted the first great migrant waves to the epic colonial adventure. Yes—the propaganda had promised—you will sign over a decade of your life to Red Planet, Inc., but by so doing, you will ensure that you and your children share in a new world. That you all will be free. As free as none since Adam and Eve. Ten years of hell to create your own heaven.

When reality finally settled in, the only part of the speeches that proved to be true was the section describing the chains. After their first decade on Mars—existing not as people but as corporate property—those still alive were actually not very surprised they had been lied to once more.

"Sorry we're late." The speaker was a tall redheaded woman, no older than nineteen. Flashing those gathered within the hidden room an edged smile, she added, "We got tied up at the boat races."

Everyone chuckled. *A lake in ten years.* Just another promise made to the Gran'olds that had been broken. The Originals were not the only ones cheated, though. The next generation grew to find not the freedom promised, but bills waiting owed by their parents— sometimes their grandparents.

"All right," announced the redhead as she made her way to the rough cavern's focal point. "Enough chatter. Let's get to work." Victoria Cobber, current leader of the Martian underground resistance known as the Resolute, dropped her humorous air as she asked, "First—do we have outside contact yet?"

"Sorry, Victoria, nothing's getting through. Word from the comm hub is solar storms are still pumping too much radiation in our direction. Nobody can cast or receive anything."

"No one? Ganymede? Callistro? The Beltbases? Bigrock? Mumbly?" Every location named received another shake of the head. Sitting on one of the makeshift benches put together decades earlier by the first Resolute members, Cobber narrowed her eyes suspiciously. "Does anyone else here find their apprehension meter going off?"

"Oh, vat this." The outburst came from a slightly older man who had arrived with Cobber. Wearing a friendly smile, he said, "I'm as knee-jerk about the League as the next guy, but not everything that goes wrong for us is a management conspiracy, Vick."

"No, not everything, Roger," the girl answered her companion softly. "But this storm—doesn't it seem to have arrived at a very convenient time? Just when we need to stay in contact with our off-world people the most?"

"Victoria," interrupted a woman in her forties, "whether it is or isn't, there's no way we can tell. Mars doesn't have an observatory. We can't check it out for ourselves. All we can do is gather what information we can from incoming ships, and so far the word from Earth is that it's a solar storm."

"Yes," agreed the girl. "And a very convenient one. But you're right—enough. Roger, you have the best contacts off-planet. Work them on this. Okay?" After her friend agreed, Cobber steered the meeting to the group's regular agenda. Membership was reviewed, working conditions were discussed, the relationship between those in the Big Above and those still cloistered in the Below was gone over—everything analyzed for changes. As the meeting went on, Victoria Cobber did not like what she heard. And everything she heard that she did not like concerned Benton Hawkes.

Unlike many on Mars, Cobber was not impressed with Hawkes. Working with words and documents instead of fighting, she slotted him as just another bureaucrat. Short as her life had been, she knew enough of her world's history to understand what dealing with company men got one. The girl did not deny that he had kept the League's forces from sweeping through the colony. Many Martians would have resisted, of course. And they would have died. The rest would have been chained and worked from then on at gunpoint. Hawkes had prevented both those unattractive outcomes. But as soon as Mars had fought its way to an advantage, he had prevented that from being used as well.

Resolute membership was dropping off. As Hawkes and the other new leaders of Free Mars continued negotiating and debating with the League, people had begun drifting back to their lives. When one of those assembled reported that people were in favor of Hawkes and President Waters's proposal to add new ways citizens could pay off their corporate debts, Cobber suddenly exploded.

"In favor of it? That's putting it pretty vatting mildly. They're dancing in the goddamned tunnels is what they're doing! Pay those bills with community service. Work in the gardens, help the child care crews, assist in the schools. The empty-heads—young and old—they're eating it up with both hands. Doesn't anyone see what they're doing? Can't anyone see past their own self-interest anymore?"

Standing, for once the young leader of the Resolute broke her personal rule against giving in to her emotions. "We're not talking ancient history here. We're not the first rebels on Mars. People tried before. They tried! And they were murdered for their efforts. And what followed? *What?!*"

"Work reductions," answered Roger. "Corporate understanding, Days of Healing. For a while." Cobber smiled, grateful to her boyfriend for cutting her off, for giving her a moment to compose herself. Once more in control, she agreed.

"Yes, *for a while*. Then the taxes were reimposed, the overtime hours were mandated again, and everything slid back to where it was. The Gran'olds were promised a share in Mars. It was supposed to be theirs by now. Ours! But every time they turned around rents went up, food prices went up. Their shares paid no dividends because there weren't any profits. Then the League raised the price of fuel so the transports wouldn't make any money. And when that wasn't enough, the taxes came down—education taxes, energy taxes, the oxygen tax—*the oxygen tax!*"

Enraged at the memories she had evoked, Cobber suddenly sucked down a deep breath and screamed: "Doesn't anyone get it? *Anyone?* This is how they rule—this is how they win. So Hawkes and Waters are making nice to the poor downtrodden Belowsters. So bloody what? We've seen it before! We've seen all they can do before and we know where it leads!"

Damnit! The thought echoed through Cobber's head, demanding she rein in her emotions. Her hands balling into fists, she told herself, I won't cry. They can't make me cry. Not ever again.

Everyone in the room waited in silence for the young redhead to speak. As much as they all believed in their cause, she was their matrix. As one of them had once said, "We're all in the same pot, but it's Victoria what keeps us boiling." After an eternity of seconds, Cobber's fists relaxed back into fingers.

"Okay," she said simply. "Quoting my mother, if you can't say anything nice about someone, better figure out how to get rid of them."

The crowd chuckled, more out of relief at the return of their leader's sense of control than her humor. She wanted to lecture them, to try and get through to them, to make certain each and every one of them knew just how dangerous their enemies were. But she also knew they had to stick to their schedule. People had jobs they had to get to, places they had to be if they did not want to be noticed, even though Resolute membership was no longer thought of as a crime.

Yeah, sure, thought Cobber. Hawkes and his dogs cleared the Resolute by decree. No one is a criminal. Fuck you, old man. We'll still keep the membership roster our little secret if you don't mind.

"Anyway, enough. We're here today to take the vote. Is there any other business we need to air before we move on?" A thin young man raised his hand, seemingly afraid to speak until Cobber recognized him. "Jason—you have a report?"

"Yes, Victoria. I got word through a barge crew that docked this morning. The art show, the one with my pieces, the one I told you about in particular . . . It's opening today. It's going to be a very big thing on Earth, a real gala . . . lots of Leaguers taking their first look at Martian art. Including Hawkes."

"Fine," she told the artist with a nod, keeping private what she alone knew his comment meant. "Let's hope they come to appreciate us as noble beings with souls capable of creating beauty. Then maybe they'll stop murdering us and charging the cost of the bullets to our children."

A part of Cobber wanted to tell everyone else what the artist had struggled for months to create specifically with Hawkes in mind. Another part of her made the same suggestion it had from the beginning—Keep the information to yourself. Changing the subject, she said "We'll all come to watch them pin a blue ribbon on you. Right now, however, we need to take our vote." All eyes shifted forward to stare at the young redhead. Her voice thin and cold, she said, "Word is Hawkes and the others are nearly finished drafting their panacea of a treaty. With the communications blackout still on, we can't afford to be caught by surprise. Hawkes's League buddies could show up at any time to announce how good everything's going to be now that they've gotten all their grand ideas down on paper."

"Yeah," called out a voice from the back. "Won't dat be swell?"

"Doubtful," answered Cobber. "So let's do it. You've all discussed this with your cells. We need to know where the Resolute stands. The best chance we're going to have is the moment the enemy makes their public announcement. They'll be expecting folk to queue up for goodies, not start tearing the place apart. So . . . which is it going to be? Do we play the cards we have, or do we fold?"

The young leader of the Resolute let her eyes skip from face to face, from person to person, demanding they vote as she wanted. Most of them did.

"Play," said Roger, immediately supporting his lover.

"Play," said the woman in her forties. As did the man behind her who had come representing the Resolute members of the Vat 18 crew, as did the delegate from the dome gardeners, the one from the reclamation level, the landing crews, and scores more. One by one, the Resolute membership cast their votes. By the end, Victoria Cobber had the answer she wanted. Out of two hundred and sixty-eight votes, two hundred and sixty-three were for revolution.

As soon as the vote had been taken, people began to move back out into the corridor. Leaving as they had come, in groups of twos and threes, the Resolute leaders dispersed out into the tunnels, making their way back up to the Big Above. As always, they left in the order they arrived. Time was precious on Mars—and no one understood the old maxim better than the Resolute membership.

"Last to arrive, last to leave," whispered Roger jokingly to Cobber. As he and his lover passed beyond the mesh, the man added, "If we're not careful we're going to develop a reputation."

"Ummmmmmmmmm, yeah?" purred Cobber. "As what?"

"Wouldn't you like to know?"

As the pair brought up the rear, moving out into the cold darkness of the old Deep Dig, the Resolute leader whispered seriously, "Yes, really, I would like to know. What is our reputation? How do the others see us?"

"How they see *us,* I don't know. But I know how they see you. You're the hope of Mars. The one who keeps things together. The one who's going to fix whatever mess that bastard Hawkes gets us into."

"That's how everyone sees me?" Cobber asked quietly, her voice teasing her boyfriend.

His voice just as low, he answered, "It's how I see you."

Cobber smiled. Everything was going as she had planned. She knew things would be hard for the Resolute in the months ahead. Just as she knew that many of them would die. The thought did not bother her, though. People had been dying on Mars since the first day they arrived. At least, the Resolute leader told herself, this time, when we die, it's going to mean something.

Then, suddenly, as the pair reached the last doorway between themselves and the Above, Cobber turned to face her lover. Gripping his arm with a frightening urgency, she whispered, "God, how I want Hawkes dead!"

"Don't worry, sweetheart," answered Roger. Taking the young woman in his arms, he whispered, "The moment our dear prime minister comes back to Mars—he's mine."

Cobber looked into the man's eyes, needing to see his sincerity—desperate to know for certain that he meant what he had said. She only needed the briefest contact to be sure. One glance told her she had nothing to worry about. If she could be certain of anything, the burning hatred in her lover's eyes assured her that her Roger wanted Benton Hawkes dead any way possible.

What she could never have guessed, however, was why.

HAWKES SHOVED ASIDE his daydream for the moment, taking a few seconds to move on to the screen within the next cubicle. The gallery had used moving walls to divide its floor space into a hundred such little spaces for this showing of electronic paintings. Displays were mounted on the outer walls of the three-sided rooms, with the more lavish pieces displayed on the inside of each U-shaped cubicle.

As he took the new vid-painting in—a constantly changing day-to-night study of a Martian landscape—Hawkes found it ironic that the whole time he had been on Mars he had learned nothing of that world's art. He realized that if he had thought about it at all, most likely he would have assumed it to run along the same lines as that found on Earth. Perhaps it might have followed this discipline or that, but essentially the prime minister would have expected it to be the same. He would have been wrong.

While electronic art had fallen by the wayside on Earth, it was the main form of expression in her colonies, because flat screens took up so little space. All they needed were chip generators and a few feet of wiring, things plentiful off-planet. Marble, charcoal, and ink were all rare on Mars. Oil-based paints had to be imported— Mars had no fossil fuels lurking beneath her crust from which they might be made. Even acrylic paints were based on hydrocarbons— something denied most Martian consumers.

Of course, thought the prime minister, watching the sun rise over the foreign landscape once more, to have noticed what kind of art they produce up there, I'd probably have to give a damn about the miserable rock in the first place.

It was not the first time in the last year Hawkes's contrary emotions concerning Mars were made obvious to him. For reasons of his own, the prime minister hated all of outer space, but the red planet in particular. When first ordered there, he had fought the assignment in every way he could. When he finally accepted his orders, it was only because he thought by doing so he could bring ruination to the world he detested so intensely.

But things had not followed along as his emotions had desired. He could have easily framed things the way the League had wished, setting Mars up to exist forever under Earth's domination. He had wanted to—even after he had learned the truth, his lifelong hatred had almost pushed him to do the League's bidding. But in the end, he had not. He had met too many good people there, too many good and honest souls who did not deserve the fate of existing at the end of Earth's tether. And so, he had turned on the League and led the Martians to freedom, hating himself all the while for doing so.

Thinking of it again only angered him, though. Pushing the recent past from his mind with practiced ease, Hawkes returned to simply staring at the landscape before him, thinking of the art he had seen around the world. Where people lived surrounded by great stands of rock, sculpture arose. Of course, there was plenty of stone to be found in the Martian colony. But until the revolution, no one had had the time to dedicate half a year to a personal endeavor—especially one as frivolous as creating art.

"Well," he said quietly, trying to temper his hatred with indifference, "maybe that'll change now."

"What's that?"

Hawkes turned toward the voice, surprised that anyone had heard him. His defensive reaction turned to relief when he realized who it was that had interrupted his musing.

"Val!" he exclaimed, delighted to find his old commanding officer behind him. "What in God dragged you away from the pleasures of life? I haven't seen you wear anything formal since the last time we were both in uniform."

"I own more than one set of dress studs, thank you," the older man said with a smile. "And I could lie and make some polite buzz about being a patron of the arts—blah blah blah—but lying is something I leave to you all in the diplomatic corps. Here," he added, extending one of the two tumblers he was carrying. "Have a drink."

Hawkes twisted his mouth into a crooked line to show his old friend that his joke had hit its mark. Accepting the offering and raising it to his lips, he smiled as he recognized its contents. Amaretto, Kahlúa, Jack Daniel's, and milk, it was a creation Hawkes and Hensen had perfected with several friends on a camping trip decades earlier.

"You're still drinking Happy Times?" asked the prime minister. Hensen took a sip from his own glass.

"Course," he answered. "Specially when I run into some old faker without enough sense to make one of his own." The two men tapped their tumblers together and drank, then both released a sigh of satisfaction.

"To be honest," Hensen said, "I'm not here by accident. I knew you'd be here and, well, screen communication gets a bit impersonal as far as I'm concerned. Besides, I wanted to thank you for cutting me in on Red Planet, Inc. Maybe I was doing a good deed helping you out, but it paid off for me too. Making someone a gazillionaire deserves a handshake, I'd say."

Hensen stuck out his palm. Hawkes took the older man's hand without a word, merely nodding. Hensen had risked not only his fortune but his life as well when he had helped the prime minister during the revolution by buying up all the available Red Planet stock for Mars. The prime minister knew that doing so had not made Hensen rich—he had been rich enough beforehand. But he had risked all for his old friend, and together they had thwarted the desires of the entire League.

Feeling a question forming in Hawkes's mind, the older man asked, "So, to paraphrase another prime minister, you feeling as if this was the day you weren't meant to see?"

"If you're asking me if I'm still worried about assassins, I'll admit I've been keeping my guard up. I don't think anyone would move before the treaty is signed, though. They'll want their piece of paper in place before they do any tidying up."

"Unless they plan to make it look like the work of the Resolute."

"And what makes you think the Resolute wouldn't still want to do it all on their own?"

"Touché," answered Hensen. Lowering his voice, he asked, "Stocking up on paranoia early this year, or have you heard something?"

"No, haven't heard anything, but let's just say I'll be keeping one eye on the exits all the same." Taking another sip from his drink, Hawkes asked, "I assume you haven't heard anything?"

"No, no," the older man answered, shaking his head. "It's just that you've spent a long time trying to put these bastards in their place. I guess if nothing else, I just wanted you to know I'm still in your corner."

"Thanks, Val." Wanting to blurt a score of responses, knowing he would embarrass both himself and Hensen with any of them, Hawkes merely nodded, adding, "Glad somebody is."

"More people than you know, probably. But enough of this maudlin talk. Tell me something about all this art. Any new Picassos or the like in this batch?"

"Honestly, I wouldn't know. Tonight's the first I'm seeing most of this, myself."

Hensen gave his old friend a stern look. "Now, Ben, why doesn't that surprise me? Let me guess . . ."

The old soldier took a sip from his drink. Then, unconsciously slipping into a slight drawl, he said, "You've let these negotiations run you ragged. You've never been between two more diametrically opposed sides and the stakes have never been this high. You're looking at yourself as the only thing standing between peace and interplanetary war, and the whole thing is making you sick and nervous. Am I close?"

"Val, I'm tired. I'll tell you the truth, this all can't be over too soon for me."

The two men moved away from the painting they were viewing. With the conversation growing serious, neither wanted to risk anyone eavesdropping on them—accidentally or otherwise. Moving about the room, the pair spoke in close whispers, one eye on where they were going, the other on the milling crowd.

"I've been doing this for over thirty years," Hawkes said as they moved off. "I know how to keep my emotions in check, do my duty, not get involved. And I did it here. The League appointed me the provisional governor of Mars. It was my duty to keep the peace, and I did it."

"That you did, my boy," answered Hensen, stifling a laugh. "If they wanted someone who was going to roll over on the Martians, they sure as hell shouldn't have sent you. But still, I think you're starting to let this game get the best of you."

"Maybe," admitted Hawkes. "But it won't be for much longer. The treaty will be fait accompli in a few weeks. And after that, old friend, it's over."

"What's over?"

"Me, my career, whatever. I'm retiring. I'm sure there's someone up there who can play prime minister in my stead. And they're going to have to, because I'm going back to my ranch, and the world—both worlds, for that matter—can get along without me. Civilization did all right on its own for quite a long time. It'll manage again."

"I'm sure it will, Ben. Maybe as well, maybe not. We'll leave those kinds of evaluations up to the history books. But are you sure that's what you want to do?"

"Oh, yes. There's no place for me in the League after what I've done. They don't want me and I don't want any part of them."

"There's always Mars. I'm sure they could use you up there."

"There's a lot of things they could use up there," answered Hawkes tersely.

When he let the comment hang, Hensen took another sip from his glass. The older man purposely dragged the action out to emphasize the silence, then said, "Don't let the past eat your soul, Ben."

Hawkes started to respond, but his old commander cut him off with a wave of his hand. "I don't want a debate. You either hear what I'm saying or you don't. Just think about it for a while. Or even better, stop thinking about it for a while. Okay?"

The two men made a bit of idle chatter after that, then went their separate ways, agreeing to meet again before the dinner to come. Not wanting to get pulled into conversation with anyone else at the moment, Hawkes turned his back on the crowd and took in the closest available screen. The one he found was a traveling tale. Most of the art on display was not static. Each vid was more like a short film; some even came with dialogue, narration, and sound tracks. Most did not, however. The majority of the electronic artists considered such things gimmicks, shortcuts that detracted rather than enhanced. Having turned to the piece he was viewing just as its tale began, Hawkes decided to view it in its entirety.

The piece seemed to be a day in the life of a Martian boy. It started with the youth staring into a mirror, obviously getting ready for the day. Then, interestingly, instead of focusing on the boy, the artist's viewpoint merged with his subject's. From then on, what the boy saw the viewer saw.

"Different," muttered the prime minister. For some reason he could not put his finger on, something in this piece was intriguing him far more than the others. For the life of him, however, Hawkes could not determine why. The boy's day was one of unrelenting grayness. Studies, work details, dull-looking meals, more of each, over and over, all of it passing by in the same stupefying gray.

Part of Hawkes's mind realized what the artist was going after. For anyone who had not been to Mars, who had not lived in her claustrophobic tunnels, the piece would be quite gripping. It was a stark glimpse into a world most of the people of Earth could not relate to on any level. Earth lived off the sweat of Mars—it did not sweat itself.

Then, the prime minister's musings came to a halt as the painting moved toward its climax. The artist had returned to the same dreary cubicle home he had started from. As the boy moved into the bathroom, the light came on and he was revealed in the mirror once more. But he was no longer a boy. A haggard, defeated elderly face stared into the mirror—into Hawkes's eyes. The sight unnerved the prime minister greatly.

I get the point, he thought, blinking his eyes against the image assaulting them. Born on Mars, die on Mars, and nothing changes in between. Life is gray and forlorn and without hope. Well, maybe with the League off their backs, some of that will change.

Hawkes watched as the haggard face disappeared from the mirror. As the dull gray home in the story faded, the prime minister thought grimly, But whether it does or it doesn't . . . I don't care. I've done just about everything for Mars that I intend to do.

And then the call was made to enter the dining room. Shrugging, Hawkes turned to join everyone else for the latest round of "rubber chicken and speeches." Then suddenly, he turned back toward the painting again. It was just beginning again and the prime minister found himself overwhelmed by the desire to see the boy's face once more. There was something familiar to Hawkes about the youth. He did not know when or where, but he could swear he had seen the boy someplace before. The boy and the old man both.

When the face disappeared from the screen, however, Hawkes turned back to the dining room queue. So the boy looked like someone he knew, he thought. So what? He had more important things to think about than that.

Scanning the crowd, the prime minister managed to locate Val Hensen just as the older man spotted him. Working his way through the crowd, by the time he reached his old commander's side, Hawkes had completely shoved any memory of the boy in the painting from his mind.

Or, at least, so he thought.

W E DON'T GET this thing runnin'," snarled Ed Keller, pointing at the tractor before him, "you can kiss a fall crop goodbye."

"Well," Hawkes answered, stepping down from his front porch with a pair of saddlebags slung over his shoulder, and a large dog running around his legs, "give it a big one for me."

Keller released a string of curses, half of them aimed at the disabled tractor, the other half aimed at his employer. The old man had served as the ranch's foreman since before the prime minister was born. With the death of Hawkes's father, the loyal retainer had stepped in and kept the ranch going. He had also taken over the raising of the younger Hawkes, keeping the boy together the best he could. Keller taught his charge mechanical and electrical repair, taught him how to plant a hillside, hold a rifle to his shoulder, track an animal across sand and rock, and a thousand and one other bits and pieces of information a man needed to survive without the rest of the world.

Eventually Hawkes left the ranch for the military. There he had come under Val Hensen's wing. Leaving the service, he directed his life toward the diplomatic corps. And after that he had become a man no one could teach—a condition that usually worked in his favor, but sometimes to his detriment. He did not care, however. Like most people, by that stage in his life he had crafted for himself a set of principles and guidelines as familiar as vices. They were the patterns he was comfortable following, and on those occasions when they led him astray, it was still simply easier to follow his old instincts than to try and craft new ones.

"Shirking your duties, eh, boss?" asked Tony Celdosso, the head of Hawkes's ranch security team.

"Look, greasy," the prime minister told the far younger man in a joking voice. "In case you haven't noticed, I've been having a rough year."

Hawkes tried to continue, but the dog jumped up against his chest, hitting him with such force that he almost knocked him over. The prime minister smiled, set his saddlebags down, and then grabbed the large-pawed mutt by the head and shook him fiercely. Just slightly less than a year old, the dog barked excitedly, barely feeling the abuse that would have rattled most men. Laughing, Hawkes picked up a handy piece of tree branch and flung it away toward the barns. While the dog raced off after it, the prime minister turned back to Keller and Celdosso.

"Look," he told them. "I just got back home last night for my first break since all this started. And I have to be back in Washington in six days to oversee the signing of the treaty. So, if you workaholics don't mind, I'll be taking the morning off. I *am* still the boss around here—right?" Before anyone could answer, a woman with short dark hair and deep green eyes stepped out from the main house.

"Hey," she cried out, "better not let Cook hear you say that."

Everyone chuckled. Dina Martel, Hawkes's chief aide throughout the Mars affair, was referring to the elderly woman who ran the prime minister's home. "Cook" was not the woman's given name. But she had gone by it for so long no one on the ranch could remember a time she had been called anything else. Ignoring the comment, the prime minister changed the subject.

"Well," he said, referring to the fact Martel had arrived a few days before Hawkes to set up his office, "you look rested."

"Oh," she answered, smiling as the dog returned, the branch firmly in his mouth, "a couple of days relaxing around this place can do wonders for a person. You ought to try it."

Hawkes nodded, wrestling the branch from the dog's mouth and throwing it even farther, getting it over the corral fence.

"That," he said in a voice loud enough for everyone in the immediate area to hear, "is what I had in mind. In fact, I think I'm going to get started right now." Both Keller and Celdosso moved forward with questions. Hawkes cut them off.

"Fellas, listen to me. I've been away a long time. Instead of stars and pines at night, I've been living in tunnels, surrounded by stone—above, below, all around. Do you understand? I need a break, and I'm going to take it. Ed, forget the tractor for now. I want you and Tony to make sure all the perimeter defenses are in tune. Even if you think they're fine, do a double check."

"You expectin' trouble, boss?"

"No," answered Hawkes. "But we weren't expecting any after I told Mick Carri I wouldn't go to Mars, either. I don't want to get caught off-sides again. You two check the system over this morning, we'll all sleep better tonight."

"But," responded the foreman, "we just went over the system from the in to the out last week."

"Then it shouldn't take you too long to do it this time."

"Uh-huh," grumbled Keller, "and just what'll *you* be doin'? In case we need to find you for some reason more important than yer playtime, that is?"

"I have a promise to keep," answered Hawkes. As the playful mutt returned again, the prime minister charged Celdosso with keeping him busy for a while. Then, turning toward the stables, he called to Martel. "You ready?"

"No," answered the young woman with a coy smile. "But if I can stay by your side through a revolution, not to mention a battle with interplanetary space pirates, I can do this." The prime minister responded as the two moved inside through the stable's large swinging doors.

"*Battling* interplanetary space pirates? When our ship was boarded, all I seem to remember you doing is a lot of running away."

"Just trying to keep up with you."

"Oh, I see."

Hawkes led a trail horse out of its stall while he continued to banter with his aide. Bridle rig in hand, he got the large black stallion to take the bit easily. Spreading a saddle pad across its back, he picked up his personal saddle and slung it over the motionless animal. He felt the pull of unused muscles in his shoulders, side, and forearm. "You know," he admitted with a smile, "it's been a while since I've gotten to do any real work."

As he pulled the cinch buckle closed, his assistant teased, "Cross your fingers. Maybe we'll get to fight some more interplanetary space pirates soon."

"Not funny," answered Hawkes. Finished with his own horse, he led a suitable mare from its stall and started readying it for Martel, telling her, "I'd have thought you'd had enough of that."

"Sorry," she answered. "But if you weren't worried, you wouldn't have Tony and Ed checking out the defenses."

"I'm not worried. I'm cautious."

"That's one word for it," answered Martel.

Frowning, Hawkes slid his foot into the stirrup and mounted in one motion. The woman stepped toward her mare with trepidation. Like most people of her time, she had never actually seen a real horse, let alone attempted to mount one. Grabbing the saddle horn with an unsure hand, she kicked at the stirrup, struggling to insert her foot. Hawkes watched the woman's floundering for a moment with growing amusement. Finally he moved his stallion closer and extended his hand, helping her into the saddle. Once astride the mare, Martel asked, "Where's the seat belt on this thing?" The prime minister responded to her joke with one of his own.

"Hope you wore your thick pants."

And then, before the woman could respond, Hawkes slapped her steed on the rump, sending it rushing for the barnyard. Martel hung on to her reins tightly, cursing the prime minister as the mare bolted. Chuckling, Hawkes nudged his own mount and set off after his still-screaming assistant. Again his body made small complaints as more long-dormant muscles were forced to life. Ignoring their protests, he urged his stallion on faster. In a matter of minutes they passed Martel and her mare, leaving the two of them far behind.

Hawkes needed the moment alone—needed the pounding speed, the familiar jostling rhythm, to drive away the weariness that had invaded his soul. Throughout his life, whenever problems had grown to where they seemed insurmountable, he had always turned to his horses to help him clear his head. Alone on his mount, ranging across his fields, winding his way through his forest, Hawkes always came away renewed, rejuvenated. It was the single greatest joy in his life.

If he had realized it was a joy he would never again know, he might have sat his saddle longer.

● ● ● A LITTLE MORE than an hour after Hawkes and Martel left the main living area of the ranch compound, Keller and Celdosso found themselves just finishing their diagnostic check of the spread's security systems. As the foreman had predicted, everything was up and running perfectly.

"Tol' him so, damnit."

"Give him a break, Ed," answered Celdosso. "He's been pulling his wire pretty thin lately. I mean, how many people tried to kill him when the revolution started? And shit—you think some of 'em still don't want to?"

"Yeah," growled Keller. "I know all that. But it don't change the fact we tol' him everything was okay an' it is. You wanta let him turn all paranoid 'bout every little thing, you—" Before the foreman could finish his thought, the security hand in charge of the monitors they had just finished interrupted him.

"Mr. Keller, Mr. Celdosso, we've got an intruder."

"Oh, paint me white and call me Frosty." Crossing the room to the registering monitor, the foreman said, "We've got the detail cranked down so low on these things they're pickin' up every damn thing that moves. So what is it this time—a deer, or a badger? I'll put five on a deer."

"Neither, sir," answered the watchman. "We've got no ground contact. Whatever it is, it's airborne."

"And moving fast too," added Celdosso, his eyes tight on another screen. "*Too* fast. Ed, get a weight on it."

"It's nothin' man-made," responded Keller, his eye on the displacement monitor. "But mass dispersion is only measurin' . . . Hell, it's below the scale—less than two hundred pounds. And lookit that weave pattern—what kind of . . . What the shit . . ."

"Mr. Keller," interrupted the watchman again, his hand reaching for the compound-wide alert system, "hate to argue, but whatever's coming at us *is* man-made."

As the ranch's alarms began to buzz all around them, the foreman shifted his attention to the monitor the security man had just checked. Not certain he was interpreting the screen correctly, he asked, "Does that say what the hell I think it says?"

"Yes, sir," answered the watchman. Reaching for his combat gear, he added, "Whatever our bogey is, it's Geiger hot."

Keller cursed once more, then headed for the door, Celdosso on his heels. They had to get to their own protective gear, and their weapons. The grid had given them all the information they needed. In less than five minutes, something fast, light, and highly maneuverable would be in the center of their compound. Something they could not identify.

Something heavily shielded, but still giving off the trace registers of nuclear power.

HAWKES POINTED TOWARD the burned and ruined gash in his mountains. Twisted girders and ugly splashes of once molten metal, thick with rust and decay, were spread out over several square miles, the surrounding vegetation barely beginning to encroach on its ugly presence. Even after all the years that had passed, Hawkes noted that the majority of the massive, rusting framework in the center of it all was still completely visible—untouched by nature.

"That's it," the prime minister told Martel. "Now that you've seen it, I assume you can tell why I call it the Scar."

The woman nodded mutely. Hawkes had long since told her of the tragedy that had changed his life—of the Martian ore ship that had fallen from the sky, killing his father, almost killing him. Hearing the story and seeing the reality, however, even so many decades after the fact, were two different things. Unlike the prime minister's resigned acceptance of the sight, Martel was shocked that after so long the forest had not grown back to cover the shattered landscape. After a minute, however, she whispered, "This is why you hate Mars so much, isn't it?"

"My mother died when I was a baby. My father was all I had— Mars took him from me. Of course I hate the place."

"No, I didn't mean that, exactly." Hawkes turned toward his assistant, studying her as she continued. "I meant the look of it—so barren, blasted, desolate . . . life struggling to get a hold, but not really able to conquer . . . I don't know about you, but it reminds me of Mars."

Hawkes began to protest her analogy, but then stopped. He had never looked at the situation that way before. Of course, he had rarely gotten anyone else's perspective on the subject. His mind racing, he could not remember ever having brought anyone else to see the Scar. Even though it covered scores of square miles, it was his father's grave. It was private. It was his.

If that's the case, a part of his mind asked, then what did you bring her here for? The prime minister considered the question. He had brought Martel there because he wanted to talk to her. Perhaps, he admitted to himself, this is one of the things I wanted to talk about.

Swinging his leg over his stallion, Hawkes dismounted. Then, after helping his aide dismount, he swallowed a deep lungful of air and conceded, "Maybe you have a point."

"Credit from the great man," Martel teased. "I'm flattered."

Although many years his junior, the woman enjoyed flirting with Hawkes. He was vital, handsome, and intelligent, and she was as willing as the next woman to admit there were worse prospects available. In fact, she thought, almost blushing, *much* worse.

"Dina," asked Hawkes, too distracted by his thoughts to notice her playful jibe, "can I ask you something?"

"Of course, Benton," she answered, noting the serious tone in his voice. "What is it?"

The prime minister moved toward the edge of the slope. While the horses grazed on the grass growing beyond the tree line, Hawkes sat down, feet over the edge.

"I don't like Mars. You've known that since you met me, of course. And you've known why. I went to Mars the first time for revenge. People were trying to kill me. They'd killed my friends, they'd killed my dog. I didn't care about the Martian people or their cause—I just wanted a little of my own back."

Martel sat on the edge of the slope as well, coming as close as she could without being suggestive. Not that she had not contemplated making a few forward suggestions to Hawkes, but she knew then was not the correct time.

It's never the correct time, is it? she thought. Always something coming between. If you want him, you'd better make a move soon, or you're going to lose him.

The woman shoved the notion away. As much as she had thought about herself and the prime minister, she knew that until he had the treaty signed and out of the way—and Mars behind him forever—there was no room in Hawkes's life for any further entanglements. Roping in her desires, she focused her attention on what he was saying, more than a small part of her hoping that it might be something leading him in her direction.

"Then I got to Mars, started to see the situation for what it really was. I realized their enemies were mine, so I turned on the League. I didn't do what I did because I'm some great champion of liberty. I did it for me. Somehow I managed to lead a revolution and come out of it still hating the people I took to victory."

"I . . . I don't know what to say."

"That's all right, neither do I," answered Hawkes, gazing out over the Scar, barely aware of Martel as he sank deeper into his own thoughts. "A piece of me saw the contradiction in that, but for the most part I was prepared to live with it. In fact, all that's really kept me going lately was thinking about retiring. For months now I've kept telling myself, Just a few more days, a few more days. A . . . few . . . more . . . days."

Hawkes went quiet then, simply staring out into space. His assistant let him do so for a moment, thinking he was merely pausing for effect. After that she let it go on, thinking that at any moment he would start talking once more. Finally, however, she reached over and nudged him in the shoulder. "Yeah—so?"

The prime minister blinked, turning toward Martel with a look of surprise on his face. Blinking several times, more rapidly than before, he finally said, "My God, I'm sorry. I got lost in thought and I . . . I mean—"

"Hey, it's okay."

"No," Hawkes disagreed. "And I'll tell you why. Ever since I went to that art show in New York—the Martian art exhibit—this has continued to happen to me. More and more often. Whenever I think about Mars now, when I try to get to the old feelings . . ." The prime minister's voice dipped downward, almost into embarrassment, as he said, "Back to my hate . . . suddenly I feel myself . . . I don't know, relaxing? Is that the word?"

"Is it?"

"I don't know. I feel my focus dissolving, as if I . . . don't have control . . ."

Again the prime minister let his words trail off, losing his train of thought. Martel stared at him, almost shocked. This was not the Benton Hawkes she knew. In an instant the young woman felt a chilled panic crawling over her. The prime minister had wanted to discuss something with her the night before when he first arrived at the ranch. She knew it—when she asked he admitted it. But he had told her he wanted to wait until the next day.

Sure, she thought. He wanted to come out here to talk. Here where his father died. Here where he's got physical proof of his reasons to harbor his comfortable hate for Mars—a whole mountainside full of them.

"Benton," she said, tightening the force of her will to keep her voice from cracking. "It's okay. Maybe, maybe you're just tired of hating. Maybe it's run its course."

"No—even if I had mellowed, it couldn't have happened over-night. One day the hate's red hot, the next day I'm all warm and fuzzy?"

Hawkes pushed himself upward, regaining his feet with surpris-ing speed. As Martel scrambled to stand herself, the prime minster continued, "No! It doesn't work that way. Not with me it doesn't. Somebody did something to me. Something happened to me at that damned show. I know it. I've had two days to think about it, watch-ing it happen, feeling the changes trickle in."

Martel walked behind Hawkes as he paced through the grass and weeds. He was not ranting, but she knew he was no longer talking to her, either. She had become a prop, a justification so he might think aloud without having to wonder if he was losing his mind. As his aide, she had grown used to the tactic.

"The last time I was here people wanted me to change my mind about going to Mars. That time they tried to strong-arm me there. What if this time it's something more subtle?"

Stopping suddenly, Hawkes brought his hands together in front of his chest. Threading his fingers, he bowed his head slightly, try-ing to force himself to step beyond his internal understanding of what was happening so that he might be able to focus on the big picture beyond.

"What's coming up?" he muttered, rubbing his braced fingers across his face. "Signing the treaty—that's it. After that Mars is be-hind me. On its own. The League and Red Planet, Inc., will have to deal with each other. So who could care what I think of Mars? Who could it be important to? And why?" And then, suddenly, he turned to Martel. His fingers falling away from his face, eyes wide open, he asked her, "*Why?!* What does anyone gain? The treaty doesn't gouge either side. It doesn't force any massive concessions. It just eases things up for the Martians. Their lives get a little better, the League still keeps its hold on everything. Instead of a war that destroys two worlds, everyone gets what they want."

"Do they?" asked Martel. Finding the courage to interrupt the prime minister, she asked, "Does everything work smoothly for both sides from here on in? Guaranteed?"

"Well, considering there are no real guarantees in this life . . . it's the next closest thing. As long as both sides can rein in their greed and megalomania—as long as nobody gets the idea they deserve thralls and are willing to risk billions of lives to get them . . ." And then Hawkes stopped abruptly, wondering if he was merely talking gibberish, or if he was actually thinking it.

People control their greed? he asked himself. Give up the idea of enslaving others? Meglomaniacs surrender their goals because lives are at risk? Just what the hell do you think the word megalomaniac means?

"I don't want to contradict you," said Martel quietly, not at all certain what had happened to the man she had worked with for so long to have changed him to such a degree. "But do you really think there's any chance of that? Of people controlling their greed and all . . . just because it's right?"

"Honestly?" Hawkes admitted quickly. "No. Not in the least."

And then, a sudden metallic whining split the air. The horses looked up, their heads turning this way and that. Their riders followed suit a second after, searching for the source of the disturbance. They discovered it almost instantly.

A figure flew out of the trees, startling them both. After a moment their eyes adjusted to the new situation, feeding information to their brains. The figure was a woman's, one wearing an Air Force uniform. On her back was strapped what both Hawkes and Martel assumed must be a flight pack of some sort. The prime minister had heard research was being done with such devices, but had never seen a working model—not one that worked as well as hers apparently did. She landed within a few yards of them.

Getting her bearings, the woman moved awkwardly toward Hawkes and his assistant, weighed down by her effective but somewhat clumsy pack. As she closed with them, she removed her helmet, one that Hawkes noted was outfitted with long-range listeners.

Then, stopping a few feet short of the pair, the woman said, "So, you don't think people are going to get over their murderous ways anytime soon, eh, Mr. Prime Minister? You know what? You're right."

HAWKES'S FIRST REACTION was to fire off any question that would prompt the young woman to identify herself—preferably before she got much closer. Then, the way a lock of her hair fell across her forehead made him recognize her.

"Major Truman . . . Elizabeth, isn't it? You headed up the security team that brought our diplomatic mission back from the Australia talks last year."

"I'm flattered you remember, sir," answered the woman, almost embarrassed. Freezing her face against even the slight rush of blood she could feel warming in her cheeks, she added, "But just as glad. Not having to introduce myself will save time."

"Are we in some kind of hurry?" asked Martel, somewhat annoyed that she had not yet been introduced, mostly annoyed at the presence of another woman.

"Oh, sorry—forgive me, ladies," interrupted Hawkes. Turning from his assistant to the major, he introduced the pair to each other, then asked, "Now, as Ms. Martel so aptly put it—are we in some kind of hurry?"

"That, sir," answered Truman, her jaw firming, eyes going hard, "will depend on what you think of the information I have for you. I could give you a verbal replay of some of it here, but the displays and recordings will require a power grid. If you'd like to receive everything at one time, I suggest we return to your home. And again, I would strongly suggest that we hurry."

"This isn't an official visit, is it?" asked the prime minister, already knowing the answer. The woman had arrived wearing a highly experimental piece of new technology—something that would not have been allowed under normal circumstances. Neither was she displaying her rank. When Truman acknowledged the prime minister's guess, he put his hand on his mount's saddle. He held his pose for a moment, wishing just once he could ignore the world. Then he said softly, "Let's go back, Dina."

Martel nodded, unable to give voice to the volatile mixture of thoughts running through her head. She had wanted their time together to count for something, to start the two of them in a new direction. Securing her foot in her stirrup after the third try, Martel watched the major silently rise into the air under her own power.

Okay, I will have to admit that this is a new direction, she thought, grunting, struggling to regain her saddle. But it's not the one I had in mind.

As Martel finally managed to flop awkwardly back atop her mount, the sight of Major Truman delicately drifting off into the trees with Hawkes's eyes following her did nothing to slake the anger rising in the back of her mind.

Oh, yeah. This is another one you played out just fine, Dina.

Taking a deep breath, the woman swallowed the air along with her pride and then gently started her horse forward. Feeling the inevitable closing in on her, she reminded herself that the forces surrounding her and Hawkes were bigger than her desires, that the prime minister was the focal point around which revolved the survival of millions of people—perhaps billions. She told herself that most likely the entire solar system was about to be plunged into war, and that Benton Hawkes was the only man who could prevent it.

Feeling the tears beginning to roll down her cheek, Dina Martel damned the politicians and the revolutionaries and the fates themselves. Then she admitted to herself what she was really upset about, and cried all the harder.

● ● ● "YOU WANT TO talk trouble—fine. Let's do it. The asteroid miners and outer explorers all port through Mars. The colony's refineries handle some seventy-five percent of the solar system's natural resources. Trying to redirect this pipeline to our lunar facilities would take years. Two months into a cutoff, the Earth would have no tungsten, no scandium, tellurium, gadolinium, dozens of others. But then, why worry about that when long before we could notice any of them had run out, half the people in the world would have died from starvation and murder?"

Hawkes sat at the head of his dining room table, listening to a recording of Mick Carri's voice. It had been made earlier in the week when the Senate majority leader had addressed a private session of select members of the Earth League. Martel sat at the table listening, as did Ed Keller and Tony Celdosso. Major Truman sat at the far end with the prime minister's audio player, working to keep the sound level constant. No one bothered her with any questions. There was no need. As usual, Mick Carri was not having any trouble making himself understood.

"Hundreds of thousands of square miles of Mars are covered with the nutrition vats. We came up with the perfect food and then we set up the factories that make it somewhere we wouldn't have to bother with them. 'Put it all on Mars!' was the cry. And we did. Looking back, I'd say it was not our brightest move. Because now it allows the right honorable Benton Hawkes and his Martians to think they have us all bottled up. If we say boo to them, they cut off the raw materials we need for building, the chemicals and minerals we need for everything from making plastics to vitamins . . . and, of course, the food we need to live."

As the recording disintegrated into static and garble, Truman boosted the power, apologizing again. "Sorry, but it was hard enough just to get any kind of equipment in with me, let alone—" She broke off as she found the proper level and Carri's voice flooded the room once more.

"But the question is, will they? Or, more specifically, will *he?* What I mean is, is there anyone in this room who thinks our self-righteous Martian prime minister would actually starve an entire world?"

Hawkes frowned. He knew where the majority leader was going. He had feared for some time that someone would see what Carri had obviously seen.

"If Mars has us over the barrel, then why has Hawkes spent the last ten months working with us to hammer out the Brooklyn Accord? Word from Mars is that the Resolute, the bastard group that started this trouble in the first place, is dead set against any treaty with Earth. And yet this Martian—for lack of a better word—*government* has been bending over backward, working like dogs, to forge an agreement we all can live with. Why?"

You're one smart son of a bitch, Mick, thought Hawkes through his growing disgust. I'll give you that much.

"Why?" asked Carri's voice somewhere in the past. "I'll tell you. First off, no one—not amongst them or us—wants to be responsible for the deaths of billions, *billions,* of people. When the United States dropped the first nuclear warhead to be used against an enemy force, the repercussions of guilt and national trauma went on for eighty years. As jaded as this weary world has become, genocide is still a dirty word."

Keller shook his head, hanging it sadly. Hawkes could tell he had figured things out already.

"Secondly, the problem with a weapon like controlling your enemy's food is that once you cut it off, you've given your opponents little choice other than to strike back with everything they have. Yes, Mars *can* starve half our world in a matter of weeks. But, that still leaves the other half to wreak havoc on them."

"But what can we do?" Hawkes identified the new speaker as the British ambassador. No one at the table spoke as the uneven audio output continued, almost cracking.

"We all know our history. A century ago the West and East had massive arsenals pointed at each other—a stalemate game that went on until the East collapsed down a hole the West damn near fell in right behind them. Are you asking us to play that same game? To try and outstare the Martians until one side blinks?"

"No, Colin. It's not going to be that hard. You remember I mentioned the Resolute before. Well, just as we have people ready to take Hawkes's navy out from under him, we have people in the Resolute as well. When Hawkes returns to Mars with a treaty that they don't want, he will be eliminated by his own rebels."

Everyone at the table stared at the prime minister. Silently he tilted his head, gesturing at the machine with both hands to indicate that staying calm and listening would be their best choice. Surprisingly, there was not that much more to hear.

"Benton Hawkes will be assassinated. So will much of the new government. At the same time, their navy will be eliminated. And then, by the grace of the very treaty the Martians insisted upon, we will be forced to impose martial law on Mars. For their own good, of course. And then—"

Major Truman shut down the player at that point. "That's it," she announced. "That's all my people could get."

"That's enough," added Keller.

Rubbing at his forehead, Tony Celdosso did not agree. "Not for me it isn't," he told the others. "There's nothing new here for us. We knew Carri was going to pull some shit. This just confirms it. We knew the Resolute still hadn't warmed up to you—this proves it."

"Haven't warmed up to him?" asked Martel. "They're going to kill him. And," she added, turning toward the prime minister, "the fact that Carri is ready to call your bluff on denying Earth food is not good news."

Hawkes sat quietly, stunned by much of what he had heard— surprised by none of it. The prime minister had lived over half a century. He had known all manner of people. He was—simply be- cause of the things he had already lived through—a hard man to surprise. But he had yet to reach the point of not being affected at all in the face of the natural perfidy of politics.

Knowing it was never wise to say anything until one had all the facts, though, he turned to the major, asking, "You don't have any more of the League's chatter for us, but you do have something more, correct?"

"Yes." She threw a switch on Hawkes's holocaster, and the space above the dining room table was suddenly filled with the image of a clumsy-looking, dull gray metal satellite. As everyone leaned in to inspect the shimmering projection, the major explained.

"There's been a megastorm raging on the surface of the sun for a while now—one that's been disrupting communication throughout the solar system, right?" Once everyone acknowledged their agree- ment, Truman told them, "Wrong. This is a boiler ship. Its name comes from its function, which is to heat the radiation in a given area. This magnifies the radiation's effects to the fourth, fifth, some- times the sixth power."

"So," asked Keller, "what're ya tellin' us?"

"Just what you think," answered the major sharply. "That the League had one put into Martian orbit eight months ago."

"All right," Hawkes interrupted calmly. "As best I can tell, we're all on the same side here. Major, let me see if I have everything in the right order. A few weeks back, you volunteered for a special duty—testing the flight rig you arrived in. While still at the testing grounds you were asked to put together a secure team for the next League meeting. Correct?"

"Yes, sir. I know most of the clearance fields that are posted in and around the capital by heart. If I'd been there I'd most likely have headed the detail myself."

"Um-hummm. So, tell me, Major—what makes a clever man like Mick Carri use security recommendations from someone who sympathizes with his enemies?"

The major pursed her lips for a moment, lowering her eyes at the same time. Then, meeting Hawkes's gaze head-on, she told him, "Sir, when you turned on the government last year, you saved everything my family had. You couldn't know that, of course, but I wanted to thank you—personally—to let you know that there were some people who thought you'd done the right thing. I got onto the detail that returned you to Washington by making all the right negative chatter. I knew they were looking for people who didn't particularly like you, so as far as anyone was concerned, I became one of those people."

Hawkes could remember the brief moment they had shared alone. Truman had seemed honest and sincere—as much then as she did now. Looking deep into the woman's eyes, the prime minister told himself, Well, you trusted her then . . .

"All right, you were able to get a sweep monitor inside an important League meeting. It didn't pick up a lot, but I'm grateful for what it did get."

"What're ya sayin'?" snapped Keller. "What'd it get? A lotta nothin' is all."

"Ed, calm down," answered Hawkes quietly. "It told me that I've got trouble—a lot more than I wanted to believe I did. Me—like some gullible idiot, I thought I was going to retire after this. I thought the lies and the betrayals and the whole dirty game was going to be behind me. It told me I was wrong, and that I'd better wake up and do something about it while I still have the time."

The prime minister placed his hands palm down on the table before him, his fingers arching as his nails dug into the polished wood.

"We know that Carri has some way to take our ships away from us. Either one of our captains isn't loyal, or the ships can be blown from long range. We don't know which it is, but we know something's wrong. We know they still have people on Mars. We know they have them in the Resolute, and we know they're ready to use them. We know they're ready to call our bluff, and most importantly . . . we know they still think they own Mars, that they can do with it what they want."

Hawkes lowered his head until his chin touched his chest. His eyes closed, he withdrew into himself for a long moment—thinking. Suddenly, too many of the tiny clues he had been ignoring raced back to fling themselves at him. Concessions granted, sly looks and conciliatory motions that could only be explained by an agenda already in place—one that would do as it pleased when the time was right.

And, Hawkes thought, we know when that is, don't we?

Lifting his head once more, Hawkes released his grip on the table. Bringing his hands together before him, he looked from person to person around him, then said the one thing most of the assembly thought they would never hear him say again.

"And we know one more thing. We know I have to get going."

"Get going?" asked Martel, fearing yet knowing his answer. "Get going *where*?"

"Mars," answered Hawkes softly. "Where else?"

YOU KNOW," SAID Truman with a trace of ill-concealed awe in her voice, "when you said bring the flight pack with me, I couldn't believe you'd be able to get it through."

"I'm used to getting my own way," answered Hawkes. Settling in as best he could on the form-molded seat, he folded his luggage bag over to act as a pillow, adding, "It may not be my best feature, but it comes in handy."

The major nodded, looking out their room's single window. They had not yet even started their ascent, but already she was beginning to feel confined. Noticing her discomfort, Hawkes inquired as to how a pilot cleared for deep-space flights could suffer from claustrophobia. She told him.

"It's not that, not a fear of enclosure, I mean. I just, I don't . . ." The woman swallowed, then began again. "We're going to be on this thing for twenty-eight hours. With someone else at the controls. I don't like not being in control."

"Well, now there's a problem I can sympathize with."

Neither spoke for some time after that, both eager for their journey to begin. Of course, thought Hawkes, it began the moment I saw and heard the information the major brought to the ranch.

The prime minister had realized that there were only a precious few days before he had to return to Washington. If he had any chance of reaching Mars before Carri and the others could try to stop him, he knew he had to leave immediately. With a deep sigh of regret, he had started snapping off orders.

Keller and Celdosso would run the ranch as they always did in his absence. If anyone called for him, they were to be stalled—so sorry, the prime minister is on vacation, the prime minister is riding in the mountains, the prime minister does not wish to be disturbed, et cetera—first by Celdosso, then by the older, gruffer Keller, and finally by Martel.

Leaving his aide behind was Hawkes's ace in the hole. Everyone knew of the strong bond between the prime minister and his assistant, of the confidence he placed in her. She was his sounding board, his extra set of hands—since the revolution they had rarely been apart. He had not liked the idea of leaving her behind, but he had no doubt she could cover his trail until the day he was supposed to be back in the capital. Perhaps longer.

Of course, if Hawkes did not like the idea of leaving Martel behind, she loathed it. Especially when Major Truman volunteered to accompany the prime minister. Far too professional to voice her concerns, however, the diplomatic aide had said nothing. She knew Hawkes was right. If he was going to attempt to head off the League by returning to Mars, then he had to leave at once. And if he was going to have the maximum amount of time to get there, then she was going to have to stay behind to throw the dogs off the trail.

Loyal to the end, Martel had thought bitterly, Why don't I loan her some lingerie while I'm at it?

But despite her personal desires, she had helped Cook pack Hawkes's bags while Celdosso and Keller had organized his escape. Using the never deactivated credentials of the late Daniel Stine, the prime minister's previous aide, the pair booked a flight for two to the Maldives as well as a tiny coach box on Skyhook.

As to the size of the accommodations, they had no choice. Anything larger would not have matched the junior diplomat's status rating and would have drawn instant suspicion—something they could not afford. Stine's old Iden card had been used solely for the purpose of utilizing his diplomatic immunity—the privilege which allowed the pair to bring an inordinate amount of secure baggage, including the major's stolen flight rig.

As Hawkes had explained it, the experimental suit was certain to have been tagged with tracer elements. Truman had covered her escape with an ejected distress beacon which she had dropped over the ocean set with a delayed timer. But the prime minister knew the Earth League and the forces they commanded. Even on the bottom of the Pacific, the beacon would be found. After that, heaven and Earth would be moved to recover the suit. Hawkes could not afford to have the top-secret rig found on his ranch. That "act of war" would be more than enough of a lever for the League to engage the conflict they so desperately wanted.

"Besides," he had said, "who knows? We might even find a use for it on Mars. Somebody has to paint the ceilings."

But that had been a half-day before. Now, as their coach box continued to belt forward on its tracks, neither of them felt much like joking. Especially Hawkes. Whereas the major was comfortable with the idea of riding the Skyhook, the prime minister was not. Because of the way his father had died, he had little use for anything that had to do with space travel. Since Skyhook was responsible for every aspect of man's colonization of the solar system, the massive space elevator made Hawkes particularly uncomfortable.

Skyhook never stopped moving. Passengers and cargo alike were jockeyed toward it on conveyor strips. One after another the cabins and cargo holds were gently rolled into their secure berths as the great belts snagged and pulled them upward to the launch platform waiting in stationary orbit far above. As he sat waiting for the almost imperceptible jolt that would indicate their room had been locked into place, Hawkes thought of how the Skyhook project had changed everything in human existence.

The prime minister had been born only a few years after construction of the Earth League's first epic project had begun. The world of nations and ideologies all his forefathers had known had quickly begun to slip away. One by one nations disappeared, replaced by businesses. War became less and less practical as the planet's available resources were consumed in the grand struggle to put the star elevator in place.

"Eleven years to build this thing," Hawkes mused abruptly. "Eleven years. But only a year and a half later people were already living on the Moon. And before that second year was out, we were raiding the asteroids and setting our sights on Mars."

"You know how people are," the major offered. "Once they get started on something, it's hard to hold them back." The prime minister eyed Truman coldly. She had not understood his meaning—did not realize which emotions motivated his comment.

Seeing in his eyes that she had made some kind of mistake, she asked, "I've said something you don't agree with?"

"You could say that, Major. I'm not much of a fan of Skyhook. From what I can tell, the Earth was doing all right for itself before the grand crusade to reach the stars got rolling. The people who started the League didn't care about any kind of grand destiny for mankind. They wanted power, plain and simple. The building of this thing gave them the excuse to tax and plunder like nothing else. 'Earth doesn't have any resources anymore.' 'We have to get off the planet.' 'Everyone has to do their share.'"

"But sir . . ."

"Don't, Major—don't read me the standard excuse list. The greedy and the grasping have always despised the individual. This was just their way to destroy their enemies without facing them.

'Global emergency.' 'Everyone must contribute.' Tax and work people for the greater good. 'We're conquering the solar system—unlimited wealth awaits.' 'Plenty for everyone.' 'A life of ease.' 'Every man a king, a chicken in every pot.' It's all been said before. Each new benefactor of mankind shills from the same handbook. And they all deliver pretty much the same goods.''

"There were changes . . ."

"There was one change. Food grown in vats. Synthetic mush—God, how disgusting. A big box delivered once a week to your residence—one for each member of the family, ready to eat in your government-allocated cubicle. And no one with any more than anyone else . . . except, of course, for the elites living off the poor idiots who bought their message in the first place."

"Like you?" A part of Hawkes took umbrage at the woman's comment. The part of him used to playing the diplomacy game held his anger in check, however, allowing him to answer.

"You mean, I assume, the fact that I still live on my own land, grow my own food . . . Yes, I'm a privileged character. I admit it. By going into the military and then the corps, I carved out a niche for myself where I could keep what my father and his father and his and his had carved out for themselves. Yes, Major, I've used my wits to keep what I want. Try to understand, though—the main thing I was trying to keep was myself."

Major Truman pursed her lips. Her first reaction was to strike back, but she quickly realized she had no actual ammunition. Hawkes had simply agreed with what she had said, merely adding his own spin to it.

And, she thought, who's to say he isn't right? The man claims he hung on to his ranch to maintain his individuality. In this cookie-cutter world, how many others do you know like him? And more important, how many others would you have thrown your career away for?

"Sorry," she offered. "You get so used to the anyone-with-more-is-bad argument you tend to forget that most of the people using it have more than anyone."

"Apology accepted," answered Hawkes with a sincere smile. "On one condition. You tell me something about yourself. We've just started a very long trip. Who is it I'm traveling with? Give me the details on Major Elizabeth Truman."

Returning the prime minister's smile, the woman felt herself suddenly relaxing. Working herself into a more comfortable position on the molded seat, she went with the feeling, glad to escape the tension they had both been living with for too long.

"I was born in Gettysburg, lived there in the Warren Harding Memorial Quarters until I joined the service. Good enough grades—bad attitude, though. Got into more than a few scrapes until finally they gave me the M-or-M choice."

"Mars or the military."

"That's the one. Probably all for the best. The service gave me a place I could bang out a lot of frustration. Shaped me into someone. My air time scores were A-ninety, but my looks kept getting in the way. No one seemed able to find an assignment for me that didn't involve showing off my legs to high-ups."

"I remember you mentioning that before," said Hawkes. "But tell me—if that's the case, how did you get the assignment testing the flight suit?"

"Easy," answered the major, patting the box containing the experimental rig. "This is the X-AC-7. The first six crashed. They were getting short on qualified volunteers."

"I see. Oh well, tell me more."

"Not much more to tell," responded Truman. "My family's mostly gone. There's no one special anywhere waiting for me. Up until recently life had looked pretty clear. Keep my nose clean, put in my twenty, retire to a quiet box life somewhere and join the local Quote society."

Hawkes's ears picked up. A onetime serviceman himself, he knew and loved the game. Breaking out into a grin, he challenged the major to a round instantly.

"Twenty-eight hours in this coffin we booked?" answered Truman. "I'm ready for a championship match. Let's go. You want to go personality or category?"

"I'm a smug member of the elite, remember?" joked the prime minister. "I think I can beat anyone. You choose."

The major thought for a moment. "I'm better at random trivia," she told Hawkes. "Let's do a category. As a poor allotment drone, I'll stack the deck in my favor and say war."

Hawkes nodded, then sat back and waited for the first round to commence. The rules of the game were quite simple. After a topic was chosen, the first player then named any person they were certain had said something memorable on the subject. If any of the others playing could give the correct quote, the turn passed to them. If not, the point went to the person who had first given the name, after they recited the quote they had in mind. As the challenged, the major got to go first.

"Joseph Heller," she offered.

The prime minister rolled his eyes. "Let's not make this too easy." When Truman merely stared, Hawkes shrugged his shoulders and continued, saying, "All right. 'I'd like to see the government get out of war altogether and leave the whole feud to private industry.' "

When the major's eyes went wide, the prime minister told her, "That's practically the Earth League's motto. How about Saint Augustine?"

" 'The purpose of all war is peace'?" She had offered the quote as a question, but Hawkes nodded, acknowledging her point. Like any good player, the woman tried to select her next quote not only as a bit of game play, but also as an answer to the one before it. With mischief in her eyes, she offered, "Menachem Begin."

" 'If both sides don't want war,' " Hawkes responded instantly, " 'how can war break out?' " When Truman furrowed her brow, her opponent reminded her, "If you want to win, don't try using my fellow prime ministers against me. That's why I think I'll give you . . . ah, Albert Einstein."

The major thought for a long moment, but could not remember anything the long-dead scientist had had to say about war. Reluctantly she conceded the point. With a smile, Hawkes quoted, " 'As long as there are sovereign nations possessing great power, war is inevitable.' " Truman nodded, then instead of returning to the game, asked the prime minister a question.

"Is that what you think, sir? That this war . . . between the League and Mars . . . that it's inevitable?"

"If I thought it was inevitable, that there wasn't anything that could be done about it, I would have stayed home and helped tend the herds. I believe in results. Not destiny."

"I believe," answered Truman, turning toward their cabin's window once more, "that things are going to get a lot worse before they get better." Looking out the thick porthole, the woman eyed the slowly receding ocean below, adding, "A lot worse."

Hawkes made no answer. He merely looked on, watching Truman watch the world fall away beneath them. Finally, the major turned back and said, "I'm sorry, sir, but somehow . . . I'm just not up for playing any games."

Unblinking, Hawkes stared into the woman's eyes. Filled with a growing anger for all the fools whose greed and hatred had upset his life once more, he answered her simply.

"That's all right. Neither am I, Major. Neither am I."

G OD, OH GOD oh God . . . I have to stop . . . have to stop . . . can't go on like this.

The jumbled blur of thoughts burned at the forefront of Hawkes's mind, echoing in his ears louder than his reverberating heartbeat. The prime minister leaned against the wall, panting, hiding in the deep shadows of the access corridor. He concentrated desperately, struggling to get his ragged breathing under control. He had been running for so long at such a frantic pace, he found he could barely stand. His legs were shaking, cramping—his joints in agony. Frigid beads of sweat dripped from his hairline, burning his eyes, chilling his neck.

"Christ almighty," Hawkes wheezed under his breath. "I hate this goddamned planet."

How long had he been back on Mars? Exactly just how long had it taken before he was running for his life? Hours? Minutes? Hawkes could not remember. Fatigue poisons flooded his bloodstream, making him dizzy—shattering his memory along with his ability to care about the answers a part of him had been seeking only a second earlier.

None of that matters, he thought. Praying he was strong enough to start moving again, he whispered, "The only thing that matters is staying alive and staying ahead of . . . of . . ."

Who? Staying ahead of *who*? He couldn't remember. Had he known before? He couldn't remember that, either. All he knew for certain was that someone or some group of someones had been chasing him for so long he could barely stand, could barely think— for so long a part of him actually longed to surrender.

"After him! Faster—get him!"

Hawkes coughed violently as he ran, his agitated stomach rebelling against him. By that point the prime minister was stumbling, lurching awkwardly, the stinging sweat in his eyes blinding him. Somehow, though, he found the strength to stagger on, half loping, half falling, but still just barely keeping ahead of the tireless mob.

All around him, his exits had been cut off. Howling people hung off balconies far above him, stuck their bodies out of windows carved in the rock tunnels, all pointing, all screaming, all of them just a part of the swelling mob bent on . . . *what?*

Your capture? Your death? You're running and you don't even know what you're running from.

Hawkes twisted to the right, then the left, but it was too late. He had nowhere to flee. He tried to ball his fingers into fists, but there was no strength left in his body. Resist the horde closing in on him? He could barely force his bleeding eyes to focus. Before he could even raise his hands to try and ward off the closing throng, they were upon him.

"Damn you!" he cursed. "I hate you, I hate all of you!"

The prime minister found himself lifted into the air by rough hands. He tried to concentrate, but he saw nothing further. Those who had borne him along now dropped him and shoved him forward into one of a series of dreary, gray cubicles housing computer workstations. The prime minister wanted to resist, but a compulsion he found he could not escape forced him to tab access into the station, which had somehow already been programmed to respond to his commands.

It only took a moment for the dark screen to flash clear. As the hostile crowd melted away behind him, Hawkes stared at the glowing square, watching the face of a young boy form in its center. As the boy's eyes opened, all around Hawkes the factory noise of the other cubicles pounded away, their pitch and bellow flooding the space around him.

Hating the growing noise with a building rage, the prime minister looked up as if it were a tangible thing he could swat away like a circling insect. When he did, he saw that the ceiling had disappeared, suddenly replaced by a red, smoke-filled sky. And then, the boy's face floating across his computer screen began to talk to him, and Hawkes awoke screaming.

● ● ● "YOU MAKE A lot of noise for one of the reserved, sophisticated set." Seeing that her humor was having no effect, the major said, "Sorry. Just thought a joke might help. Are you okay, sir?"

"Yes," answered Hawkes, his growing anger keeping him from feeling foolish. "And thanks for the joke, even if it doesn't seem like I appreciated it. Since we'll be together for a while, I should let you know that I've been having a series of disturbing dreams for some time now."

"Anything you'd like to talk about?"

"No—but I suppose I should." The prime minister struggled to rearrange himself on the molded plastic seat. The Skyhook berth was so uncomfortable he was not certain how he had managed to fall asleep.

Make do, he told himself. Make do.

Then, still digging his fingers into a knotted spot in his shoulder muscles, Hawkes told the major, "I've been having these dreams for some days now. And, to anticipate you—no, I'm not normally known as a man who has nightmares. But yes, I do think I have an answer."

Hitting the wrong nerve, a sensitive spot below his shoulder blade, the prime minister cried out. Major Truman moved behind him at that point, shoving his hand gently aside. "I'll do this," she told him. "You keep talking."

"Thank you," said Hawkes. Then, consciously willing himself to relax so the major could work on his cramped muscle, he said, "A few days ago I was at an art show—all Martian art—electro-screen work, flicker-vids. One piece in particular attracted me like none of the others. I didn't think much of it at the time, but I've been seeing bits and pieces of it in my dreams ever since."

"And you think someone did a fidget with it? Sublim-tinker?" When Hawkes tried to turn and stare at the major, she turned his head back, reminding him, "I've been doing security work for quite a while now. Tinking vid-screens hasn't been very practical for years. Too easy to spot. I'm certain the gallery would have been swept before the show. Routine these days."

"But," Hawkes responded, inspiration filtering through his voice, "what if this is something new? You're talking about subliminal message countering—stopping general wave patterns from reaching innocent mass targets. But what if this vid wasn't tinkered to affect the masses? What if it had a specific target?"

"That's a lot of work—hundreds of concentrated hours—just on the *slight* off chance of having it pay off? You're talking real dedication on someone's part."

" 'Diligence is the mother of good luck,' " quoted Hawkes, " 'and God gives all things to industry.' "

"Benjamin Franklin . . . and I still say that for anyone to go to such lengths is stretching things a bit thin."

"Oh, you mean that people don't do things like that?"

"Not often," answered Truman.

"Yes, I suppose you're right. That would be almost as foolish as stealing a piece of top-secret military equipment and taking it to a man who is targeted by the government for assassination—and then trying to get it off-planet while you help him try and avert an interplanetary war."

The major did not respond for a long moment. When her hands stopped working on Hawkes's shoulder, he moved his arm to see if the kink in his muscle had disappeared, turning to face the woman behind him at the same time. When he did, he found her face almost embarrassingly close to his.

Speaking in a softer tone than before, she told him, "You know, if we're right about all of this, it's possible that when we reach Skyhook Station there'll be troops waiting for us."

"Cheery thought," Hawkes answered sarcastically.

"I was just thinking, since these could be our last moments . . . as free patriots . . . perhaps we should . . . *relax* a little."

The prime minister looked on with appreciation as the major let her uniform blouse fall off her shoulders. Grateful for the chance to "relax a little," Hawkes reached forward and took the woman's hand, drawing her to him.

Then their lips met, and for a while, Mars was forgotten. For a while.

KEEP MOVING, PLEASE. Many wait to follow you. Keep moving, please. Keep moving . . ."

The automatic voice continued urging the crowd forward. Hawkes and Truman, working to stay anonymous within the center of the herd identity, moved as those around them moved, putting genuine effort into maintaining a drab uniformity with the trudging swarm. The pair had managed to disembark from their Skyhook berth, as well as ride out the entirety of their connecting shuttle flight from the stationary satellite's docks, without being noticed.

Since most all of the prime minister's fellow passengers were as exhausted as he and his companion from the ascension up the great elevator, it was no real problem for them to remain unrecognized on the short trip to the Moon. All they had to do was surrender to the honest fatigue eating away at them and let the indifference of those around them do the rest. Their arrival at Lunar City posed new problems, though.

Hawkes had secured both their Moon shuttle and their Skyhook tickets while still on Earth. Passage off the Moon could not be booked anywhere, however, except in Lunar City. That meant repeated possibilities for exposure—making their way to the exit ports, booking passage, then finding a place to stay and surviving unnoticed until whatever flight they eventually found was ready to leave. Depending on the current cycle of the planets, as well as the type of ship they could find, that waiting time could be anything from an hour up to several months.

"Them's the breaks," Truman had offered lightly. Hawkes had answered her with a polite smile. Anything beyond that, like speculating on things he could not control, struck him as pointless.

Exiting from the windowless shuttle terminal, the pair came into a long tunnel area lined with observation ports well shielded from above. For protection against the fierce meteor showers that plagued the atmosphereless Moon on occasion, most of Lunar City was built underground. It had been decided somewhere along the line, however, to risk dedicating that one heavily reinforced stretch of tunnel to the task of giving new arrivals a taste of the lunar surface. Truman readily understood why.

"Lord, but it's magnificent out there," she whispered. As the sliding sidewalk moved the pair forward, the major's eyes stayed riveted to the passing windows, taking in every aspect of the silent gray landscape beyond.

"Yes, quite true, I suppose," answered Hawkes. "If you're big on vacant desolation. In the meantime, let's not get too carried away. You've seen all this before, so let's keep to our objective, shall we?"

"I'm happy to keep to our objective," the major answered with a touch of a snarl, "but you could let me take a peek. I don't know where you get your information, but you're the only one in this party that's been on the Moon before." Hawkes's eyes narrowed as he turned toward his companion.

"You said you were checked out on deep-space missions," the prime minister said. "How does someone do that without coming through here?"

"Our ships left directly from the Skyhook docks. We blasted straight out into the Deep Dark. The Air Force pays people to work, not to pretend to be tourists."

"Um-humm, that's interesting." Hawkes pulled in a deep breath, tucking away the new bit of information while he reworked their next move out in his head. He had thought Truman familiar with the Moon, had assumed her acquainted with how operations worked there. In some ways he had been counting on it. Of course, he had been in Lunar City several times himself, but the circumstances had been somewhat different.

Yeah, just a little bit, he thought. Both ambassador and prime minister Hawkes carried a lot more weight than fugitive Hawkes. But still, this shouldn't make that much of a difference. We just need to find someone headed for Mars—someone who doesn't ask many questions.

Hawkes shoved such hyperbole from his head, reminding himself that "fugitive Hawkes" was still a bit of an exaggeration. No one was searching for him—him or his companion, for that matter. Not on the Moon, anyway. Not yet. There were people searching for the major back on Earth, but they were dragging the ocean, not checking airports.

Who says so?

Hawkes considered the brief thought as it flashed through his head, then decided perhaps he should give it the attention it deserved. The prime minister had learned decades earlier to question himself every time he felt complacency setting in. He had seen overconfidence topple far too many powerful people—had counted on it in his enemies too many times—not to give it the respect it deserved.

Telling Truman to enjoy the lunar landscape view for a moment, he pulled Stine's Iden card from a pocket in his weathered leather vest. Walking to the nearest prompt box, he slid the slender metal rectangle into the proper slot, waited for the acceptance click, and then indexed the menu for the latest news from Earth—headlines first. In less than two minutes he returned to the major's side.

"Let's go."

"What is it?" asked Truman as Hawkes grabbed her by the arm, moving her along forcibly. "What's happened?"

Marching as quickly as he dared, trying to get himself and the major out of the open without attracting too much attention, the prime minister answered her in a harsh whisper.

"You're not as dead as you thought you were."

"What?"

"Somehow the Air Force has determined you and the X-AC-7 aren't under the briny Pacific after all."

"Already? How? I mean, what did it—" The prime minister cut the flustered woman off.

"I don't know," he told her. "Once I tapped that particular headline, I called for any relevant broadcasts, but none of them were giving out that kind of information. Doesn't matter, though. The bottom line is, the Air Force doesn't believe you're dead. They think their rig is in one piece and that you have it. Oh, and on top of that, there's a reward for your capture."

Hawkes stopped to take a breath. Then, reeling in the panic he could feel trying to take control of him, he repelled it with indifference, telling the major flippantly, "So, I guess it's welcome to the Price on Our Heads Club."

Truman stopped walking, seemingly staring back toward the area of the tunnel where the observation ports lined the walls. She was not, though. Hawkes could see in the woman's eyes that she was lost in thought—in his opinion, a dangerous landscape to be wandering at that moment. Drawing close, he whispered in her ear, "Time for daydreaming later. Right now I suggest we get out of sight and start planning how we're going to get out of here altogether."

"Could I have a moment, please?"

The prime minister felt a cold wave of frustration flash through his body. Years of diplomatic interaction kept it from showing on his face or in his voice, however. Lightly, his tone as pleasant as

that of a waiter trying to coax a difficult patron up to a more expen-
sive choice, he said, "No, if you don't mind, we really should—"

"Damn you!" snapped the major. "I just lost my whole life." Not
reckless enough to be foolishly loud, she hissed her words under
her breath.

"I knew it was coming—okay? I'm not an idiot. But now that it's
here, it's a bit of a shock. I wanted to do the right thing . . . I
just . . ."

"Now listen, Liz—please." Hawkes slid his forefinger under Truman's chin, tilting her head upward. There were no tears in her
eyes, but he could hear them in her voice, knew he only had seconds to head them off.

"I know these aren't the words to cheer you up—but you're right.
You did throw your life away. Your *old* life. Everything of your
past—your home, parents—it's all cut off for now. For *now*. Later,
maybe you'll be able to get some of it back. But first you're going to
have to live long enough to get the chance to find out what you can
salvage."

Truman remained silent, but nodded her head. She began moving again, still shouldering the canvas bag housing the stolen flight
rig. Somehow it seemed heavier than it had before. She knew
Hawkes was right, knew that nothing attracted attention like a crying woman. Knew as a soldier that for anything else to matter she
had to survive first. As they walked, though, she took a long look at
Hawkes from the corner of her eye.

Studying his face, she remembered their previous meeting, a
handful of seconds engineered by her so she could tell him how impressed she was with him. They had come together at that past moment because he had thrown away his life to do the right thing. She
had made the opportunity to talk to him happen because at the

time, it seemed his career, perhaps even his life, was forfeit, and she wanted him to know that at least some people cared—respected him for what he had done.

Now, she had done the same.

All around the pair, the tunnel began to narrow as it arched downward. The dull plas-metal slidewalk had begun to dip sharply, descending into the lunar underground. The pleasant airiness of the observation stretch, with its brightly colored tourist amusements and potted tree–lined restaurants, quickly disappeared from view, replaced by simple but functional gray concrete and burnished girders.

Everything changes, thought Truman as the slate-hued grimness enveloped them. Just that quickly.

Turning her head slightly, she looked over her shoulder, watching the lights from above recede behind them. As they neared the bottom, she nodded her head, her lips drawing into a straight line at the same time. Then the pair reached the point where the slidewalk came to an end. Hawkes stepped off, heading in the direction of the fewest lights and thinnest crowds. The major followed him without hesitation.

I did the right thing, she told herself. I know I did.

Suddenly the canvas bag on her shoulder no longer seemed so heavy.

THIS HAD BETTER be important."

Gladys Beckett dragged herself to the edge of her bed. For a tiny moment she had not been able to actually believe that her comm system was calling her. She had tried to tell herself it was an evil dream, a mistake, a malfunction, a conspiracy, anything other than something she had to deal with in the middle of the night. Finally, however, she had forced her eyes open. She was not happy to do so.

"Goddamned important," she growled bitterly.

As chief of office operations for the Senate majority leader Beckett worked long days. Six days a week—minimum—she spent at least ten hours toiling for the greater glory of the United States Senate, the Earth League, and ultimately her boss, Michael Carri. Many days she worked far longer.

That was why once she had left the office—once all the fires had been put out or at least securely contained—she liked to be able to think of the rest of the meager handful of minutes allotted her each day as her own.

Thus she did not like intrusions into her private life. And especially not at two o'clock in the morning. Fumbling into her robe, she cursed the Knockdown she had taken before she went to bed, cursed her job, cursed the communications industry in general and whoever was leaning on her comm line in particular. Pushing her hair out of her eyes, she tabbed the monitor on her nightstand to life. Seeing a face she did not recognize, she reined in her true feelings and simply muttered, "Who are you, and what do you want?"

"Colonel Raymond Thomas, sir," answered the face on her screen. "One of my subordinates has brought something to my attention . . . ma'am . . ."

"Something," asked Beckett as her eyes grazed her clock once more, "that couldn't have waited a few more hours?"

"I don't believe so, ma'am," answered the colonel. "That is, not if your boss is interested in what Benton Hawkes might be doing right now."

Beckett snapped awake. Adrenaline splashed into her system instantly. Anger was slapped away by gratitude, personal feelings washed away by duty. Snapping on her comm's recorder and scrambler with one motion, her face rearranged itself instantly, drowsy hostility shattered by attentive warmth. Blinking the last sleep out of her eyes, she stared at the round military face on her screen and crossed her fingers.

"He just might be, Colonel. It's possible he just might be interested at that."

● ● ● FORTY-SEVEN MINUTES later, Gladys Beckett and Colonel Thomas were at the home of Michael Carri. While the colonel waited in the foyer, the majority leader's chief of operations conferred with her boss in the privacy of his study.

"And you think this is a level sale?"

Carri stood in his pajamas and robe, slippers on his feet. Usually, the senator was not one to be seen with even a hair out of place, giving Beckett great cause to smirk at her boss's present appearance. His hair was rumpled, his face still dull from lack of sleep, and he needed a shave; it was not a state she saw him in often. Not allowing her amusement to show, however, she answered him in the positive.

"Oh, yes—I think he's got something, sir," said the woman, the gleam in her eye cueing Carri that she thought it was a great deal more than a simple "something." Crossing the room, Beckett wet her fingers, then ran them through her boss's hair, smoothing it. She straightened the lapels on his robe, adjusting the collar of his pajamas as well.

Carri stood for the grooming, welcoming it. Reaching within himself, he stirred his resources, forcing himself awake. In an age of intense electronic spying and sabotage, he knew that there were numerous situations that called for people to forgo the comm for face-to-face meetings. He also knew there were few things that would prompt Beckett to wake him in the middle of the night.

"It's Hawkes, isn't it? What the hell would some low-level bird colonel have on Hawkes?"

"Why don't we let him present his material, sir?"

His eyes suddenly gleaming, Carri answered, "Get him in here."

Sliding open the study's hideaway doors, Beckett summoned Colonel Thomas. Within seconds, the military man was outlining what he had discovered.

"Mr. Senator," started the colonel, "I'm part of the detail assigned to recovery of the Air Force's new developmental assault carrier. That's the AC series, the X AC 7 to be exact. It went missing some—"

"Yes," answered Carri, "I've read the reports. Experimental flight rig, went down over the Pacific. Correct?"

"No, sir. That's what we were initially led to believe, but we no longer feel that is the case."

Carri's impatience growled within him. But he knew Beckett would not have allowed him to be disturbed for anything that was not vital, and he was politician enough to keep himself in check.

Thomas outlined how they had recovered the distress beacon the major had ejected from the flight rig, as well as the delayed timer she had used to buy herself extra time. Carri had known of this. The X-AC-7 had been labeled stolen earlier that day. What further the colonel had discovered, however, Carri had not known.

"I was searching the major's past for some lead as to why she might have done what she did. Family, friends, past assignments, hints of money problems, the usual. At the same time, some of our people discovered radiant trail readings cutting across the Pacific Northwest. Nothing definite, but it helped me narrow things down. Approximately a year ago, Major Truman was part of a detail assigned to deliver then ambassador Benton Hawkes home from Australia . . ."

"I knew it!" shouted Carri. "Previous contact, and traces of the stolen top-secret equipment found headed toward that bastard's ranch . . . I knew it was Hawkes, it had to be!"

"Sir," reminded Beckett, "this is still a bit thin. I mean, as convenient as it would be for us to find that Mars was engaging in interplanetary espionage . . ."

"No, no, Gladys," answered Carri warmly. "I won't be jumping any guns too quickly." Extending his hand to Thomas, the majority leader told him, "Fine work, son. And correct you were to come to us right away. Why don't you have a seat? I think we're going to need you to start a few balls rolling in a minute."

Sitting back, Carri smiled. Everything had been so easily laid out before. Get Hawkes to sign the treaty, maneuver his own people to kill him, then use that to justify breaking up the new government on Mars once and for all. Simple. Neat. But too easy. Too boring.

. As far as the majority leader was concerned, Hawkes needed to sweat. Bad. He needed to run scared—to dodge death by inches, but to never escape its reach. Carri wanted his old antagonist to feel the hand of fear clawing its way through the skin and muscle of his abdomen, all the way into the depths of his guts. He needed to know the kind of pain Mick Carri wanted him to know. The pain of loss, of humiliation. And especially of defeat.

No bullet in the head after another one of your puking moral triumphs. Not for you, Benton. Not this time. You need to know that someone's pulling the trigger—and you need to know it's me.

"Gladys," said the senator warmly, "why don't you get us a round of cognacs—I feel a toast coming on. And then, why don't you buzz the Hawkes ranch, and let's talk to our old friend. If he's there."

● ● ● "I'M NOT, AH, certain, that I can locate the prime minister at this time, Ms. Beckett."

Martel stared at her comm screen, at the steel-smooth face staring at her, demanding to be able to put through a line from Michael Carri to Hawkes.

They know something, thought the prime minister's aide. But how? And what? And how much? They weren't supposed to be after him for days yet.

"Ms. Martel," answered Beckett, "I'm not certain I see the problem. Mr. Carri needs to talk with the prime minister now. This is of vital security interest to both Mars and the Earth. I would think you'd move heaven and all the stars to find him, not just hem and haw like a schoolgirl."

"Ms. Beckett, I've dispatched the ranch foreman as well as the head of security here to find him. The prime minister *is* on holiday now. Since he's not in his quarters, our suspicions are that he's gone for an evening ride. If he took a bedroll with him, we might not see him until morning. Maybe not for days."

"Under normal circumstances, of course," answered Beckett.

"But I would assume that if he's out riding in the mountains, in the dark, your security chief could find him simply by consulting the ranch's motion battery. Six, eight hundred pounds of man and horse . . . I'm certain he'll show up."

"If you could just tell me the nature of this emergency, Ms. Beckett, I'm sure—"

"We've gone around in this circle three times, Ms. Martel," answered the majority leader's operations chief. "It's almost as if you don't want us to speak to the prime minister. You seem flustered, Ms. Martel, worried. Is something wrong? Has something happened to the prime minister?"

"Nothing is wrong," snapped Martel, instantly knowing she had spoken too loudly, too defensively. And as understanding filled the woman's face, Mick Carri moved into view on her comm screen.

"Good morning, Ms. Martel. I hope we haven't inconvenienced you too greatly."

"Senator," answered Martel, bracing herself for an even worse haranguing. "As I was trying to tell your assistant . . ."

"Ssshhhhhhh," said Carri, putting a finger to his lips. "It's all right, my dear."

"But Senator Carri . . ."

"No, no, you can stop now, " said the majority leader. A brandy snifter in his hand, he smiled warmly. "No need to embarrass yourself. Or to incriminate yourself. We know Benton is on his way to Mars with Major Truman. We just needed your confirmation."

"But, sir . . ."

"Now, no more lies. You've done your job, you tried. Now I suggest you all just sit back and herd cattle, or grow corn, or just do whatever it is you do out there."

Carri held in the laughter he wanted to let loose. He wanted to leap upward, to dance on his desktop, to scream from the rooftops that finally, *finally,* Benton Hawkes was going to pay—fully and completely and for the rest of his life. Containing himself, however, he added simply, "Now, I doubt Benton is carrying any receiving equipment powerful enough to break atmosphere, but please, feel free to send him a message. We have a blanket ring of listeners positioned—just waiting to listen in."

"Senator Carri, you don't understand," answered Martel desperately. "You have to listen . . ."

As the woman pleaded, the comm screen went blank before her. She did not bother to try to reestablish the connection. She knew Mick Carri well enough to know that she would not get through. Folding her hands, she closed her eyes and whispered a small prayer. It was a tiny gesture, but it was all she could do for the prime minister at that point.

From that moment on, Benton Hawkes was on his own.

S O, THAT SETTLES it—right?" asked the prime minister, fingering the prop cane by his side.

"Yes, sir, Mr. Stine. Ol' Scout can get you to Mars."

Hawkes nodded, smiling cheerfully, pretending to believe every word offered by the unkempt man across the table from him. Scratching at his soiled uniform, unshaven, his hair greasy and stringy, he was not the kind of pilot who inspired confidence within his passengers. But it had been three days since the prime minister and Major Truman had arrived on the Moon and the beginning of desperation was forcing their hand.

"So," asked Hawkes as nonchalantly as possible, "not to hurry you or anything, but when do you think we could leave?"

Somehow, Carri and the League had learned not only that the major was alive, but that she had reached the prime minister as well. Hawkes could not contact his home, had no idea what had actually happened. The news services said that no formal charges had been made. No matter what the government-owned spin on the story was, however, the prime minister knew the League would be looking for him as well as Truman. And it was also more than obvious where they would be looking.

"As you must know, getting to Mars from the Moon—it's not like catching the crosstown floater."

"Yes, of course," replied the prime minister easily. He was not boiling just below the surface, masking over anxiety. That was for amateurs. True, there was a small box in the back of his mind where he had locked away his fear and tension. He could feel them both—could hear their suggestions buzzing in his brain. But they were safely contained where they could not leak into the atmosphere, possibly tipping off the pilot that Hawkes might have some ulterior motive beyond those he had already admitted to.

"Once you start deviating from the standard Hofmann transfer orbits, you just play havoc with the payload-to-fuel ratios." Hawkes had worked the man carefully, first pushing a story about wanting to get to his dying son's side, then finally coughing up the truth.

"I know, that's why the next regular Mars run isn't for over a month. But with this revolution going on, a shrewd man can making a killing if he can get to the right people in time. It's going to be like the Wild West up there, Scout."

Hawkes picked up his drink, hoisting it to just in front of his lips as he added, "You ought to think of getting in on some of it yourself."

"Oh—but, sir," answered the pilot with a wicked tone, "isn't that against the law?"

"Why, yes," admitted Hawkes. "About as illegal as piloting unscheduled flights to Mars."

Both men chuckled, clinked their glasses together, and then drank deeply. Wiping his mouth with the cuff of his flight suit, Scout admitted, "Ah, right you are, right you are. But as to that matter, I thank you, but those high-run games aren't for a Jim like me. Stick to what you know, me dad always said. No offense, sir, but I think I'll take the ol' man's advice on this one."

"If more people listened to their fathers' advice," Hawkes told him, "it might be a better solar system. But since I have people to answer to, I do have to ask for your best rough estimates. When do you think we can get a flight out of here? And more importantly, when will it get us to Mars?"

The pilot bit lightly at his lower lip, pulling the skin tight. He worried it for a moment longer, then answered, "To be honest, I'd have to go do some math, see where my crew is . . . We wasn't expecting to be shipping out quite so quick. But if any of them has lined up some offset cargo that . . . I mean, enough to compensate . . ."

Hawkes put a finger to his lips. "No trade secrets. You do what you have to. We can meet here again at . . . ?"

"Tell you what," answered Scout, acting as if he had just had a stroke of genius. "You sit tight right here. Let me see if I can trace down my second. I might have some kind of answer in just a minute. Whaddya think—can you wait?"

"For the best drinking partner a man could find in all of Lunar City? I wouldn't dream of moving."

The pilot laughed, tossed off the rest of his drink, and then moved over to the wall that housed the restaurant's communications bank. As he did, Major Truman moved from her place at the bar to take his seat, asking as she sat, "Getting anywhere with this one?"

"He'll take us to Mars, for an outrageous price of course."

"Of course," agreed the major.

"Yes. And also if he can line up some other illegal cargo of one sort or the other."

"What kind?"

"I didn't ask," answered the prime minister, his eyes studying Scout's back as the man talked animatedly into the wall unit he had chosen. "I'm not certain I like this setup all of a sudden."

"It'll get us to Mars, won't it?" asked Truman.

"Maybe, maybe not. Our friend might be playing up the criminal side of his act because he thinks he has to appear dishonest to put a dishonest client at ease. But when dealing with people like him,

I'm always reminded of what Teddy Roosevelt said about working with crooks. 'A man who will steal *for* me will steal *from* me.' "

Scout turned and looked at Hawkes. The prime minister hoisted his drink and saluted the pilot, suddenly finding he was having a harder time keeping his smile in place. Distrust was flooding him, pouring through his system. Without warning, fear had escaped the box he had stuffed it into earlier and was now running through the halls of his mind, throwing all the panic switches it could find. Setting his drink down abruptly, the prime minister told the major, "Let's go."

"What? But what about—"

But Hawkes was already up and out of his seat, halfway to the door. Truman began to follow him, when suddenly Scout abandoned the communications wall, hurrying after the prime minister. He caught up to him at the door.

"Okay, let's not have any trouble, Mr. Hawkes." The prime minister sighed. Changing his eye color and hair color, wearing clothing like nothing he had ever been photographed in, walking with a cane—all of it useless, a ruse seen through by the first cheap grifter he tried to hustle. Looking down, Hawkes was shocked to see a tiny, two-burst needler in the pilot's hand. The Moon's antiweapons regulations were so severe that the sight left the prime minister clearly startled.

You're losing your touch, Benton, he told himself. Sagging his shoulders, he assumed the posture of a man who had surrendered. He gave the effect a moment to register in Scout's mind, then drove his elbow into his would-be captor's throat, grabbing the man's wrist at the same time. The pilot's finger tightened on the trigger of his weapon instantly. Hawkes turned the needler just as the first dozen tines erupted from the barrel, driving themselves into the communications panel.

A shower of sizzling blue and gold sparks flashed up the wall, followed by thick plumes of purple-tinged smoke. Flames erupted next, as well as bursts of current which scorched the wall around the ruined communications panel until the automatic dampers finally cut in. By that time Hawkes and Truman had reached the tunnelway outside the restaurant. But, surrounded by the other patrons fleeing the turmoil, they were spotted by the crewmen Scout had called from his panel.

"There—get 'em!"

The prime minister pulled his captured weapon around, firing at the center of the cluster of men moving toward him and the major. The compact needler released its second round, driving tines into two of the approaching quartet. All around them people screamed and ran. Defense sirens sounded, filling the tunnel with their numbing screech.

Hawkes wasted valuable time wiping the needler clean before dropping it. The Lunar City peace officers would be on the scene in seconds. To be caught with a weapon was an offense from which even his diplomatic immunity might not protect him—if he even still possessed it.

One of Scout's men who had not been hit closed with Hawkes during the brief instant. The prime minister swung his prop cane up above his head, threatening to use it as a club. The smuggler, a monster of a man standing a good ten inches taller than Hawkes, did not seem to be impressed.

"Big reward for you—Mars boy," he sneered, flexing his fingers in a threatening manner.

Hawkes swung his cane wildly at his opponent's head. The thug bent low, dodging the blow with ease. Unfortunately for him, the prime minister was not targeting his skull. Wanting the man to duck, Hawkes looped the cane back and then brought it in along the ground, snagging his opponent's ankle. A sharp pull left the attacker on his back, stunned and bleeding.

Across the tunnel, Truman was facing off with the three others. Thinking their larger companion could handle Hawkes, the last remaining unwounded thug and his bleeding companions had taken after the major.

"We just want to turn ya in for the reward, sweetie." Slipping a length of conduit piping from his jacket, the smuggler brandished it menacingly. "We don't need to mess ya. That's up to you."

"Oh," responded the major. Dropping her defensive pose, she hesitated convincingly, answering, "Ummmm, I understand. I mean . . . in that case . . ."

And then, sensing she had put them off their guard as far as possible, Truman shifted her weight onto her left heel. Pulling her right leg up at the same time, she shot it out at waist level, driving it several inches into the midsection of her central attacker. Plucking the pipe from his hand as he fell past her, she swung it with all her might, slamming it against the side of the next-closest assailant's head.

"Fuckin' bitch!"

The last man managed to grab the major from behind, catching her in a fearsome stranglehold. Pulling her body against his—needler tines still piercing his muscles—only aggravated his wounds, but he did not care. Directing his anger at Truman, he exerted greater and greater pressure, doing his best to kill her then and there.

"Die, you bitch," he snarled. Blood surging up around his wounds, he growled against the pain. *"Die!"*

The major groped weakly for a hold she might use against her attacker, but his rage had motivated him too well. He had her too tightly, too securely—and then his fingers released so suddenly that both Truman and the thug fell to the ground in a tangle. From the amount of blood sluicing out of the man's skull, it was obvious only one of them would be getting back up. The major looked up to see Hawkes standing over them, his prop cane shattered.

"Thanks," she offered in a gravelly whisper, all the voice she could manage. Pulling her roughly to her feet, Hawkes merely nodded and then started them running from the area. Truman got going as best she could, quickly regaining her strength. The pair managed to clear the area seconds before the lunar police reached the scene—an arrival that automatically closed down one hundred meters of the tunnel in each direction from the restaurant.

Having escaped for the moment meant nothing, however. Hawkes kept their pace up, pushing himself and the major as hard as he could—trying to cover as much ground as possible without attracting too much attention. As bad as things had been before, he knew they had just gotten infinitely worse.

By trying to hire Scout with his Stine Iden, the prime minister had just ruined that cover identity. He would have to use the old Iden card within the next few minutes to get as much hard bank as he could before the smuggler was questioned and the faux identity was nulled. Their Stine-secured quarters would also have to be cleared out—fast. Hawkes knew it was only a matter of perhaps half an hour at best before everyone with access to a news comm would know that he and the major were on the Moon.

Which means every two-bit piece of crap like Scout and his

trained monkey act will be searching for us, thought Hawkes. And after the mess we left back there, most likely they'll be ready to kill us without hesitation.

The prime minister slowed their pace by half. They had reached a proper residential section of the city where running at any pace would draw curious eyes. Moving along crisply, his eyes scanned Truman for any evidence of bruises others might spot. As he did so, however, anger began to boil deep within him, slamming out in all directions, growling for blood.

Another quick glance showed him that dark purple blotches were already beginning to form around his companion's throat. Turning away, watching the tunnelway ahead of him, Hawkes placed the lightest of pressure against the violence he could feel growing within him. He was not trying to dispel it; he only wanted to keep it simmering.

Why is it, he wondered, that every damn time I try to reach Mars, someone gets it into their feeble little brain to get rid of me? Well, all right, you bastards, you want to kill me—fine. Come on . . . try it.

Eyes narrowing, teeth closing hard, breath heating, Hawkes kept walking—the fingers of one hand clenching and unclenching with every step.

Please try. For once, I feel like killing someone myself.

EXCUSE ME, SIR, who did you say you were?"

"Benton Hawkes, prime minister of Mars. I'd like to see the administrator if it's not too much trouble."

"Ah, I don't . . . Let me see what his schedule is like today—now, I mean . . ."

"Of course," answered Hawkes casually. "Take your time. He's not expecting me. I just happened to be in the area and thought I'd drop in. Professional courtesy and all. You know."

The prime minister smiled at the middle-aged Asian woman, trying to put her at ease enough so she could announce him to her superior, but not enough to allow her to think he could be put off. He understood her difficulty in making a decision. Unofficially, Hawkes was a wanted man. Officially, however, he was an honored dignitary. If she announced him to her boss, the main administrator of Lunar City, she would be officially opening formal channels between Mars and the Moon—involving the administrator in the prime minister's affairs.

All in all, thought Hawkes, something the man probably wouldn't want done. Unfortunately, I can't be concerned with other people's worries right now.

"I wouldn't want to tell you how to do your job, of course," said the prime minister, concentrating intently on the woman. His voice dropping a single notch down from the jolly tone he had used to announce himself, he suggested, "But don't you think the easiest thing to do would be to just buzz him and tell him I'm here?"

The aide looked up, her eyes locking with Hawkes's. He could tell from her expression she had already finished sorting through the better lies she kept in her mental file for driving away undesirables. Before she could deploy her top choice, however, the prime minister struck first.

"I do hope he can make time for me," he said. The words alone would have been those of a hopeful beggar, but Hawkes had wrapped them in a tone easily recognized by the main assistant of any politician. Holding her breath, the woman waited for the threat she knew would follow. Hawkes obliged her, adding in a relaxed voice, "After all, I'd hate to see Lunar City deprived of its food barges for the next quarter."

"Excuse me, sir?" The woman was losing ground, rapidly falling out of her element. Trying to give her more of an excuse to pull out of the race altogether, Hawkes pushed at her harder.

"Oh, you know," he added smoothly. "I'm here on the Moon, just trying to get back to Mars—not bothering anyone—and you've got people running around trying to kill me. I thought it best I come here and get it straightened out right away. After all, any place that allowed one of Mars' elected officials to be murdered by street vermin . . . well, I don't know . . . There's already talk of cutting off Earth's food supply. I'd hate to see such a brutal policy get extended to Lunar City as well."

"Yes," a new voice interrupted, a velvet sound laced with only the briefest hint of doubt. "I'm certain it would break your heart." As Hawkes turned, an older Asian man with close-cropped black hair came forward, introducing himself. "I am Chon Zheng Lin, head administrator of Lunar City. Why don't you stop threatening my poor assistant and come inside to harass me for a while with your genocidal threats?"

"Why, Mr. Lin," said the prime minister with no trace of sarcasm, "what a kind offer."

Stepping around the assistant's desk, the prime minister followed the administrator into his office. Lin disposed of the usual amenities as quickly as possible. Then, once both men were seated, each with a saucerless cup of a hot beverage close enough in consistency to green tea to actually be tea, the administrator got the ball rolling.

"I am a very busy man, Mr. Hawkes. I do not believe Mars has any intention of allowing the twelve-point-three million people here to starve to death. I also do not wish to test this belief, however. Not this early in our relationship."

Hawkes nodded politely but without signaling any kind of commitment while Lin took a sip from his cup. Then, still holding the delicate, thin-walled ceramic between thumb and forefinger, the administrator added, "Although I like to trust my judgment and, like most Chinese, I do enjoy gambling, I would not like to gamble with that many lives. All this noted, would you like to tell me what it is you want?"

"Certainly." Hawkes lifted his own cup and took a sip. The tea was ferociously strong, leaving a bitter aftertaste. It was nothing the prime minister could not handle, however. Peoples from every corner of the Earth had been feeding him outlandish dishes for decades, looking to see how much the outsider could take. He doubted the Moon held any surprises for him.

"I want to get to Mars." Hawkes paused to admire the cup's simple but elegant pattern before he set it back down. "I want to make it a decent place for people to work and live. I wouldn't mind doing the same for Earth. But, one planet at a time. What do I want? I want people to stop shooting at me. I want to retire to my ranch and be left alone. I want to get through the nightmare I see brewing on the horizon without having an interplanetary war start."

"You want many things, Mr. Hawkes."

"All men want many things, Mr. Lin. I just happen to have a list ready." The administrator made no acknowledgment of the prime minister's statement, taking another short sip of tea instead. Finally, however, he set his cup down and stared at Hawkes, his look much like that of a school principal wondering how to keep the upper hand with a particularly unruly student.

"Why don't you give me a more immediate list, Mr. Hawkes? One complete with whatever number of things you mean to extort from Lunar City—whatever it is we need to provide you so that you don't feel it necessary to starve us into submission."

The prime minister regarded Lin coldly. It was readily obvious that the administrator had no intention of playing games with him. There was an undercurrent to the man's attitude, however, one Hawkes could not seem to get a handle on. Despite his words, the prime minister was certain that Lin was in no way worried about the lunar population starving. He was also certain the administrator's attitude had little to do with whether or not the arrival of the food barges could be halted.

Interesting man, thought Hawkes. I wish I could afford to like him.

The notion was one that had come to the prime minister many times in his career. Sadly, most of the finer minds he had come in contact with throughout his life had been assembled by fate as roadblocks. Knowing he had no time to waste looking for detours, though, Hawkes decided to forgo subtlety and head straight for the point.

"I need to get myself and one other person to Mars. Yesterday if possible."

"The other being Major Elizabeth Truman, the spy and traitor, I presume?"

"That's what they're labeling her today?" asked Hawkes rhetorically. "Yes, her and myself. We'll travel on anything, pay any price. All I'm asking is safe passage."

"I'm afraid, Prime Minister," answered Lin without hesitation, "that that is out of the question." Hawkes protested immediately, but was cut off.

"Please," added the administrator, "whatever arguments you might have, they are useless in this situation. The League has already made it quite clear you are to be found and held. Now that you have made a public display of coming to my offices, what choice do I have?"

"No one knows I've been here but the woman outside, and if I'm any judge of personnel, she's as loyal to you as you could ask."

"True. So, you would like me to endanger her as well as myself for your convenience. I see." Lin sat back in his chair, his hands folded gently on the desktop before him.

"Tell me why we should both do this. And please—I will be direct—I am not searching for personal gain. Although any reasonable man must admit that most likely he does have a price, I do not believe you have sufficient time available to you to discover mine. If you wish my help, I suggest you convince me there is some compelling reason for me to assist you. To risk my life. My assistant's. To jeopardize the entire stability of Lunar City . . . to aid two dangerous criminals against all reason."

Lin sipped his tea once more, then added quietly, "Please, convince me."

Hawkes did his best. As quickly as he could, he gave Lin the history of Mars since he had become involved with its destiny. He outlined what the League had done to the colony over the decades and how the revolution had tried to combat that situation. Throughout the prime minister's speech, the administrator's face remained expressionless. Whatever Lin might be thinking, he had no difficulty keeping it to himself.

"We don't have to deal with the League on their terms anymore," Hawkes offered. "Our worlds could unite, set boundaries for the entire solar system. Look at what the League has done to the Earth. The planet has never been so overpopulated or underdeveloped. The forests and jungles, even the farmland that existed just fifty years ago—most of it's been purged."

"Ah, you're going to tell me about how the near eight billion residents of the Earth live, aren't you?" asked Lin. "I'm about to receive a description of the crate houses—families living in single rooms, one stacked atop the other, ten thousand to a unit. You're going to ask me to pity them their meaningless existences, sitting and waiting for the government to feed and entertain them on a daily basis. Being a clever man, I'm certain you mean to remind me as well that while they live thusly, trapped by their own greed and fear, every citizen in Lunar City toils like a slave to make certain these precious voters can live without working."

"It had crossed my mind," admitted Hawkes.

"No doubt." Rising from his seat, Lin motioned toward the door to his outer office, telling his guest, "Walk with me."

The pair exited the chamber together. The administrator stopped at his aide's station to tell her, "I've not been here yet today. You have not seen me. You have not seen anyone."

"It's terrible when you get to be my age," answered the woman without looking up. "The things you can forget . . . and the talking to yourself. Sad, really."

Hawkes smiled. He had liked the fact that the administrator's assistant had not caved in to him earlier. Now he enjoyed her easy attitude. In some ways she reminded him of Martel—in others, his ranch's old retainer, Cook. Judging Lin by the quality of the personnel he kept around him, the prime minister allowed himself a short breath of hope. He did not think he was going to be able to win Lin over easily, but he was suddenly certain the administrator would not turn on him.

"I understand your position," Lin said as the two men moved down an empty passageway. "The Earth is both a frightening and frightened place. A toxic, imperialist charade where the rich pretend to serve the poor and the poor pretend to enjoy their lives of contained and managed freedom."

Although calm, Lin's voice was thin and cutting. Hawkes recognized the naked hate the man had for the Earth. It was the same tone that, until the very recent past, the prime minister had always reserved for Mars.

"You think that if we were to put up a united front against the League, they would finally act reasonably. If they saw all the outer points lining up against them, then surely, *surely,* they would have to come to their senses."

Hawkes listened politely, his respect for the administrator growing. He found his attention divided, however, between listening to what Lin had to say and wondering where the man was taking him. As they continued to walk, the prime minister noted that the corridor they were in had no side branches, no offices, shops, homes, or even doors leading off anywhere. It was merely a very long, white-lit corridor, extending on to some point Hawkes could not yet determine.

"It will not happen. The League does not care about anyone. The conditions under which it subjugates its peoples should make that clear. When they need workers, bodies are found. When they don't, they are pensioned and returned to their cubed little worlds. Science extended our time too quickly. In less than a hundred years they doubled normal human life expectancy . . . without giving a thought to what everyone was going to do with their extra decades."

The prime minister nodded. "Perfect breeding ground for dictators. Too many people with so little hope."

"Yes," agreed the administrator. "Which is why we now live in an age of unlimited abortion, mandatory euthanasia, extermination squads, sterilization clinics, managed war . . . The League can now use any tool it desires to prune the population. And no one will care because everyone agrees that there are too many of us. No matter what we might hope for, the League will do what it wants with Mars, Mr. Prime Minister, because it is in the position to do what it wants with everything."

Hawkes realized the corridor had a slight curve to it when he noticed the edge of a doorway coming into view farther ahead. As the two men drew closer to it, the harshness slowly dropped from Lin's voice. Easing their pace momentarily, he turned to the prime minister. Pulling a set of extremely sheer glare goggles from inside his jacket, he handed one to Hawkes.

Instructing him to put them on, the administrator slipped the other pair over his own eyes as he said, "I have something to show you, Mr. Prime Minister. It is something that has been seen by no more than a handful not born and raised on the Moon. I need you to understand what we are trying to do here . . . what it is I want for my people. And, I have decided I might trust to your discretion."

And then, before Hawkes could inquire as to why Lin felt he could trust him, or say anything at all, the administrator tabbed a stud on his wristband and the door before them slid silently open. A blast of sticky heat rolled out of the chamber beyond. Hawkes stepped in through the growing humidity, and then suddenly found himself unable to move.

HE VIEW IS better if you move all the way to the rail."

Hawkes barely heard Lin's words. Staring forward, the prime minister found himself facing an enormous cavern, a crystalline hollow measuring miles across, receding farther away than he could calculate. Massive arrays of solar relays had been installed throughout the gigantic hollow. Their light reflected by the staggering fields of crystal, the effect created was that of an open field at noon on the clearest of days.

"I don't . . . I don't understand."

"This is Geode Hall, Mr. Hawkes," Lin explained softly. "The chamber was discovered decades ago. It's existence has been kept a secret from the League, from Earth, even from most of Lunar City since the beginning. Look more closely. Study what you see. Understanding will come."

Hawkes advanced slowly to the railing, his feet dragging despite the excitement growing within him. The prime minister was awed by the massive intensity of the cavern, overwhelmed by its fierce, colossal presence. Miles of glittering gemstones stretched out before him, pillars of crystal yards long stabbing up through the ground, out of the walls and the ceiling, each new place his eyes rested more dazzling than the last.

What is all this? wondered Hawkes. And why is he showing it to me? What is it I'm supposed to understand? That the Moon has the universe's largest diamond mine? That that's why he can't help us? That the fact he controls this is what makes him different than the League . . . different than Mick Carri?

Hawkes gripped the metal rail before him, stretching himself as far as he could out over the chasm below, searching for the meaning behind Lin's last words. Then, suddenly, he found it. Slowly, as his eyes continued to adjust to the brilliant conditions inside the chamber, Hawkes began to realize that not every inch of the cavern was covered in crystal.

In between the acres of brilliance he made out massive dark patches. Swaths of fruit trees, rows of crops, stands of brush and grass—from the runt scrub needed to feed livestock to towering masses of bamboo. As the prime minister's eyes darted from wonder to wonder, Lin spoke softly behind him.

"This is why Lunar City has cleaned the Skyhook for practically nothing. Every gram of dust, every piece of hair, every discarded scab, every bit of snot-smeared tissue, is gold to us. This is why we clean the ships that land here so thoroughly. This is why we will survive."

Hawkes could see dozens of workers below him, trimming, planting, harvesting, every stage of the cycle of life boiling along simultaneously. He heard the call of cattle and the grunts of pigs. Beyond their noise, he swore he could hear ducks and chickens as well.

"The total space before you comprises nearly fifty square miles—eighteen of them dug out by us. Natural sunlight collected on the surface is wired down here—magnified electronically, reflected by the crystals to every corner and terrace. Our growing season is every minute of every day, every day of the year. We feed half our people with real food, Mr. Hawkes. Before there is another administrator in my place, we will feed everyone."

The prime minister felt a wash of emotion rolling through him As he sensed his eyes beginning to mist, a part of his brain blamed the dense humidity of the chamber and the close-fitting goggles he was wearing. The part of him not so worried with appearances rejected the explanation, however, freely admitting that the sight below had moved him deeply. After a period of time he could only guess at, Hawkes finally turned back to the administrator. For the moment, all thoughts of his own fate, of his need to escape the Moon, had been shoved from his brain.

"I'm honored to know of this," he told Lin, his voice almost cracking with emotion. "Thank you for your trust."

"Thank you," answered Lin, "for not disappointing me." Removing from his pocket the small needler which he had had aimed at Hawkes's back since they first entered Geode Hall, the administrator admitted, "If you had given me any sense that you did not realize what this meant to us, you would have been recycled for fertilizer before dinner."

The prime minister nodded. He did not speak, for words would have been useless. He understood. Indeed, in Lin's position, he had no doubt he would have acted the same himself. Hawkes could also not be bothered with useless recriminations in the face of what he was still witnessing. To do so would simply have been to waste the opportunity. Until that moment, he had thought such projects to be Herculean, ridiculous dreams not worth harboring. Suddenly, however, he was filled with more than dreams of what might be done with Mars. Suddenly, he had facts.

We already have domes in place, he thought. And unlike the Moon, we've got sufficient mass to generate the gravity necessary to hold an atmosphere. What they've done here in a couple of generations, we could . . .

"Mr. Hawkes," the administrator interrupted, "as pleased as I am with your reaction, I feel it my duty to remind you that you do not have the time for reverie at the moment."

"I'm sorry. You're right, of course." Hawkes brushed at his hair, pushing the perspiration building within back away from his forehead. Taking another deep breath of the thickly humid air rushing at him, he continued, "It's just that you've suddenly given me . . . hope. Hope for so much. I mean, if you could accomplish this much, *this* much—*here*—there's no telling what we could—"

The prime minister caught hold of himself, suddenly realizing the totality of what Lin had just told him. Collaring his enthusiasm, he choked it off savagely.

"Now you understand why I can entertain no alliance with Mars," the administrator said softly. "You are a weak world, and the object of the League's wrath. They will come at you with everything they have, wasting more of their resources, their people, their time."

Backing out of the great chamber, Lin slid his goggles off with an unconscious gesture, then indexed the proper sequence to close the entrance door once more. Hawkes removed his goggles and handed them back to the man, listening to what he had to say, waiting for his judgment.

"We are too close to the future to risk it foolishly. With luck, the League will burn itself out and we will be left with a reasonable world. If we join with you, we would become naught but a buffer between you and the League, and our destiny would be one of pain and ashes only."

As the two men returned along the way they had come, the prime minister did not debate Lin. He realized any additional arguments he might try to make would be only specious or self-serving. His respect for the administrator of Lunar City had grown to the point where he could not bring himself to insult the man with useless haggling. As they neared the end of the plain-walled corridor, Hawkes extended his hand to his host. Lin did not take the offering, however.

"Another time, Mr. Hawkes. I would not want to give you the

false impression that we have become friends. Not yet, anyway. You see, I plan to use you to my own advantage."

"Oh," answered the prime minister, readying himself for anything. "How's that?"

"I will help you and your companion leave the Moon. As I stated earlier, it is in Lunar City's best interest if the League continues to focus its attention on Mars. Your escape will not bring us troubles—I have sufficient resources to keep Mr. Carri and his jackals at bay."

"Not to count a gift horse's teeth," countered Hawkes, "but all I wanted in the first place was passage out of here. You decide you're going to do that, but first you show me your greatest secret. Why not just send me on my way and be done with it? Can I ask your game, Mr. Lin?"

"One can always ask, Mr. Hawkes." Both men smiled politely. The prime minister could not begrudge the administrator his tactics. He thought he might have some idea of what Lin was up to, and he had to admit, if he was correct, he would have played things the same way himself.

Show me what's possible and send me off to do it. Bond the next guy as an ally against the future without committing yourself to him. Set Mars up as a buffer for the Moon when I tried to set you up as a buffer for us. Pretty slick, buddy.

"Go to this café," said Lin, handing Hawkes a card from his jacket. "You will eventually encounter a man named Thorner. It may take some time, but do not worry—he will find you. And, he will be able to get you to Mars."

The administrator made to return to his office then, but Hawkes touched his shoulder, pulling at him to wait.

"You wrote this card out before I ever showed up. You were expecting me."

"Of course, Mr. Prime Minister," answered Lin. Stretching his hands wide, he smiled as he said, "This is my city. Where else were you going to go?"

Hawkes's eyes narrowed. His respect suddenly doubling for the smaller, older man, he told him, "Remind me never to play cards with you. All right?"

"If that is your wish," answered Lin. Then, without a further word, the administrator returned to his office, leaving Hawkes alone in the hallway to make his own way from there on.

If he could.

WELL, THOUGHT HAWKES, casually tipping his drink back as if he were the most carefree man in Lunar City, there's no doubt they've made me. The question is, what do I do about it?

The prime minister allowed his eyes to glance at the clock on the wall of the Valkyrie Café once more. He had been in the restaurant waiting for the administrator's Mr. Thorner for over two hours. The Valkyrie was a dimly lit place in one of the scruffier sections of Lunar City, the kind of establishment where most of the clientele were actively avoiding someone. At first Hawkes had hoped that aspect of the Valkyrie might work to his advantage. For a good while, it did.

You can do one of two things, Benton. Either you keep sitting here, hoping they'll do the same. Or you leave, hoping they won't follow. Oh, and choose good—you only have the fate of the whole solar system riding on every move you make.

The part of the prime minister's brain urging him to take some kind of action spit its words caustically. Its venom did not bother him overmuch—he was too used to it. Hawkes had never been one to let anyone off easy—himself included. But as high as the stakes had been in some of the games he had wagered on in his time, none compared to those on the table at which he was currently sitting.

No, he told himself bitterly, I've never been in a tighter game than this one. I've had better hands to play, though.

After parting company with the administrator, Hawkes had made a quick call to Major Truman to let her know he still had things under control, and then proceeded to the Valkyrie as instructed. He had lingered over the meager menu, ordered his meal, and then eaten it as slowly as possible. After that he moved on to dawdling over cup after cup of some sort of coffee substitute and nibbling at a dessert square he swore was simply fried and breaded food substitute coated with icing—all the time waiting for a man named Thorner who Lin had promised would find him.

But no one named Thorner had approached him. Indeed, outside of the waiter and the busgirl, no one had approached him at all. But he had been found. The prime minister had kept as close an eye on the pair as he could without revealing he was aware of them. Close enough to see them studying a hand screen imager. Close enough to read their lips and catch the words "kill" and "reward" and "easy." Quickly reviewing his options in his head, Hawkes decided his time was running out. If he was going to make the first move, he was going to have to make it soon.

Well, he told himself, sucking down a deep breath at the same time, nothing ventured . . .

Needing to catch the two men watching him off guard with whatever move he made, he made the only one he could think of guaranteed to be unexpected. Instead of waiting for the thugs to come to him, or showing them his back, he went to them.

"So, boys—what'll it be?"

The pair kept in their seats, both somewhat stunned by Hawkes's approach. As the prime minister slid into one of the two empty chairs at their table, he took their measure quickly. One larger than him—thickly muscled—the other several inches shorter—far lighter. But slyer-looking. Nastier.

"Come on, come on, speak up. You've been staring at me for an hour. Don't be shy—out with it. You want an autograph, right? Something for the kiddies."

"What in dust are you jabbering about?" asked the smaller man. The larger said nothing, obviously waiting for cues from his partner. The fact was not lost on Hawkes.

"Look, I'm a Jim, you're a pair of Jims," the prime minister told them with a nasty wink. "We're all chums here. Buy me a drink and I'll tell you all about it."

Hawkes spread a wide smile across his face, open and disarming. At the same time, however, he stared deeply into the smaller thug's eyes, filling his own eyes with a moment of grinding hate. The sight startled the man so badly he moved his hand unconsciously toward the left side of his jacket—telling Hawkes all he needed to know.

"Made you look."

The prime minister's hand shot out, grabbing the outline of the thug's weapon through his jacket. Then, yanking hard, he shouted, "No, Roscoe, for the love of God—*don't do it!*"

Heads turned. The smaller thug flopped toward the table, squawking to his partner to stop Hawkes. His face hit the metal top harshly, two teeth splintering, one falling loose in a sluice of scarlet. Some people stared. Many instantly moved for the exit. As the larger man reached for the prime minister, Hawkes squeezed the outline of the weapon he could feel, blasting the second thug with his partner's weapon. He kept the trigger depressed until he felt the weapon empty, shouting the entire time.

"He didn't mean it, Roscoe—he didn't mean it. Don't kill him! Don't do it!" Then the prime minister backed away from the table, pointing and shouting, "Jezz-it, Roscoe, you killed him! I'm getting out of here!"

The café's two large bouncers moved forward on the smaller thug.

Hawkes scrambled away from the table, beginning a travel arc he planned to use to merge him with those heading for the outside. By the time the small man bleeding at the table could tell his story, the prime minister figured he would be long gone. Unfortunately, he figured wrong.

"Hol' it up, trik-boy." A rough hand attached to the dark voice slammed into Hawkes's shoulder, knocking him backward. He stumbled awkwardly, nearly falling. Focusing quickly, he realized he now had three new antagonists.

Bad to worse, he thought. Getting his feet solidly under him, he muttered aloud, "Just bad to goddamned worse."

"You could say that," answered the man who had struck him. Hawkes quickly took his measure. The man was younger, lighter than the prime minister, standing a good seven feet tall. His hands were large, thickly callused from years of hard labor. And if he could not stop Hawkes all on his own, he had two friends behind him who seemed capable of finishing anything he started.

"Your move, old man," said the central thug. "Hard or easy. All I want is to collect the bank for delivering you proper. We don't even have to lay hands on you if you play nice."

Can't surprise this bunch, thought Hawkes. *They're ready to pounce. Might as well give them what they expect.*

"Sorry, boys—in school I was labeled as 'does not play well with others.' "

"Up to you," answered the larger man without emotion. "Take him, me Jimmies."

The men to either side of the central thug moved forward. Less than a minute had passed since the prime minister had made his move at the other table. People were still shouting all around him, still running about—patrons looking to avoid entanglement or paying their bills, workers trying to contain the situation, struggling to even understand it.

As one confused couple stepped in between Hawkes and his attackers, the prime minister made his move. Stepping back to allow them passage, he feigned an intent to use them as a shield, then sprang forward, moving between the central thug and one of his lackeys. The two men turned, grabbing for Hawkes. He caught hold of the smaller man's wrist, wrenched it painfully, and spun the man around, slamming him against his boss.

"Nice move," said the central thug, unperturbed. Reaching out faster than the prime minister thought possible, the larger man grabbed Hawkes's arm at the elbow and squeezed, digging deeply into the nerve. The prime minister cried out, half from surprise, half from overwhelming pain. Flopping wildly against the agonizing grip, Hawkes managed to snag a large serving plate from one of the recently vacated tables nearby. He swung it around, hoping to catch the larger man in the head. The thug easily backhanded the greasy platter from the prime minister's grasp.

"I wanted to take it easy on you, old man," offered the thug with what sounded like honest sympathy. "You're supposed to be an okay Jake. But I guess some of us never learn."

"True," came a new voice. "Some of us don't."

Large splinters and bits of bracing slats bounced off Hawkes's back as the central thug's head stopped the chair they had recently been a part of. The big man's grip loosened. The prime minister pulled his hand free and then staggered backward, desperate to put some distance between himself and his attackers. As he watched, a heavyset man with a close-shaven skull and several days' growth on his face slammed into one of the other thugs, sending him flying.

Hawkes nodded with appreciation, stepping forward toward the central thug, who was just beginning to stand once more. Threading his fingers, the prime minister made one large fist of his hands and then swung them with all the strength he had left, slamming them against the larger man's head and sending him stumbling off into the nearest wall.

"Not so 'old' yet, flathead."

And then the siren drones sounded. Grabbing Hawkes by the shoulder, the newcomer said, "Kitchen. Let's move."

As the two ran for the back of the Valkyrie, the prime minister asked, "And you are . . . ?"

"Curly Thorner. I hear you want to go to Mars."

The heavy man slammed his weight against the kitchen door, bending it off its automatic track just enough to allow them to squeeze through to the other side. A number of the cooks and their assistants made to move forward on the pair, but Thorner grabbed the edge of a nearby table stacked twenty deep with dirty dishes and heaved, overturning it in their direction. Molded plastic covered with the slop of twenty score meals spilled over, sending the workers jumping to get out of the way.

"You're late," Hawkes spat, not certain whether he was grateful or annoyed with his rescuer.

"Yeah, true enough," admitted the heavy man. "But you know, better late than never. Right?"

The two men hit the back door together, passing into the hallway behind the café, crashing into a crowd of mixed passersby. They untangled themselves quickly and moved off without offering apologies, Hawkes hoping to avoid being recognized by anyone else, Thorner simply because apologies were not part of his style. The pair ran until they had rounded several corners, putting what seemed to be enough distance between themselves and the Valkyrie. Resting against opposite walls, both men panted, straining to catch their breath.

"You . . . you can," gasped Hawkes, "get me . . . and someone else . . . to Mars quickly?"

"Not all that quick," answered the man. "Only got . . . got a Yamato Special. Take a couple . . . couple extra weeks. But it'll . . . get us all there."

"Couple extra weeks?" repeated the prime minister, his heart rate calming, breathing returning to normal. Deciding annoyance was for fools, he added, "Well, as a wise man once said, better late than never. Right?"

Thorner smiled. It was a happy but somewhat delirious grin, a broken line that made his shaved head resemble a cracked egg. Stepping away from the wall he had been resting against, the heavy man shook himself, then answered, "Right. So, when you thinkin' about headin' out?"

Before Hawkes could respond, however, the noise of angry voices and hurried footsteps sounded behind them from the direction of the Valkyrie. Looking ahead in the opposite direction, the prime minister began moving again.

"How about now?" he asked.

"Good plan," answered Thorner. His eyes lighting up, he slapped himself in the face several times, shouting, "It's great. Totally great—I love it."

The two men ran, plunging deeper into the back lanes of the dingy residential area they had entered. Thorner led the way, making jokes and then laughing at them as they raced along. As they made good their escape, the prime minister could not help but wonder what kind of lunatic Lin had sent to him.

Everything about this Thorner seems so, so . . . goofy, thought Hawkes. Relaxing somewhat as he hopefully categorized his rescuer as essentially harmless, he put his energy into his running, thinking, Oh well, as the old saying goes, any port in a storm.

Which was just the impression the heavy man had been carefully laboring to make.

THERE WE GO," announced Thorner, indexing the last of the necessary automatic controls. "We're on our way. Next stop, the big red planet."

"Nice ship you have here," offered the major. Sitting back in the copilot's seat, she added, "She's small, but in decent shape. You could keep busy with a rig like this. What's her displacement?"

"Oh, you know, standard L-class weight on full speed, Q or better at half."

Truman nodded, honestly impressed. "High ratios for a Yamato, even a Special. You been tinkering?"

"Little ol' me, a humble asteroid miner, play around with spanners and dink wire?" Thorner grinned at the major, running one of his meaty hands over his close-shaven skull. "Ohhhhhh, it's a possibility."

Hawkes sat back, distancing himself from the conversation. His interest in mechanics stopped after whatever knowledge he needed to help keep the basically low-tech vehicles and machines on his ranch operational.

A man can only know so much, he thought, and right now, what I know is I'm tired. Damn tired.

Truman challenged the pilot, daring him to take her on an inspection tour of his engine room. Slapping his hands together gleefully, Thorner replied happily, "Here we are, not three hours into a three-week trip, and already this comely beauty wants to drag me down among the rings and valves and cracklin' steel. Ahhhh, this is my kind of mercy mission."

"Why's that?" asked the major with mock innocence, quickly warming to the heavyset pilot.

"You and me, wandering in and out of the bells and whistles, hoping—dreaming—daring all . . . Ya-haa, Lord have mercy."

Truman rolled her eyes with exaggerated force, but laughed nonetheless. Then she stepped back to clear a path from the control board, saying, "Okay, lead on, grease monkey. And if you get out of line, don't waste time begging the Lord for mercy."

"Ohhhhh, mama," sighed Thorner, turning to Hawkes at the same time. "Don't you just love her?" He turned away just as quickly, though, dancing for the exit from the front cabin, singing and doing a passable soft-shoe. "The steel in her eyes, the fire in her thighs, oh, how she reminds me of Granny. Sweet . . . beloved . . . Grann-an-anna-an-i-eeeeeeee!"

And then the pair exited, still joking and laughing. Hawkes sighed as the door slid shut behind them, cutting him off from the happier atmosphere they had created for themselves.

"Glad someone's in a good mood," he muttered, staring at the once again sealed door, or more specifically, at the image the ship's captain had attached to it. It was a black-and-white reproduction of a Earthly city scene, one at least a hundred and fifty years old. Its focus was a wrecked automobile with three men standing around it in ruined tuxedos. All of the trio were scratching their heads as if deeply puzzled. Each of the three had a distinctly different haircut, something the prime minister assumed was meant to be humorous.

Hawkes was certain that the image was supposed to inspire mirth. The picture fairly shouted out that anyone who knew who the three men were would be highly amused by the scene. Not knowing the trio, however, the prime minister was left with the basic image itself— confused men standing over a chaotic vision of destruction without the slightest sense of what had caused it or what to do about it.

Hoping to get in a short nap before Truman and their host returned, Hawkes closed his eyes, whispering to the trio, "Gentlemen, I know exactly how you feel."

● ● ● "YOU ALWAYS MAKE that much noise when you sleep?"

Hawkes brushed at his clothing, as if smoothing out nonexistent wrinkles might chase away his embarrassment.

"Sorry," he told Thorner. "I've been having bad dreams lately."

"Space bugs," offered the miner. Hawkes simply stared at him, not understanding his comment, not wishing to understand. Looking to change the subject, the prime minister did ask a question that had been bothering him.

"Earlier you said it was going to take three weeks for us to get to Mars. The longest it's ever taken me before is fifteen days. Why the extra time?"

"You've been pogoin' around on liners. This is an ore scout. She's a good ship, as tough and faithful as gravity, but she's built for haulin' loads, not haulin' ass. Sorry for the delay, but like they say . . ."

"Yes, I know," interrupted Hawkes. "Better late than never."

Thorner laughed, then expanded on his explanation. "Actually, the *Stooge*—that's my ship's name—she can outrun a lot of what's moving across the lanes these days. The problem is really just seasonal. Mars is outside the optimal direct trajectories right now—and movin' farther every minute. Good for us miners . . . puts the factories closer to the prime astie fields everybody's pretty much workin' these days. Lotta big loads gettin' flung down from Mumbly right now—Ganymede too. Harder gettin' there from Earth, though."

Turning back to his controls for a moment, the miner ran through the standard checklist of setting inspections merely as a matter of practical routine. While he eyed his ship's current levels, he added, "Still a lot better than the old days. First flights to Mars took almost a year—one way, mind you—and that was at peak season."

"The first flight to Mars," Hawkes reminded his host, "exploded before it got halfway. But then that didn't stop people from going, did it?"

"Hey," laughed Thorner casually. "I guess ya can't keep a determined group of chuckleheads down."

"Point taken." The prime minister went silent, not knowing what else he might add. He found Thorner to be something of an enigma. His humor was bizarre and primitive, but somewhat entertaining. Hawkes did not believe, however, that the miner was usually quite the buffoon he presented himself as.

Testing his theory, he asked, "Curly, why the jokes? Why so much nonsense all the time? You keep shoving this persona at me, but I get the sense that underneath it there's a different man lurking somewhere, masking himself away. Why?"

"You get right down to it, don't ya?" answered Thorner.

"I'm sorry," Hawkes said. "Sometimes I forget I'm not in charge everywhere I go."

"That's okay. I don't mind. I pretty much do it on purpose just to see who'll notice." The prime minister said nothing, waiting for the miner to continue. Understanding that he had been given the floor, the heavy man took it.

"Bein' an astie miner ain't easy. It's a turd-faced life where everything sluices—big-time. You'll find a lot of miners come on ding-cracked. Half of it's just that people pretty much expect miners to be shock cases—short on dampenin' rods, if you know what I mean."

"And, what's the other half?"

"You chalk-jump your way through the Deep Dark for a few years, see if you have all your bolts tight when you get back. Livin' off-world—*any* world—it ain't no picnic. You ain't turned your nose up at me yet, 'cause people can bathe on the Moon. Not here, though. You wait—we're all gonna be pretty ripe in a couple of days, then you'll get a taste of this life."

"Well, everyone has it tough these days, Curly," the prime minister answered. Not overly concerned with anyone else's problems at the moment, he hoped to pay a bit of lip service to Thorner's grievances and then steer the conversation in some other direction. The asteroid miner did not oblige him.

"You got it all figured out, don't you?" snapped Thorner. As Hawkes looked up, the miner roared, "You show me anyone outside a leper that's got it worse than an astie humper and I'll kill the bastard!"

"Really, I'm sure the prime minister didn't mean anything, Curly," offered Truman, trying to placate the large man. It did not seem to help.

"No, I'm sure he didn't. No one ever does. People complain about their lives—let 'em live in an Io box." When Hawkes and the major stared blankly, Thorner explained, "They're survival huts—about the size of a coffin. You fit it over some crack in the ground and you live under it while you survey a rock. Your mates'll be back for you in a month. What's the big deal?"

"Curly, no one's looking for an argument with you," Hawkes responded, not knowing what else to say.

"Yeah, yeah, it just makes me sore. Miners grub their way through the Belt like mealworms lookin' for the goods. You start out knowing that it's just gonna take you a few weeks, maybe a month or two, and then you're gonna lom across the big one—a hundred-tonner cast in gold, a two-mile float ball crusted with diamond. Deep in your soul—you *know* it. But months turn into years and all you end up with is a rip in yer suit and a quick death lost in the dark."

"We all gamble in this life," Truman answered, a touch put off by Thorner's sudden self-involvement.

"Yeah, we sure do. Astie miners gamble their lives—a million seconds at a shot—nobody to talk to, breathing the same regurgitated air till you want to puke, eating pills, drinking Palcher substitute, and diggin' rock till your fingers break and you hate the sound of your own voice from having talked to no one but yourself for the last year."

"Look on the bright side," the prime minister answered. "At least no one's trying to kill you."

"That's only 'cause most days none of us would try to stop them."

Hawkes made to answer, then closed his mouth. He did not know enough about the life of the asteroid miners and the men harvesting minerals from the moons of the outer worlds to argue with Thorner. Nor did he wish to argue—with the heavyset miner, or with anyone else for that matter. Sensing the shift in the prime minister's mood, Thorner turned around in his seat, his own mood altering suddenly as well.

"Look," he told his passengers, "don't get me wrong. I got nuthin' against you, or what you're tryin' to do, or Mars, or anything. In fact, it's pretty much the opposite."

"How much the opposite, Curly?" asked Hawkes, curious as to where the miner was headed.

"Administrator Lin didn't send me to you 'cause he pulled my name out of a hat. He and I got a few beams triggered at the same target. I got a lotta pull with most of the other freerunners, for whatever that's worth. We alla us'd like to line it up with someone—anyone. But . . . Mars, Lunar City, Skyhook Station, it's always the same. 'Miners smell,' 'They ain't fit human.' People just want us to drop our ore, collect our pay, spend it, and get the hell out."

Hawkes nodded absently, lost in memories brought to the front of his mind by Thorner's angry speech. He had never actually thought about the asteroid miners before as anything but scattered opportunists, motley scavengers working for themselves.

Hawkes wanted to say something to cheer up Thorner. He liked the big man, was grateful to him for saving him from the hands of the League, for volunteering to get him and the major to Mars.

Of course, a voice from the back of the prime minister's mind added, He did it because he wants to drum up some respect for asteroid miners. And he's going to keep beating that drum until we get to Mars. Every time you see a helping hand, Benton, you'd do well to remember that everyone has a plan. Everyone.

Right, he thought. Everyone but me.

And, at that moment, Hawkes suddenly realized just how long it was going to take them to reach Mars.

OH, MY LORD, but it's good to see you again, Benton. Things are just a mess here."

The speaker was Samuel Waters, onetime manager of Red Planet, Inc., the corpor/national that controlled every aspect of the Martian colony. Now, he was the freely elected president of the planet and possibly, thought Hawkes, the most grossly overworked man in the entire solar system.

"It's good to see you, Sam," offered the prime minister. "If it's any consolation, things are a mess back home too."

"It is, you know," answered Waters. "A consolation, I mean."

Hawkes surveyed the changes in his fellow administrator. Like almost all second-generation Martians, the president had always been a thin man, the skin of his face sallow and tightly drawn. Hawkes was shocked to see how those conditions had been exacerbated by public life.

Not quite forty, Waters looked perhaps twice his actual age. He appeared almost drained, his form bent and weak, his pallor practically jaundiced. The prime minister was heartened, though, as his old friend smiled and said, "I hate to admit it, but I actually find it somewhat comforting knowing there are other people with problems right now."

"Especially when it's the SOBs who gave you your problems," interjected a woman entering the spaceport meeting room. "Isn't that right, dear?"

Hawkes and Waters turned to find the president's wife, Glenia, approaching. The last time the prime minister had seen her, she had still been comfortably insulated from the rest of life by a pleasant layer of fat—practically sinful by Martian standards. He noted that she had lost quite a few of those pounds in the preceding months.

"Glenia," the prime minister told the advancing woman, "you look positively wonderful."

"Yes." She beamed, doing a short twirl to show off both her newly shaped figure and the old dress she had finally been able to slip into once more. "Trying to keep this new democracy you gifted us with has kept everyone hopping, but as you can see, it has had some side benefits." Hawkes nodded in friendly approval. He started to make a comment to that effect, but the president cut him off, snapping tersely at his wife.

"Glenia, I asked you to wait for us at the office."

"Oh, for God's sake, Sam, things aren't that bad yet. And I did bring Norman with me." A stocky, big-shouldered man older than all the others present stuck his head around the corner.

"As if I'd let this vagabond land on Mars without bein' here to check him out." Norman Scully, the colony's chief of security, entered the room, his hand extended toward Hawkes. "Welcome back, Mr. Prime Minister."

"Thanks." Hawkes's eyes were immediately drawn to the security man's pistol belt. Noting that Scully was carrying not only a revolver with the holster's cover unclipped and drawn back, but a half-dozen small rectangular leather pouches that indicated extra cartridges, Hawkes asked, "Expecting trouble?"

"Yes," answered Waters. "That's why I'm so . . . let's just say upset that Glenia didn't wait for us at the compound." The president's wife started to make a remark, but Hawkes gently interceded.

"People—please. Can't we postpone any state-level discussions until I've at least introduced my companion?"

The Waterses both fell silent, embarrassment flashing across their faces. Crossing the room to where Major Truman stood waiting, Scully extended his hand.

"You could wait forever for one of these politicians to say anything." Shaking the woman's hand briskly, the old security officer introduced himself, then said, "Welcome to Mars, Major."

"Thank you, Mr. Scully." Nodding her head, her eyes linked to his sidearm, she asked, "If you are expecting trouble, and you have another one of those . . . ?"

"Always ready to deputize a good Navy man. We'll fix ya up soon as we get back to the compound. Which, unless we have some reason to stand around here I don't know about, should be our next destination."

No one argued. Scully sent several of his men to the Stooge to secure Hawkes's and Truman's bags. At the prime minister's request, he also told them to expedite Thorner's landing clearances.

Hawkes and the oversized asteroid miner had spent a great deal of time together on the voyage to Mars, discussing ways the asteroid miners and the Martian colonists could help each other. The prime minister wanted to put Thorner and Waters together as quickly as he could to discuss some of those ideas. Also, he had grown somewhat fond of the miner, despite the large man's sometimes bizarre sense of humor, and wanted to spare him the lengthy rigors of Martian clearance processing.

As the party moved through the secure hallway, Scully dropped his casual mood. Well in advance of the moment they would reach the public area, he told the new arrivals, "I do have to caution you both, things have been in kind of an uproar around here."

Patting the weapon on his hip, the security man added, "I

haven't been runnin' around with this blunderbuss strapped to my leg for fun. Thank God I ain't had to use it, but we've got a lot of upset people here, grumblin' to everyone around them . . ."

"Which just makes more upset, grumbling people," interjected Hawkes. "Yes, I've been there before. I was a diplomat a long time, Scully, and if there's anything I know, it's that—sadly—there's nothing that throws people for a loop more than a sudden dose of freedom."

The small crowd reached the exit doors at that moment. Scully motioned his men into position, two to lead the way to the roller that would take them all to the presidential compound, two to bring up the rear. The prime minister and Truman both noted the tension in the four men's shoulders, the constant scanning movements of their eyes.

Well, thought Hawkes, at least they're not walking around with their guns out and at the ready. Yet.

And then the secure doors slid open, revealing the crowds of sullen, angry people moving beyond the entrance to the spaceport. The prime minister was struck as if by a physical blow at the boiling unrest he found in every action and motion of the newly freed citizens of Mars. An average person would not see the differences, of course, but Hawkes was a career diplomat. Reading the mood of masses of people was one of his specialties. The shock of it bothered him, though.

When the prime minister had left Mars a few months earlier, the colony had been populated by people eager to embrace a world they had finally won the right to rule for themselves. Now he returned to a confused and bitter populace, their simplest actions seething. Stepping through the hatch into the waiting roller, Hawkes found a seat, then looked out his window at the worker directing traffic in and out of the port.

The woman's face was tired, pinched. Her appearance was of someone worn out and on edge—frazzled. But not by overwork. Stress of some sort was pulling at her—her and apparently everyone else in the new democracy known as Red Planet, Incorporated. Taking a last look into the worker's eyes, Hawkes then remembered the weapons of his guards neatly tucked away in their holsters and wondered if perhaps the security men were not being a touch too optimistic.

● ● ● "BENTON," SAID TRUMAN softly as the roller moved through the Martian tunnels. "After all you've told me about Mars, I . . . well, let's just say I'm surprised."

"You're not the only one, Liz," answered Hawkes. The sadness in his voice surprised even him—especially him. He knew that the dreams which had plagued him since the art show had slowly been altering his old feelings toward Mars, but this was different. The prime minister had spent nearly his entire adult life moving from one troubled spot to the next. Dealing with disrupted and even broken populations had ceased to affect his outlook decades earlier.

Now, however, he felt pity, even the beginnings of despair, brewing within him. Leashing in his feelings until he could deal with them, he took another short glance out his window, then turned to Waters, asking, "What's going on, Sam? Everyone out there looks either angry or nervous. What happened?"

"Victoria Cobber," answered the president, his hand pressing gingerly against his obviously upset stomach. "She's what happened."

"Should I know this name?" asked Hawkes.

"No," Scully told him. "When you left the last time, she was just

another face in the crowd. Since then she's spent her time orga-
nizin' protests, gettin' petitions signed—if there's a demand on
Sam's desk, her name's signed to it somewhere."

"Well, that is what democracy's all about, Norm," Hawkes answered comfortably. "We are supposed to be responsive to the
people and their needs. That's the big difference between us and
the League, remember?"

"Could be maybe we shouldn't have billed ourselves as being so
different then." The prime minister turned back toward Waters,
asking what he meant—already knowing. The president confirmed
his guesses.

"Cobber—she wants everything and she wants it now. All past
civilian debt erased. Surface parks opened—now. Dome habitats
for every family that wants to move outside—now. Government
health benefits—free. Medicine and food—free. Education—hours
and years—both to be expanded. All free. And she wants a say in
what gets taught in the schools. Says there's too much League history. Just wants Martian history taught. And the—"

"Sam, please." Hawkes dropped his voice down into a quiet
plea. "Calm down. For your own good. You're letting this turn you
into a wreck. I'm not trying to tell you this woman isn't a problem—
I just don't want you to turn her into even more of one than she actually is."

"Easy to say, Benton," answered Waters, his voice growing testy.
"But I'm the one who's had to live with it. You've seen the signs
pasted up everywhere from the spaceport to here. We're on the
verge of anarchy. And you'll get a taste of it, just as soon as she
finds out you're back on Mars."

"Guaranteed," agreed Scully with a grim nod.

Fumbling in one of the pouch pockets built into his belt, the president dug out a pair of pills, which he swallowed dry. Grimacing from either the taste or the difficulty of getting them down without any liquid, Waters turned back to Hawkes as soon as he could speak again, adding, "She's been demanding a meeting. Especially with you. Told us she wants to see you to present her ultimatums the second you returned."

"Well," answered the prime minister, "then I guess we'd better set up a meeting with her."

"You've got to be kidding." Waters rolled his eyes, then chuckled. When he did not hear anyone else laughing, he stared at Hawkes. Shaking his head, he told the prime minister, "We're ninety percent sure she's with the Resolute."

"We've worked with the Resolute before, Sam," Hawkes reminded the president. "If it weren't for them, none of us would be alive. No—have her notified that I've arrived . . ."

"Don't worry—she'll already know," Scully said with easy assurance.

"I figured as much, Norm," answered Hawkes. "That's why it's in our favor to appear to be cooperating. Trust me, everyone—we've got bigger problems coming our way than this woman. But having the Resolute against us during the next few weeks would be a critical mistake. We've got to get the people behind us—quickly. And I mean everyone. So set up a meeting with the captains of both our shield vessels for early morning, and then a luncheon with Cobbler and however many she'd like to bring."

Hawkes looked into Waters's eyes, searching for the man's true feelings. The prime minister knew things had been hard on the new president. He had never wanted to be a politician. Public office had never been considered as one of his goals—he had neither expected it nor trained for it.

Whenever the new government did not run like a business, Waters found himself almost hopelessly lost. The fact that his managerial skills availed him little as a leader had not sat well with him, for there are few men who do not like to think of themselves as capable of ruling a world. Despite his inexperience, however, Waters knew he was the president, knew that how things ran was up to him.

Hawkes understood his friend's problem. Unlike any other man who had ever lived, Sam Waters did have an entire world to rule. The prime minister had faith, however. Knowing that no matter what happened, he would not find an ego too large to work with within Samuel Waters, Hawkes said softly, "We'll handle Cobber. And we'll handle whatever's coming."

"And if we don't?"

"Well," answered the prime minister, stretching his palms apart before him expansively, "then we can take our act out of town. Run you in the primaries on Io. Ask not what the asteroids can do for you, ask what you can do for the asteroids."

Everyone chuckled—including the president. Relief slowly filtering through his system, Waters indexed the proper control on his mobile comm and contacted his staff secretary, ordering that the two meetings be set up as per Hawkes's suggestions.

After that, the prime minister rubbed his hands together. "All right, now let's get on to what I've been waiting for. Let's head for the main dome." All of the Martians stared blankly, none of them speaking. Somewhat confused, Hawkes asked, "What is it? What's wrong with the dome?"

"Sorry—I thought you would have guessed."

"Guessed?" Sudden agitation pounding at him, the prime minister barked a touch too loudly, "Guessed what? What's wrong?"

"The solar storm, the one that's been tearing up communications throughout the system—the radiation on the surface . . . it's too much for the workers—too dangerous. Been burning people right through their suits. Even a lot of the plants haven't been able to take it. We haven't been able to send anyone out for sky work for months."

The prime minister listened to the words, understanding them easily enough. What he did not understand was his reaction. A terrible sorrow billowed within him at the thought of the domes still empty of people—still unobtainable. He could feel his heart racing, his breath going short, strangling in his lungs. And then suddenly, his mind barked at him—

Pity? Pity for Mars? Is that how *you* feel?

Catching hold of himself, his fingers tightening so fiercely that his nails broke the skin of his palms, Hawkes banished the sudden mood.

Enough, he told himself. This has gone on long enough! I know what this is about, and damnit, I know who did it to me. Well, now that I'm back here, I'm going to get it undone. And I'm going to get it undone right now.

"Sam, I want to ask a few favors."

Waters took a moment to answer. The rapid changes he had just witnessed in Hawkes had caught him off guard. Trusting the steely look that had filled the prime minister's eyes, however, remembering it from the days when—side by side—they had changed an entire world, he was quick to let Hawkes know that a few favors between friends was never a problem.

"Glad to hear it. First, I'd like it if you and the first lady could take the major here to our quarters. Glenia, you could certainly give her a better perspective on how women manage on Mars than I could, and at the same time you could pump her for news from Earth."

"It would be my pleasure, Prime Minister," answered the president's wife.

"Fine—you two get acquainted. Liz, you learn as much as you can pronto—I need you beyond tourist familiarity by noon tomorrow if you're going to be any use to me."

"No problem, sir," answered Truman, finally beginning to warm to the prospect of life on Mars.

"Excellent. After that, I'm going to need to borrow Norman from you, Sam."

"For how long, Benton?"

"I've got people trying to kill me again and—you know—I don't seem to like it any more now than I did the last time." Turning to the old security man, Hawkes said, "I need someone who knows this planet inside out. Someone I trust at my back. You've been here since the first ships, and if there's a tougher man on Mars, I haven't met him. Feel like running around trying to keep me alive for a while?"

"It'd be my pleasure," answered Scully. Staring Hawkes in the eye, he asked, "And somethin' tells me you'd like to get started right away."

"Mind reader too," joked the prime minister. "That'll come in handy."

Scully grinned with appreciation, ordering his man to stop the roller at the same time. As the main bus came to a halt, its two side vehicles quietly slid to a stop in near-perfect synchronization. Tabbing the hatch, the security man jumped out, communicating with his men in the rear shield car at the same time, ordering them to transfer to the roller. Then, while Hawkes gave a few last-minute instructions to Truman and said his goodbyes to the rest of the party, Scully commandeered the smaller, faster side vehicle. Moments later, the roller had moved on, leaving Hawkes and the security chief on their own.

Strapping themselves into the small combat vehicle, Scully tabbed open the speeder's locational guide as he asked, "So, I know you got some kinda bug up your behind that's makin' you itch. Where is it we gotta go to get it scratched?"

Turning to the security man, Hawkes let his eyes narrow and his heart go cold as he answered, "The place where dreams are made."

So this is what a Martian artist's studio looks like," said Hawkes, moving between the tables filled with various bits and pieces of electronic equipment. "Fascinating."

The prime minister's eyes roved the single room, wondering how anyone could even live in such a small area, much less create art in it as well. Hawkes had, of course, seen literally millions of people not only in similar conditions, but in states so much worse that the artist's home would have seemed to them a residence approaching a palace. Even after all the millions, though, it still tore at him to see people shut up in boxes.

One room, he thought bitterly. Living room, bedroom, kitchen and dining room, and art studio. One body—one room. One stinking tiny little windowless square to rot in. Communal bath down the hall. Enjoy your stay.

Shutting his thoughts away in a place far smaller than the cramped home in which he was standing, Hawkes randomly picked up one of the tools heaped in a box on the table next to him. Fingering it absently, he walked over to a blank screen hanging on the wall farthest away from him, noting somewhat sadly that it only took five steps to reach it. Pointing toward the dark screen with the tool, he asked, "A work in progress?"

"Yes, yes it is," answered the young man, still somewhat dazed at the prospect of having the prime minister of Mars wandering through his studio. "Would you care to see it?"

"Would I care to see it?" The prime minister turned to Scully, laughing. Holding himself as if he had never heard anything so amusingly understated, he replied, "My dear boy, what do you think I've come to Mars for?"

"What you came to . . . what you . . . I mean," the young man gasped at his next breath and then went silent, trying to control his sudden stammering. As he did so, Hawkes continued to retrace his steps, making the same pitifully small circle over and over as he pretended to ramble.

"It's just so . . . energizing," said the prime minister with an enthusiastic twinkle in his voice, "to be in the home of a real artist. Someone who actually still creates. In all this stale, dull solar system . . . when you finally come across someone who still feels they have something to say . . . well . . . But excuse me, I'm sorry. I don't mean to fluster you, obviously, but it's just all so exciting."

The young man knew what Hawkes meant, of course. Nearly fifty years earlier the Earth League had canceled all the copyrights in the world and confiscated every bit of existing entertainment. Movies, radio broadcasts, television productions— every bit of previously created art, both high and low, became the property of the world government.

It was meant as a supportive gesture—every home would now be filled, twenty-four hours a day, with free entertainment. Just ask the system for anything in the encyclopedic listing and it would begin playing on the designated screen within seconds. For free. To a people frightened of walking their own streets, living on budgets that became more restrictive every year, it seemed a blessing. A hundred and fifty years of taped entertainment—centuries of paintings and statues and architecture waiting to be reviewed— there was so much to watch it almost made making new vids pointless.

That, of course, was in the first days of the policy. By the time League Vid Net was eight years old, the last corporate studio closed its doors. The major independents held out for another twenty-two years, struggling to exist much the same way they always had, but eventually, with no return whatsoever to be made on their products, they all faded away as well.

Now, art of any kind was back in the hands of the people, with no means of mass exposure open to anyone except those anointed by the occasional patron to be found among the elites. People like Benton Hawkes—prime minister of Mars.

Forcing himself to finally regain his composure, the enormity of what was at stake firmly at the front of the artist's mind, the young man asked, "Excuse me, sir, but I actually don't understand. I have my hopes—sure. But if you please, could you tell me . . . why did you come to Mars?"

"Why did I come to Mars?" Hawkes molded his face into a comic mask of inane confusion, then turned from the artist to Scully and back again as he asked, "Are you joking? Is he joking? Are you? Joking, I mean?"

"No, no . . . I . . ."

"You *are* Jason Harris, aren't you? Scully, we did come to the right place, didn't we?"

"Mr. Prime Minister," offered the security man offhandedly, doing his best to appear uninterested. "You've forgotten the solar storm. We ain't received no news on anything that's happened on Earth for months, unless it's come word-of-mouth by way of a ship's crew or somethin'."

"Oh, oh, yes—of course." Hawkes continued to stroll through the crowded room, his feet routinely finding the same twenty-two spots. Rounding the same corner for the fifteenth time, the prime minister spoke over his shoulder to Scully, actually aiming his comment at the young artist. "Then he doesn't know anything about the prize—does he?"

"Prize?" asked the artist hesitantly, but with understandable curiosity.

"Why, your prize, of course, from the art show in New York." Turning to face the artist, the prime minister carefully held in his true desires, maintaining his foppish pretense as he led the young man onward. "Your piece, that day-in-the-life thing. Splendid, splendid work. It's caused the most delightful stir—has all the intelligentsia stampeding to see it."

"It does?" asked Jason, honest humility cautiously asking the logically required question the rest of his mind wanted to forget. "Really? Me?"

"Well, of course, you," answered Hawkes. Catching the artist by the shoulders, he said, "Your work is the toast of New York. Which actually . . . I suppose, come to think of it, makes it the toast of . . . everywhere."

Jason struggled to concentrate on the prime minister's words, even as his mind went racing off in a hundred other directions at the same time. As the young man's knees went suddenly weak, Hawkes caught him and then passed him to Scully, who helped him stagger to his couch.

As the artist sat there, still trying to comprehend all he had heard, the prime minister asked, "So tell me—from what I gather, just as on Earth, for the most part nobody is a full-time artist on Mars anymore—correct?" When the still-stunned Jason agreed, acknowledging that all of his artistic endeavors had to be done on his breaks, in the evenings, or during whatever other free moments he might find, Hawkes continued, "So, the piece you did for the show . . . how long did that take you to complete?"

"Not really that long, actually," Jason announced with pride. "Less than two months."

"Oh, I can't believe that," answered Hawkes with mock amazement. "Not even two months? *That* piece?"

"It's true," Jason insisted. "Tell me, though—the critics, they really liked my work?"

"They loved it. But back to what you said—less than two months? It can't be. Can't."

"Oh, no, sir—honest."

"Oh, please." Hawkes rolled his eyes, arching his eyebrows at the same time. "It's simply impossible . . ."

"No, I did it. I did it—"

"Why, the subliminals alone . . ."

"No," protested the artist without thinking. "That was the easiest part. I . . ."

And then, suddenly, Jason Harris understood. His head snapping up, he stared directly into Hawkes's eyes, letting the prime minister see all he needed. Realizing what he had just been tricked into admitting, the artist whirled around without hesitation, bolting for the door.

"Sit."

Scully caught the far younger man by the collar. With a simple snap of his wrist he flung Jason backward, aiming him so that he fell into his couch. The artist hit face first, floundering awkwardly in its pillows until he managed to right himself after a few seconds. Turning around, he found the security man standing over him, arms folded across his chest.

Staring at the young man as harshly as he could, the security man told him, "Stay," then turned and walked to the other side of the room.

Sitting down next to the artist, Hawkes said, "Well, now that we've established what's really going on . . . let's you and me talk."

● ● ● "I HAVE TO hand it to you," Hawkes said, sitting back comfortably in the artist's best chair. "It was a clever plan. Bold and risky, well thought out and well executed." Lifting the glass of water Scully had provided him while Jason outlined the story of what he had created, the prime minister saluted the young man. "Here's to your success, Mr. Harris. May the gods continue to smile on you."

Hawkes drank from his glass, all the while staring at a copy of the electronic painting that had shaken him so in New York. The artist had filled the piece with subliminal messages all aimed directly at the prime minister. General influencers hidden beneath any electronic work would have been discovered when the artwork first arrived at the museum, but Harris had not targeted the mass public—just Hawkes.

"What's going to happen to me?" asked the artist.

"Don't worry," answered Scully in a chillingly friendly tone. "I'm sure there's a dark hole around here somewhere we can drop you in."

The first of Harris's goals had been to force the prime minister to return to the Martian colony. The second had been to break down Hawkes's passions concerning Mars. The facts of the senior Hawkes's death, as well as his son's subsequent hatred for the planet, were well known. The subliminal messages implanted in the painting had been geared to work with the story, both aimed at breaking down the prime minister's resistance to the Martian plight.

"A dark hole might not be necessary," offered Hawkes.

"Yeah, sure," Harris spat angrily. "All I have to do is sell out the Resolute to you and I get to go free—right? Man, Victoria had you pegged from the on switch."

"Victoria Cobber, I presume?" Scully asked rhetorically. Harris groaned as he realized what he had said, leading the security man to comment, "You ain't really cut out fer this kinda thing, are ya, son?"

Sitting across from the young man, Hawkes looked into the artist's eyes, then back at the painting that had inspired his rash of nightmares. As the painting recycled to the beginning again, the prime minister studied the face in the mirror carefully, suddenly realizing where he had seen it before.

"That's me!" he cried, caught off guard for one of the few times in his life. "My God—that's me when I was a boy."

"Yes," Harris admitted sullenly, not seeing what he could possibly gain by lying at that point. "I downloaded a photo I managed to find in the League Library Link. 'Famous People as Children.' I animated it, used it for the boy in the painting. Then I took a Martian vid-shot of you, ran a wrinkle scan, you know, aged it up. That became the old man at the end. Except I switched the eyes."

"You switched the eyes?" the prime minister repeated with curiosity. "Why?"

"An old man's sad eyes evoke one feeling, a child's sad eyes evoke something different. I wanted the horror of lost dreams and lost youth mixed together. So I dubbed the young eyes in on the old man's face."

"I told you he was an artist, Scully," Hawkes said to the security man. "So, son . . . what do you think happens next?"

"What do I care?" answered Harris mournfully. "I let you make a fool out of me, and I've put you onto Victoria. What does it matter what happens to someone that stupid?"

"Well, first off," Hawkes told the artist, "no one ever makes a fool out of us, we only make fools out of ourselves."

"Thanks," the young man spat bitterly.

"Yeah, and I wouldn't worry too much about your friend Cobber," added Scully. "No offense, kid, but we didn't need you to get onto her."

"All right," Hawkes told the security man, "leave him alone. I've got what I wanted."

"What?" demanded Harris. Getting to his feet, the artist snapped, "That's it? You blow in here, dish me through the whole cycle, then . . . nothing?"

Scully began tabulating a list of Harris's crimes, but the prime minister cut him off. Turning to the artist, Hawkes told him, "Listen to me—you set out to change my mind about Mars. Fine—you win. Mission accomplished." The young man backed off a step, suddenly confused.

Pitying him despite the torment he had caused, Hawkes told him softly, "I was filled with hate for Mars for a long time. Longer than you've been alive. But it was the misdirected anger of a child. A spaceship killed my father, so space was bad. Years later, I knew it was the greed of League directors that had caused the accident, but it was too late. My hate for Mars was reflexive by then. And besides, I worked for the Earth League. It was far more convenient to simply let my hate stay aimed at the target it knew best. You said you

143

wanted to change my mind about Mars. Well, it needed changing, so thanks."

The prime minister extended his hand, waiting for the artist to take it. The young man, somewhat stunned by the sudden shift in the situation, was slow to move. Finally, however, he took Hawkes's outstretched hand, shaking it respectfully.

"I'm sorry if I caused you any—"

"No," interrupted the prime minister. "Don't say it—no need. Once my old attitude toward Mars began to slip away, the nightmares did as well. That hate was an anchor, one dragging me down deeper all the time. Thanks for the air."

As Hawkes and Scully moved to leave, the artist suddenly realized that it sounded as if there would be no penalties for his actions. The prime minister confirmed his hopeful suspicion. Emboldened by the revelation, Harris asked the pair, "Hey, what about my prize?"

Hawkes chuckled. Admitting that the award had only been a ruse to catch the young man out, the prime minister put his arm on Scully's shoulder and told the security man, "You see, he is a real artist."

The two men laughed all the way back to their vehicle.

HAWKES SHOOK HANDS with the captain of the U.S.S. *Roosevelt,* and then with the captain of *Die Berlin.* The two military men had just finished bringing the prime minister up-to-date on the current situation. Neither officer had anything much to report. Things had remained quiet in the Martian orbit since Hawkes's last trip to Mars. At least, as far as anyone knew.

Making apologies for the short notice he had given both captains, the prime minister invited them to stay planetside for a few days. Both officers understood that the invitation was not a request and so accepted, thanking Hawkes and President Waters for the sudden shore leave. After the captains had left the president's office, the real meeting began.

"All right," the prime minster started. Turning to Waters and Scully, he asked, "What do you think? Which one of them is selling us out? Norman?"

"Got me," answered the security man. "If we'd leveled with them, told them what we were after and interrogated them like real suspects, maybe I'd have an answer for ya. This pussyfootin' around, though . . . what can I tell ya? Diplomacy ain't exactly my long suit."

"I understand, Norman," answered Hawkes with a degree of honest sympathy. "But at this stage of the game, we can't afford to let the League know how many of their cards we've seen. It would be a lot better for us if we could isolate our traitor without letting anyone know what we'd done."

"Couldn't we just relieve both of them of their commands and be done with it?" asked Scully.

"We may have to," Hawkes admitted. "But I'd certainly like to hold off on such a measure until we had to use it. How about you, Sam? Any ideas on our captains?"

"What do I know about these things?" complained the president. Stretching his neck one way, then the other, he worked at releasing the kink in his back. "I'm no good at this. They both answered all the questions okay enough. From what I just heard out of them, they're both clean."

"Yes. Well, I hate to admit it," answered Hawkes, "but I have to agree with you both."

Scully excused himself at that point, wanting to be in the outer office when the Resolute members arrived. The prime minister and Waters could not fault his judgment. After he had left the room, the president asked Hawkes, "You think your information might be wrong?"

"No. I trust Major Truman implicitly." The prime minister reached for his water glass. Staring at his reflection in its side, he said, "One of those two is just a very good actor."

"Yes," drawled Waters, trying to imply something to the contrary with his tone. "Someone is."

"Sam, you have something to say . . . you can just say it."

"Awww, Ben, I'd think you'd be tired of hearing me say it—politics and intrigue and all just isn't what I'm good at." The president pointed at the door through which the captains had exited.

"If one of those two is a spy, sitting back waiting for the chance to turn on us—to murder us with our own battlewagon—then I can't see it. I'm sorry. On the other hand, trying to be a crafty and suspicious leader, I have to ask . . . Just how much do you know about your Major Truman?"

The prime minister regarded Waters for a moment—coldly, at a distance—as if for that split second the president were someone he had just met. Not giving voice to either his surprise or his anger, though, he allowed his negotiating skills to take over.

"Sam, Cobber and her delegation are going to be here soon, so I won't waste time fencing with you. I take it you've noticed how, shall we say, friendly Liz and I are, and you're wondering if I'm making an old fool out of myself over some woman who could easily be a League spy—something like that, more or less?"

"Not that I want to start anything, but—yeah. Something like that."

"Don't worry about it," Hawkes told the other man earnestly. "I have to admit there was a moment where I gave the same notion some thought myself. But that woman almost died getting here, same as myself. If she's working for Mick Carri, she's pretty damn loyal about it."

"I get you," answered Waters quietly.

"And yes, I like her a lot," the prime minister told his friend. "She threw away her career—maybe her whole life—to help me keep mine. I've learned a lot about her in the last three weeks. I know one shouldn't put a lot of stock in shipboard romances . . ."

"Didn't want to make an issue out of it," replied Waters, cutting Hawkes off. "We've all had people turn on us we never expected. I guess . . . A man hates to admit it, but . . . I guess I'm just scared."

"We're all scared, Sam," the prime minister said softly. "But, if I can ask, there seems to be something else bothering you about this. If you're worried about the major, you could have her clearance restricted, or—"

"Oh, no—no, nothing like that," Waters answered, flustered with embarrassment. "It's not her."

Confused by the president's tone as well as his response, Hawkes asked, "Well, what is it then?"

"I guess it's just that, Glenia and me, we sort of figured you were headed toward settling on that nice Martel girl."

The prime minister's head snapped slightly, momentary surprise flashing through his eyes. Before he could say anything, however, the comm on Waters's desk hummed softly. The president acknowledged the machine verbally, opening the connection.

"Mr. President," came the voice of Waters's chief aide, "the Cobber party is here." The president ordered that they be shown into his office. The two men glanced at each other, and then turned toward the door. As they waited, the prime minister heard Waters's comment in his head once more.

We sort of figured you were headed toward settling on that nice Martel girl.

Funny, thought Hawkes. Now that I think about it, I wonder why I didn't.

Then Scully returned, ushering Victoria Cobber and her party into the president's office, forcing such thoughts to be shelved for another time.

● ● ● "NO, HAWKES—*YOU'RE* the one who doesn't understand!"

The prime minister sat back in his chair, pressing his spine deep into its padding, forcing himself to relax.

Remember Massinger's law, Benton, he told himself. "He that would govern others, first should be the master of himself." His hands flat on the table before him, his eyes barely able to contain the anger boiling within him, Hawkes managed to maintain his calm.

"Miss Cobber, please—believe us—there isn't anyone in this

room who trusts the Earth League. We know they won't honor any treaty unless they believe Mars not only willing but able to hold them at bay, as well. But we *can* make them believe this—it's the kind of game that takes years, sometimes decades to play out to its end, but in the long run, it's better than war."

Hawkes wanted to stop. They had been arguing in circles for hours. Despite his skill as a negotiator, pointless bickering still made him weary. He could feel the tension tightening the muscles in his face, the strain starting a dull throbbing in his temples. Knowing he dare not break off, however, he strove to keep any sign of the growing pain out of his face as he offered, "Perhaps we've made the wrong impression. No one here meant to give you the idea that we wouldn't fight in Mars' defense if we were attacked. All we said was that it would be best to avoid interplanetary war if it was at all possible."

"No—no wrong impression," one of the men with Cobber answered. "We understand you, Hawkes. You want to talk the League into submission. Make a deal with them—one that gives them everything they want and sells Mars back into slavery."

"Roger is right," Cobber added. "But even if he isn't, it doesn't matter. What is important is making the League pay for their crimes against Mars."

"They have to pay and pay hard," the young man shouted. "Martians have been dying for thirty years at the League's hands. Now it's Earth's turn. We've got to bomb them out of existence, foul their precious oceans and poison their atmosphere. Let them melt down polar ice for drinking water. Let them breathe out of tubes and live underground. Let them have a taste of the hell they made here for us!"

The prime minister turned back to the young redhead, letting

Roger rant as he tried instead to gauge exactly what had happened since the meeting began. At first, Cobber had seemed somewhat receptive to the treaty that Hawkes had been crafting over the previous year. She had listened politely as he explained its various provisions, answering her questions carefully and honestly. Then, somehow, things had gotten twisted around and suddenly everyone on the other side of the table was demanding a war.

No—not *somehow*, thought Hawkes. I know exactly how it happened.

Looking over at Cobber's boyfriend, Roger, the prime minister quickly scanned his memory of the meeting so far. Although the young redhead had proved to be quite a firebrand on her own, he quickly realized that it was her boyfriend who was truly fanning the flames.

"Pay for their crimes?" asked Waters. The prime minister regretted his momentary pause. While he had taken a second to think about what was going on, the president had risen to the bait being thrown out by the Resolute leader. Hoping for the best, Hawkes sat back and let Waters continue.

"Are you just dim? How exactly are we supposed to fight the League? We've been god-blessed lucky so far, and it's taken every trick we've been able to finagle to get us here. In case you people hadn't noticed, Mars is in no way ready to repel the kind of forces the League could send against us."

"That's just the kind of talk that's going to send us back into chains," snapped Cobber. "Three hundred years ago, England was the mightiest nation on Earth. No one could stand against them. Certainly not thirteen small colonies with no navy and no real army. Those early Americans knew the odds, but they fought anyway. And they won. They stood against the most far-flung empire in the world, and they defeated it. Don't try to scare us, President Waters. We're ready to die for our world."

"Well, you better be," answered the prime minister. Deciding that Waters may have done them a favor by turning the debate headlong into the truth, he let his voice go cold as he told the Resolute delegation, "Because that's what will happen. You'll die. And most likely, no matter who fights and who doesn't, you'll take the entire colony with you."

"Don't try to scare us," snapped one of the others.

"I don't have to try," answered Hawkes. "I just have to explain a few things. Those American colonists, they lived on the surface of their planet. They had thousands of square miles to hide in. They lived in a world where it took weeks to move a sizable party two hundred miles. They also not only had as an ally the second-largest empire in the world, but they profited from the fact that their foe had just finished with years of war in Europe. *Their* enemies were tired and they were civilized. Two things the League is not."

Rising from his seat, hoping that breaking the usual rules of negotiation might work for him under such different circumstances, Hawkes let his voice notch upward emotionally as he continued.

"You start a war with the League, you're not going to have it as easy as the colonies did. Red Planet, Inc., is focused in one small area. Two or three nuclear bombs get dropped anywhere in our general area and it's all over. We live in a trap here—this colony is well mapped. Its exact coordinates are pinpointed to the inch. If we start a war, we've got nowhere else to go when the trashers start to fall. We've got nowhere to hide, no atmosphere, and no allies."

"So that's it." Everyone turned toward Roger. Not looking to anyone else, the young man spoke only to Cobber as he said, "They're giving up already. You wanted to give them a chance. You gave them one. And here's what they give us. We're defeated before we start. We've got no choices. Best to crawl back in our holes and do what we're told. Go away. Behave."

Goddamnit, thought Hawkes. He had gambled and lost. He had worked long and hard to bring the revolutionaries before him around to his way of looking at the situation. Obviously, however, he had not worked long or hard enough. What the Resolute might do next was anyone's guess.

Goddamnit, he cursed himself once more. I really am getting too old for this.

"I'd hoped you might understand," the young redhead said as she stood up. "But you can't. You weren't born here. This is just a job to you. Well, it's our lives, and if you won't help us get them back, we'll take them on our own."

Neither Hawkes nor Waters spoke as the three Resolute leaders left the room. Letting go a deep sigh of frustration, Scully muttered, "That went well."

Ignoring the security man's comment, the president tried to apologize for losing his temper. "You warned me, but I lost it. I can't tell you how—"

"Forget it." The prime minister cut him off. "As soon as you did it I crossed my fingers, hoping for the best. Nothing else was getting us anywhere. I'm not very surprised things went the way they did."

"Didn't surprise me none," Scully agreed cynically.

"What I'm surprised at is that little Cobber girl," replied Waters. Scratching at the back of his head, he continued, "Even with all that's been going on, I still expected her to be more reasonable. She always used to be so sweet."

"It's not her," offered the security man. "It's that boyfriend of hers."

"You noticed that, too?" Hawkes asked rhetorically. "She did seem willing to listen, to reason things out. But that Roger character—he kept feeding her the right lines, hiding in the background, pushing her buttons. Who is he, anyway? What's his story?"

"Don't know, really," admitted Waters.

"Maybe we should find out," offered Scully.

"Maybe we should," Hawkes agreed. "I'm always a little suspicious of men who sit back and let their women take the heat for them. I'll stake high odds he's the one who's really pushing for this war."

"Yeah" said the security man in agreement. "And I wonder why."

"I'm sure we could all make some guesses," answered Hawkes. "But we can worry about him later. Now I want to talk to you two about that boiler satellite wrecking our communications."

"But, Benton," Waters asked with hesitation, "isn't it just like the captains? If we destroy the satellite, won't the League know that we know? Won't we just trigger the war we spent all morning trying to prevent?"

"We gotta do somethin'," insisted Scully. "As long as the surface is bein' radiated, then the Resolute's got a point about the fact the surface ain't been opened yet."

"Nice quandary," mused the prime minister. "The domes can't be opened because of the radiation, but the radiation can't be stopped without alerting the League. The Resolute will start a revolution if the domes aren't opened. The League will start a war if they are."

Spreading his hands wide before him, Hawkes asked, "Any ideas, gentlemen?"

"Maybe," asked Scully, "we don't have to knock the thing out?

Maybe we could just secure it and then find a way to disengage it. You know, stop the radiation flow, but let it keep puttin' out a signal like it's still workin'."

Hawkes and Waters looked at each other with surprise. Turning to the security man, the prime minister smiled. "Norman, that's not half bad."

His enthusiasm growing in the face of the day's first bit of hope, the president clapped his hands together, applauding Scully's idea. Then, not wanting the moment to pass, he immediately began to outline ideas on who they could send, what ships they might use, and when they could leave.

He was only a few moments into mapping out his plan when suddenly the comm on his desk snapped on. Waters was just reaching to answer the insistent hum when his door opened. Major Truman stepped through, holding a deadly two-hand needler at the ready. Not turning her back on the outer office, she shouted over her shoulder to the three men inside.

"Meeting's over, gentlemen."

"Liz?" Hawkes asked while he stood, his hand going for the concealed sidearm Scully had given him the night before. "What's going on?"

"Is it the League?" demanded Waters.

"Don't need the League," the major snapped. As a furious background noise grew in the distance, she told them, "We've got a riot on our hands."

"The Resolute," said Scully, unlimbering his own side arm. "As soon as they knew things weren't goin' their way, they flagged in a blow-up."

"Whatever," answered Truman, "it's Dodge City out there. So grab your socks, boys. The palace is about to be couped."

19

IKE!" SCULLY SCREAMED into the president's desk comm. "Answer me, mister! What's our situation?"

"We got big bad wolves huffin' and puffin' at everything in sight, boss," answered the surprisingly calm voice at the other end of the comm. "Half in the Above—areas two, five, ten, thirteen, and sixteen—and half down in the Pit-an'-Bang, mostly around reclamation and processing sector D."

"At least they're not crackin' their skulls in the damn Down Below," snapped the security chief. "That's somethin', anyway." Hunching down over the president's desk, Scully took command of Waters's office, barking questions and orders as quickly as he could make them understood.

As rapidly as possible he determined how many of his people were already out trying to contain the situation, where they were concentrated, what types of weapons were being used on both sides, what kind of mayhem the rioters were engaged in, whether hostages were being taken, how many people were involved, whether they were working in concert or simply running rampant, and a dozen other details before he turned to Waters.

"Sam, the merry idiots are movin' like they might swing through this area. I'd feel a lot better if the young lady were to get you and the prime minister the hell out of here."

"Sounds like a good plan to me," offered Hawkes, heading for the door. Waters and Truman fell in step behind him, hurrying to catch up to the prime minister before he ran off without them. As they all raced down the hallway, Hawkes told his companions, "We've got to stop this any way we can."

"Why?" asked the president. "I mean, yes—of course, we don't want a riot going on any longer than it has to, but you mean something more, don't you?"

"It's the treaty, Sam," answered Hawkes. "It calls for the League to intercede in any problem the Martian government can't handle on its own. Typical friendship clause. But it would be easy to blow out of proportion as a justification to declare martial law."

"And we know whose courts would rule on their right to do it," agreed Waters sourly.

"Even without communications to Earth," Truman added, "if one of the captains in orbit *is* with the League, he could already have orders to deploy his troops and take over the planet if something like this were to happen."

"Especially if it was planned for it to happen," the prime minister growled angrily.

"My God, Benton," Waters gasped with the shock of sudden realization. "There are thousands of troops here in the Above already. They were moved down from the ships to save on fuel and such."

"Get us there," ordered Hawkes. "Fast. If this isn't what our friends in the League are up to, it'll goddamned do until something better comes along."

● ● ● VICTORIA COBBER HURRIED as quickly as she could. Roger had come to her with disturbing news. Earlier they had parted company after the meeting with the government. Bad enough they had revealed themselves to be members of the Resolute, she thought. To show up late for their shifts, to give the damn League any excuse to censor them, would have been simply foolish.

But long before she could reach even the level of her workstation, she had heard Roger's voice behind her, shouting for her to stop. The young woman had wheeled around, frightened by the urgency in her lover's pounding approach. She was not the only one. People hurried to clear out of the running man's way, those not capable of moving fast enough found themselves knocked violently aside.

"Roger, oh my God, what's wrong? Is someone chasing you?"

"I wish . . . wish it were . . . that simple." The young man collapsed, half against the wall, half against Cobber. His chest heaving, breath pounding in and out furiously, he gasped his words out in staggered bites.

"Told others . . . what happened. Should've listened to you. Too angry. Riots, riots starting. Not just Resolute."

"No, no." The redhead blanched, shock and terror draining the blood from her face. "We can't fight among ourselves. You said that's just what they'd want."

"Heading for the barracks," gasped Roger. Holding his sides, seemingly in terrible pain, the young man closed his eyes and hissed, then said, "Couldn't stop them. Maybe, maybe . . . you head them off . . . talk to them . . ."

For the first time in months, Victoria Cobber suddenly felt as young and helpless as any nineteen-year-old might in her situation. She had been strong for so long, had been everyone's pillar of support, never daring to show any kind of weakness. Now, all her fears tumbled outward, images flashing through her mind of all the monstrous ways she could die in the kind of violence a riot could unleash in an enclosed underground world.

Cobber remembered the riots during the revolution a year earlier, remembered the carnage and insanity that had ruled the mobs.

She also remembered that it was Hawkes and Waters who had put an end to them. Then, a part of her mind reminded her of her role in creating the current situation.

Shame filled her suddenly. Right or wrong, she knew that if people were being hurt, or maybe dying, she was as responsible as the government. Helping her lover slide to the ground, she told him, "You rest here. I'll go see what I can do."

And then she had turned and run back the way she had just come, praying she might arrive in time to stop the mob from getting themselves slaughtered—praying she might be spared as well.

● ● ● THE SCENT OF smoke drifted through the tunnels. Though it was not yet visible to the naked eye, the troops at the head of the column nonetheless began to note its presence. Already uneasy, the thought of being trapped in an underground fire tore at their nerves. There had already been whispering in the ranks. Many of the marines were confused—they had abandoned the Earth League to live as Martians. Now suddenly there was a riot in progress—one threatening to destroy the entire colony—and they had been ordered to quell it any way possible.

"I don't get this," muttered one trooper to the man next to him. "I thought we were all on the same side now. I thought things were good here. What in hell could these people have to riot about?"

"Got me, man," answered his friend. "But if the choice is them or us, it don't take higher calculus to figure the answer."

"There they are!"

As the voice rang out ahead of the marines, their commander instantly ordered his people to assume defensive cover. As the front-line troops dropped down behind their portable shields, those to

their rear scrambled into the doorways and passages along the receding length of the tunnel. While the marines prepared for whatever might come next, the voice continued to shout.

"You see—they're on the march already. They say they want to
be Martians, but the truth is they want to be the *rulers* of Mars. They
didn't stay as our friends—they stayed as our *watchdogs*! Fellow
Martians, if that's the case, then let them watch us take back our
planet—starting here . . . starting now . . . Mars for Martians!"

The marines watched silently as the hallway before them filled
with shadows, soon followed by the dark shapes of people advancing on their position. None of the soldiers wanted to hurt anyone.
They had left behind all they owned, their families and their homes
and their world, to stay on a planet without sunlight or oceans, simply because it had seemed the right thing to do.

"Mars for Martians," chanted the approaching crowd. "Mars for
Martians, Mars for Martians . . ."

"Captain!" shouted one trooper on the front lines. "This is crazy.
We're being attacked by the people we gave up everything for.
We're supposed to be defending them!"

"Tell that to them, Meyers," answered the officer, pointing at the
advancing rioters. "Now button it and stand ready."

"Mars for Martians, Mars for Martians, Mars for Martians . . ."

Those in the fore of the mob began hurling things at the waiting
troops—bottles, pipes, building blocks, shoes, anything they could
fill with anger and mindlessly heave. Most of the objects bounced
off the plas/teel shields maintained by the frontliners. Those which
made it past did little damage.

"Mars for Martians, Mars for Martians, Mars for Martians . . ."

"Steady, people," ordered the captain. Turning toward the crowd,
he spoke into his amplifier. "Drop your weapons and return to your

homes. I repeat, drop your weapons and return to your homes. No one wants to harm you."

"Mars for Martians, Mars for Martians . . ."

"I repeat, no one will harm you if you drop your weapons and return to your homes. Drop your weapons and . . ."

Fingers tightened around triggers on both sides of the rapidly shrinking space separating the two factions. Some of the rioters began to waver, sudden fear mixing with common sense, reminding them on several levels at once what they were doing. Many of the marines could feel the same emotions, praying nothing would happen, quietly begging invisible forces to let the coming trial pass them by.

"I repeat, drop your weapons. Drop . . ."

"Mars for Martians. Mars . . ."

And then, for no readily discernible reason, all of the lights in the tunnel shut down, instantly plunging everything into the horribly complete darkness known only in the underground. From no one knew where, the first shot was fired. Sadly, it was followed by others.

●

● ● ● "THEY'RE SHOOTING ALREADY!" Hawkes redoubled his efforts, pushing himself to his limit. He had sent Waters off to try and reach the colony's communications hub, with Truman for protection. If Waters was going to be of any help, it would be there, getting on the comm grid and talking sense to his fellow Martians, keeping them in their homes until the danger had passed.

The prime minister had opted to continue on to the barracks. He had talked to the troops before—his speech had been instrumental in persuading many of them to stay on Mars. If anyone had a chance of keeping them from making things worse, it was him, and he knew it.

Just a few problems, Benton, he thought, forcing himself to stagger on toward the sounds of the conflict. People who are out of breath don't make the best orators. Then there's the fact that people who are murdering each other usually don't want to listen to anybody.

And then, Hawkes saw a pitch-black length of tunnel before him. Moving on toward the sounds of the battle, he arrived at a balcony directly above the fighting. Straining to see through the darkness, he struggled to catch his breath while listening to the din of screams and gunfire echoing through the corridor. Hoping the lights could be reactivated from central control, the prime minister indexed the tab on his wrist comm that connected him with the communications hub. Silently thanking God that Waters and Truman had already arrived there, he explained the situation he had found.

"Norm'll know what to do," said the president. Instantly linking himself through to his security chief, Waters related Hawkes's dilemma.

Needing only a moment to check the problem through the hub's computer network, Scully punched in a simple sequence, then told Hawkes, "The lights in that sector read as full-functional. They just got switched off somehow. I'll have 'em back on in a second."

And, as promised, the flash panels in the ceiling all clicked on at the same moment, their sudden return blinding everyone below. Stepping up to the railing once more, the prime minister peered down to see what damage had been done. So unprepared was he for what the darkness had hidden, he found himself wishing it would return.

The dead were everywhere—marines and civilians alike. Pools of blood covered the tunnel floor, ragged smears of it splattered against every wall. The terrible smell of spent gunpowder mixed with the screams of the dying, choking and repelling any fortunate enough to still be only witnesses and not victims.

Reeling away from the sight, the prime minister turned to search for a way down to the lower level. He was not worried about further violence at that moment. From what he could see, the mob's spirit had been broken, the results of the first exchange of gunfire enough for them.

Having far fewer projectile weapons than the troops they had attacked, the mob's ranks had been shattered. Now people wandered aimlessly. Some hunkered down over their friends and loved ones, others simply knelt where they were and cried. Tentatively, despite the fact that some of their own ranks had been slain by the mob, the marines began moving out from behind their shields, offering help to the crowd.

Ignoring the growing stench of smoke still flowing through the tunnel, they gave what assistance they could to those who only minutes earlier had been ready to kill them. Most accepted their charity without question. Most—but not all.

"What are you doing?" screamed one Martian in the middle of the crowd. "They're still the enemy. They're still the ones who murdered everyone all around us." Running forward, the man stomped savagely in a large pool of blood, shouting, "This blood was spilled by them! And if we don't stop them, they'll spill more, and *more*, until Mars is in chains again!"

"No, that's not true," shouted one of the officers still behind the marine lines. Moving forward, he insisted, "Our orders were to secure the immediate area. To make sure no one tried to break into the weapons that have been stored. That's all. We didn't want to hurt anyone."

"Didn't want to hurt anyone?" The man standing in the bloody pool laughed, tears flowing down his face. Stooping down, he smeared his hands through the blood on the floor. Then he rose again suddenly, spinning around with his palms outstretched, shouting, "You didn't want to hurt anyone? Then who did this? Tell me, you bastards, *who* did *this*?"

"You did it to yourselves!"

Everyone's head turned toward the new voice. The speaker pushed her way forward through the hindmost ranks of the crowd, her red hair alone identifying her to most of those around her. Moving toward the man standing in the blood, she pointed to the marines and shouted, "This isn't their fault. They didn't start a riot. They've pledged themselves to Mars, and until they do something that breaks that pledge, they're as Martian as any of us."

Victoria Cobber took the bloody hands into her own, trying to calm their owner. Coughing from the smoke in the air, she let the moment pass, then began pleading with the man—with everyone in the crowd—once more begging them all to listen to reason.

"The League is our enemy. The *League*! We can't fight them with bricks and pipes and we can't fight them without thinking. Destroying our own homes doesn't help us. But it plays right into the League's hands. This is what they want us to do. This is how they plan to—"

But then, a new voice screeched out over the young woman's words, drowning all the noise in the tunnel, riveting everyone's attention with a single word.

"Fire!"

Instantly pandemonium tore through the crowd. As the desperate figure ran through the ranks of the mob, heading straight for the troops, everyone else joined in, the marines themselves turning back the way they had come. In the center of the tunnel, the bloody man jerked his hands free of Cobber's grasp. Desperate to flee the scene, he knocked the young woman to the ground so ruthlessly one might have thought he had done so on purpose. Cobber hit the cold concrete badly, slipping in the blood beneath her as she tried to stand, falling again.

As the crowd surged forward, she threw her hands over her head, praying that she might not be trampled by the mindless horde. As she cowered, someone dashed out from the sidelines and managed to throw himself over her before the main body of the panicking mob reached her. Smoke began to fill the tunnel, terrifying the crowd all the more. Cobber could feel her protector taking the brunt of numerous blows, people kicking, stepping on, falling over him.

Then, after a few moments, when the horde had thinned enough for them to make their escape, the man grabbed Cobber by the shoulders and said, "Come on. We've got to get out of here."

Allowing him to pull her up to her feet, the redhead followed his lead, letting him guide her to the same side tunnel from which he had emerged just before he came to her rescue. Even as he shoved her through the door, both of them could hear the warning sirens of the fire crews approaching in the distance.

Realizing they could safely take a moment, the two leaned against the wall in silence, gasping to catch their breath. After only a moment, though, Cobber turned to the man and said, "Thank you, Mr. Prime Minister. I guess I owe you my life."

"Possibly," answered Hawkes through gritted teeth. Knowing

from the pain tearing through his side that one of the clods who stepped on him had done some sort of severe damage, he told the girl, "Now . . . maybe you could do me a favor . . . and save . . . mine."

After which he slid to the floor, closing his eyes, trying not to scream.

20

"I DON'T KNOW WHY you look so glum, Benton." President Waters stood next to Hawkes's bed, nodding his head and smiling at his friend. "I said that the doctor is releasing you. You're okay—fit as a fiddle."

"Yes," answered the prime minister in a low, faraway voice. "I always seem to manage, don't I?"

"Don't get melancholy on us now. You don't have the right." Waters shook his head, not understanding what could be upsetting Hawkes. "Men our age, the type of punishment you took yesterday—ruptured spleen, lung punctured in two places, all the rest . . . A generation ago you might not have even been alive today. Hell, a decade ago you still would've been in the hospital for weeks. How much luckier can a man be?"

"Yes," answered Hawkes in a whisper. "Now we have medicines and surgery that can keep a man alive and robust until he's a hundred and fifty. The only problem is he has to live in a world that doesn't know what to do with him."

"This is Mars," Waters reminded the prime minister. "We have all sorts of uses for talented people. So get out of bed and stop feeling sorry for yourself. We've got work to do."

Hawkes looked around the small hospital room. His eyes stopped at the mirror and took in his surroundings, reflected back at him from the glass—tiny bed, one chair, small stand extended out from the wall, runners bringing it alongside the bed. Everything functional, sterile, unadorned. And, in the center of it all lay the prime minister of Mars, small and fragile, taped together and dressed in synthetic linens, as sterile and unadorned as everything else.

And functional? he wondered. Well, I guess we won't know the answer to that until we experiment a little, will we?

Hawkes sat up. The action set off a slight dizziness, a reaction to the drugs he had been given after the riot in the tunnel. He held his throbbing temples, waiting for the accompanying pain and nausea to pass. The discomfort shifted, oozing through his head, searching for a place to hide. Taking a deep breath, the prime minister closed his eyes and began the process of shoving the pain away from him.

Even as he did so, however, Hawkes's mind stayed fixed on his thought of a moment earlier. After the fires in the tunnel were extinguished, the prime minister had been rushed to the hospital. His life had been saved easily, as were the lives of most who had been injured during the struggle. And that, thought Hawkes, is part of the problem.

As the distress within his head finally faded, the prime minister opened his eyes again and slowly made his way out of bed. As he reached for his clothes, he told Waters, "I meant what I said. One of the biggest problems we all have is the fact that life has gotten too long for everyone."

"I've never looked at it that way," answered the president, not understanding where his friend was going with his thought.

"Haven't you?" Hawkes asked as he pulled on his pants. "We've all got double the lifetimes ahead of us our grandfathers had. Double. At least. But at the same time, we seem to have only half their options. Engineer—you got handed a good career for a Martian, and you made the most of it. Eventually, you rose up to head the management team here. Now you're the president. That makes you one of the lucky ones."

Pulling his shirt over his still-solid, but bandaged frame,

Hawkes added, "I'm not trying to say you don't deserve what you earned, or that you should feel guilty about anything. But what about the little guy? What about the people whose lives aren't so interesting?"

"I'm not sure what you mean, Benton."

"I mean, just what does a man *do* for a hundred and fifty years? People with boring jobs, boring spouses, boring children . . . what do they do? We're the first members of 'the eternal generation.' We're not halfway to the end and already we're starting to crack under the pressure. People are just beginning to understand what it means—retirement at a hundred and thirty . . . Think about it, Sam."

Hawkes worked the buttons of his shirt. He remembered the clothing of a few decades back, the sheer-wear that took only seconds to put on. The fad had not lasted long—just long enough for the buying public and the manufacturers to discover that no one wanted their life speeded up any further.

"Imagine you're just some guy with some fundamental job— welding sheet surfaces or tightening bolts or something. That's it. That's what you do. It's boring, but it pays the bills. Now think about doing it for ten, maybe eleven decades before you get to retire."

Sam Waters shuddered slightly. Suddenly he knew where the prime minister was going. Most people had started to become aware of the situation Hawkes was describing. The problem was, no one had any answers for it.

"Of course," the prime minister continued as he straightened his tie, "the sheet-welding and bolt-tightening jobs don't much exist anymore, do they? Especially on Earth. We have robots to handle that kind of work. So as jobs disappear, people are pensioned off, stuck in a box somewhere with unlimited tele privileges. Just sit here, watch the screen, eat your mush, and leave us alone—for the rest of your life."

"Okay," answered the president softly. "That aspect of it—sure, I've thought about it. Everyone thinks about it. But what are we supposed to do?"

"Worry," answered Hawkes. "Because that kind of boredom with life is what creates tyrants like Mick Carri. It's what fills ships with men and women ready to fight wars because the alternative is too awful to think about. That's our real enemy, Sam. That's what we're really up against."

Staring at each other, neither Waters nor Hawkes said anything for a long moment. Finally, the president blinked. Making a short noise with his lips and teeth, he told Hawkes, "All I said was that we've got work to do."

"And all I'm trying to say," answered the prime minister, "is that we've got a lot more work to do than you think."

"One way or the other," said Waters as he opened the hospital room door, "don't you think it's time we stop all this gabbing and get down to actually *doing* some of this work?"

Nodding, Hawkes stepped through the doorway out into the hall. Immediately met by a pair of Scully's guards who fell into place, one to either side of the prime minister, he turned back to Waters and smiled sourly, admitting, "Yes, it probably is."

The prime minister shook his head sadly. Seeing the armed men to either side of him, knowing why they were there and how long they would remain with him, Benton Hawkes finally admitted to himself what was coming. Starting down the hall, he repeated, "It probably is."

● ● ● "YOU'RE CERTAIN OF this?" President Waters asked the question of Scully automatically. He had no doubts of his security chief's abilities—he simply did not want to believe him.

Neither did any of the others present. Hawkes; Truman; the head of the workers' union, Ace Goth; and the Resolute's Victoria Cobber all sat in silence, waiting for the security chief's answer. He did not make them wait long.

"Certain as we can be," answered Scully. Turning to Hawkes, he added, "After I saw how banged up you were, Mr. Prime Minister, I figured you weren't just trampled by the crowd. Didn't sit right— why you and nobody else? It took a bit of lookin', but we found several people who saw what was happenin' while you were protectin' Cobber with ycr body."

The young leader of the Resolute closed her eyes. She understood what was being said, and where responsibility for the attack on Hawkes was being placed.

"You were attacked by Rcsolute members," Scully continued, as if to confirm the woman's fears. "Three of them—we have one in custody along with a confession. Those guys on you were tryin' to kill you and make it look like an accident. If Cobber here hadn't called fer help as fast as she did, this meetin' would be missin' one participant."

"And there would have been little crying in the streets over my shuffling off this mortal coil."

The prime minister went quiet for a moment, joining the others in the room in uncomfortable silence. He had suspected that those kicking him in the darkness were assailants. He had not wanted to believe so—it was a truth that made the future of everyone on Mars that much more difficult to manage. Accepting it, however, as just one more problem to be surmounted, Hawkes shoved his anger aside and addressed the assembly.

"All right—listen, everybody. We've got to turn things around and we've got to do it now. And the first thing we can do is stop worrying about where the blame goes. If all of the Resolute wanted me dead, yes—this meeting would be one chair lighter. But the Resolute has been infiltrated before, just as every other group in history has."

Hawkes gave Cobber a short direct look, letting her know he meant what he had just said, and what he was about to say.

"I think," he told her, speaking to everyone, "that you'll find the League was behind what happened yesterday, and I'm not just talking about what happened to me. But no matter *who* did *what* . . . I trust everyone here. If everyone else does, I say we get down to business."

"I agree," offered Goth. "But what business comes first?"

"You have the ear of the people on this planet if anyone does, Ace," said Waters. "What business would you suggest?"

"You want my opinion," answered the union boss, "get the domes open. You want people to think you're serious, get them onto the goddamned surface—pronto."

"Our Mr. Goth makes sense," said Hawkes. "At least, that's how *I* feel. Is there anyone here who doesn't agree?"

"Hell, everyone knows we need to get the domes open," answered Waters. "The question is still the same, though. *How* do we do it with that satellite frying the surface of the planet?"

"We turn it off."

All eyes turned toward Major Truman. As the rest of the assembly yielded her the floor, she continued, "I've been giving this some thought. If we destroy the boiler, the League will know it."

"And if that happened, they'd probably step up whatever invasion plan they already have in the works," suggested Waters. Turning to Hawkes, he asked, "What do you think?"

"I think you're right," answered the prime minister. "So, tell us, Major—what do you propose to get us around that fact?"

"I believe all we have to do is simply find the boiler, then shift its program so that it continues to collect radiation but doesn't release it."

As the others began to warm to her plan, the young woman added, "I'm willing to bet we could leave a hot box near its external output monitor and structure its surveillance signal so that whenever its onboard records are relay long–scanned—"

"What's that?" interrupted Goth.

"Series scans set up at intervals, timed to pinpoint the boiler whenever it was shut down. Normal scan systems can't operate with so much radiation around. Relay longs have more power behind them . . . but they can still only read what's there. If we can set things up right, they'd still read that the system is working the way it was designed to."

"You know, girl," said Scully, a wide grin on his face, "there could be a future for you in planetary security if you were so inclined."

The major smiled back at the old man. "I'd have to see your benefits package."

"And who would run this little mission?" asked Goth. "My guess is that if we need to keep this a secret, and we're down to only trusting each other, then finding a ship to pull this off might be a bit of a risk."

"You have a point," admitted Hawkes.

"A point?" responded the union leader. "We're talking about getting someone to risk running straight into concentrated bursts of solar tidal blasts. Where I come from, it could take a bit of asking to find a ship's captain who fits that bill."

"It just so happens," answered the prime minister, a bit of a grin crossing his face as well, "that I just might know someone."

"Someone with a ship," asked Truman, " 'as tough and faithful as gravity'?"

"That would be him," admitted Hawkes. "Yes, that would be him."

O H, SAILIN', SAILIN' over the bounding main . . ."

Curly Thorner manipulated the main controls of the *Stooge*, moving her as close as he dared to the radiation field filling the void between his ship and the still-invisible boiler satellite. Although the boiler had not released a burst in several days, the general area Thorner's computers had designated as its approximate location was still heavy with lingering radiation.

Truman sat in the *Stooge*'s copilot chair, feeding the asteroid miner navigational bits as she anticipated his needing them. Crowded in and around the few remaining seats to the back of the control bridge, the rest of the mission's crew simply waited for the pair to find the elusive satellite.

Aside from the ship's captain, however, no one seemed interested in making any noise at the moment. One of Thorner's crew had signaled from the sensor control room lower in the ship that the *Stooge* should be rapidly closing on the unseen boiler. Nervous anticipation kept all on board besides the captain staring out through the Yamato Special's front view port as if somehow they might be able to spot the satellite before the ship's probes. Concluding his song with a spirited flourish and surprisingly on-key burst, Thorner turned to his passengers to comment on their obvious nervousness.

"You know, for spacefaring heroes you're an awful quiet bunch."

"No, no," answered Scully. "We just didn't wanta gab through the entertainment."

"Oh—that right, Bennie?" Hawkes raised both eyebrows in mock irritation. He allowed very few people to even address him as "Benton," let alone "Bennie." But he had started to take a liking to the oversized asteroid miner. The fact the man had volunteered his ship and himself to their current mission without hesitation counted a long way in the prime minister's book.

Of course, Hawkes reminded himself, that might have more to do with the way he feels about Liz than any general tendency he has toward the heroic.

The prime minister frowned, wondering for a split second where he got the right to be jealous over another man's attraction to the major when he himself had not tried to lay any particular claim to her affections. Knowing he could not thrash out the problem there on the *Stooge*'s bridge, however, Hawkes turned his attention back to Thorner, answering his question with a minimum of sarcasm in his voice.

"Oh, absolutely. But while we're waiting for your first encore— and keep in mind, Curly, we *are* willing to wait—can you give us any idea how long this is going to take?"

As a low noise from the console captured Thorner's attention, the major fielded the question.

"If the calculating computer is on the ball, it should be any time now, actually." Without looking up from her console, Truman reminded the others, "Remember, since the radiation is released in waves from the satellite to simulate the erratic nature of a solar storm, Curly's crew have had to work out a sort of inverted triangulation, plotting a backward course toward the boiler."

"Yeah," added the asteroid miner. "I'll admit it's a pretty chancy bastard geometry at best, but with all the trace radiation in that field out there, we have to find a back door around it or we could get ourselves cooked."

"You mean if they was to send off another wave toward Mars?" asked Scully.

"This close," answered the major with a nod, "and of course, it's still only an assumption that we *are* close, it would cook us like Sunday dinner."

"Our assumptions are good," added Thorner. Thumping his console with satisfaction, he announced, "Because, sweet hips, we've found it."

The bridge buzzed with excitement. Waters and Goth, neither of whom had said anything for the last hour, suddenly crowded forward, straining to make visual contact. Indulging the mild chaos, the captain pointed them in the right direction. As Thorner set a circular course to bring the *Stooge* safely in behind the boiler's stream activator, Waters allowed a full-blown smile to cross his face for the first time in days.

"I can hardly believe it's going to be this easy. We just dock with that thing, throw a few switches, and that's it. It'll be over. The damned radiation will stop, and we'll finally be able to open the domes."

Turning to Scully, the president was hard-pressed to contain his emotions. "We're going to do it for them, Norm. Just like it was always promised. We're going to give everyone we know the sun again. Dirt beneath their feet. The smell of heat and steam growing things up out of the ground. Maybe our grandkids . . . Maybe they'll even know what wind feels like."

"Ahhhhh . . ."

Thorner made the brief noise, then stopped, listening intently to what his crew was telling him through his headphones. The single sound froze everyone. The dark tone of the asteroid miner's drawn-out syllable alerted everyone to the fact that something was wrong. They were now simply waiting for him to tell them how wrong. In a voice far humbler than Hawkes had ever heard the large man use, he told them.

"I'm sorry to tell you this, Mr. President. But I guess it ain't gonna be that easy, after all."

"Why?" asked Hawkes. "What's wrong?"

"Something we didn't think of . . ."

As his voice trailed off, Scully provided the answer. "There's a crew on board, ain't there?"

Thorner nodded.

"Now that we're close enough to see it, the ship's sensors can give us more pertinent feedback," explained the old security man. "Stuff like heat groupings, heartbeats. How many are there, Curly?"

"My crew rechecked the data twice. They say there's a minimum crew of twenty. But the boiler shielding could be masking more. Maybe twice as many more."

The implications were lost on no one present. Several of them began speaking at once, running over each other's words. In the moment of silence that followed, Ace Goth spoke up.

"So?" he asked. "So what? We found the damn thing once, we can find it again—right? What's the big deal? All we need to do is get back to Mars, get some more people, get some weapons, and then search the damn thing out again and teach 'em what it means to be a good neighbor."

"Ummm, maybe not."

Everyone's attention turned from Goth back to Thorner. Biting at his lower lip, the miner remained hunched over his console, studying the figures his crew was feeding to him over his main monitor array. Checking them in his head and with the secondary gauge computer at hand, he told the others, "We haven't had a burst from that thing out there for a while—right?"

"Watch chief back home made it about three, four days," confirmed Scully.

"Looks like they've been savin' it up."

"What do you mean, Curly?" asked Hawkes.

"Our scan of their systems shows that they've got a helluva load stored in the assembly cells. And . . . there's a lotta machinery sliding around out there, like they're making some kind of realignments."

"Curly's crew thinks they're getting ready to send a huge blast toward Mars," explained Truman. "Maybe the biggest yet."

"No way we could outrun it," the asteroid miner added. "We can't beat it back and if we got caught in its path we'd get fried. Period."

"So," asked Waters, "what do we do?"

"I don't know," answered Hawkes, staring out the forward port at the ever-nearing boiler. As they drew closer, they could see the acre-wide holding collectors being shifted along their tracks. "But whatever it is, it looks like we'd better do it fast."

22

HEY, WHERE THE hell's the relief team?"

Captain Faingnaert was not in a good mood. He and the rest of the crew of Solar Collector Station 8 had been scheduled to burn the surface of Mars two days earlier. But massive problems with the hydraulic motivators in the forward wing assembly had delayed the firing.

"Does anyone here have an answer for me?"

"Sorry, sir," snapped Lieutenant Dell, the captain's chief aide. "No, sir. They should have returned from the final outside check twenty minutes ago. Best guess is that they got hung up somewhere along the line and they're still outside."

Faingnaert sighed with frustration. Manning the boiler satellite was an important assignment, but not a glamorous one. The amount of radiation solar collectors dealt with not only disrupted contact with Earth but made all outside contact impossible. Crews sent to the hull for observation or in work details remained out of contact until they reentered the satellite. Period.

The captain was a good officer. Understanding the uselessness of bluster, he told Dell to stand by and wait for the crew's final confirmation that they could release their scheduled burst. After that, he was just about to begin the precountdown sequences, when the noise started. At first it was only a slight, distant clanging, a hollow rattle that began as a background disturbance but slowly built to the point where everyone in the control room could hear it clearly.

"Okay, now someone tell me what *that* is."

"Sir," answered Dell. "It sounds like somebody . . . banging on the outside of the satellite."

"What would any of our people be doing that for?" The captain stared at the back of the room, his mind making the obvious connection instantly. "That's coming from the rear—from the docking bays. We don't have anyone out there—our crews are all in the front down along the . . ."

Faingnaert let his voice trail off. His first thought was that someone dispatched from the League had come to investigate the delay in their firing. He dismissed the notion at once. Not only had they had longer delays during their mission already, but the schedule was an arbitrary one set completely at the captain's discretion. Making the deadline pleased his sense of order, but missing it by two days would not have caused anyone to be sent out to the boiler.

No one *could* have made it in this amount of time, he thought. Which returns me to the question . . . what the hell is going on around here?

"Mr. Dell . . ."

"Sir!"

"Pick a four-man detail and meet me in the docking area in five minutes."

The captain returned Dell's salute and then exited from the control room. All the way down the long metal corridor leading to the docks, he listened to the continuing noise, searching it for signs of a pattern that might betray its origin. It was obvious that whoever was creating the racket knew their way around space hardware. Anyone who could hammer on the outside of a satellite and make it heard throughout the inside understood their deep-space construction.

But also, he thought, anyone who doesn't have our entry procedures built into their ship's bridge command probably doesn't belong here.

Patting his sidearm, an affectation he had allowed himself that suddenly seemed quite useful, he said aloud, "Luckily, the Navy has a remedy for that."

● ● ● THE FOUR-MAN detail stood to the rear, two to each side of Faingnaert and Dell. All four had their shotguns at the ready. The lieutenant had ordered the weapons assigned due to the heavy-wall nature of the docking bay. They were the perfect weapons for such an area—if weapons were needed.

Dell realized they had no concrete proof the boiler was under assault, of course. But, as one of his instructors in the academy had put it, "Issuing an apology is a lot easier than writing a letter to a good man's widow."

Besides, thought the lieutenant as he stood his position with the others, listening to the banging still coming from the other side of the docking door, somebody explain to me how this can be something harmless, and then we'll both know. After all, leave us not forget that Solar Collector Station 8 is as top-secret as they come. Unless whoever is out there is from the League, they aren't going to live long enough to worry anybody.

"Okay," said Faingnaert, his eyes darting left to right, his ingrained training making one last unconscious check to see if there was anything more he could do. "Open it."

The six soldiers waited as the slow process of cycling the air lock began. All of them scanned the monitor intently as the first of the three massive roll plates slid back into the wall of the satellite. Two of the guards shifted their weight uncomfortably as the second plate rolled back out of the way. In seconds, whatever was outside the boiler's air lock would have access to the ship. There would still be another three roll plates in their way, of course, but . . .

"It's two people."

"What'd you expect, Zudiack—Martians?" asked Dell. Then, as several of his men covered their snickering, he added, "Little green ones. You comedians know what I meant."

"Eyes front," ordered Faingnaert. The six watched the two environment-suited figures—one large, one small—stumble into the air lock. The chamber's internal atmosphere began to stabilize as the second plate rolled back into place. By the time the third plate was shifting, the two figures within were helping each other off with their helmets.

"I'm popping the hatch on our visitors," announced the captain. "Any speculations?"

"I caught a glimpse of their ship in the background," offered one of the guards. "Looked like a miner. Yamato Special. Hard ship to hide any armaments on. They could be legitimate."

"True enough," agreed Faingnaert. "But legitimate *what*?"

No one had an answer as the monitor revealed the first of the roll plates to the interior of the satellite beginning its pullback. The soldiers waited out the long moment, studying the pair on their screens.

The larger figure was a man, bald, overweight, sweating, panting. The smaller was an attractive woman. She seemed panicked, exhausted. What the two were doing at the boiler's dock none of the six could explain, but they were all beginning to feel a bit more relaxed. But only a small bit.

There were still too many unanswered questions, too many possibilities that something was wrong, for any of the men to relax completely. No one in the half-dozen lowered their weapons from their defensive positions as the last barrier plate began to roll back into the wall. Indeed, as the big man staggered forward, most of them went to the ready.

"Oh sweet Jesus, oh God, oh man, oh man, oh man—did I ever think we'd bought it that time." Curly Thorner lurched into the holding chamber, staggering wildly, seemingly oblivious of the weapons being trained on him.

"I mean, after what we found, to just die in space. That would have been too much."

"Sir," asked Faingnaert with stiff formality, "I must inform you that you have—"

"God, oh, thank you, God. Thank you." Curly's body folded as he spoke. As if all his strength had disappeared, he collapsed onto the floor, staring at the ceiling of the holding chamber. Working the clasps of his environment suit's gloves, he continued to babble, ignoring all attempts made by the captain to communicate with him.

"I mean, I mean . . . Jesus shit, who wants to die after they've found Baxter's nugget? Riddle me that, man."

"Baxter's nugget?" Faingnaert asked, his tone more condescending than interested. Thorner's manner had softened the captain's defenses, but little else. Not seeming to notice the shift, however, the asteroid miner went on, half answering the boiler's commander, half merely continuing to rant.

"Ten years every pisshead ore jockey and astie jumper has been searching for it. Three kilometers wide, pack density at plus eighty—*plus* eighty. Baxter found it, radioed everybody in the system, but never made it back to Mars. It's just been out there all this time, rollin' round the sun—waitin' for me! When my threshold motivator conked, I thought the curse was true. Drifted for days. Food and water, zimmy, gone—thought I was gonna go just like Baxter."

Thorner looked up. Staring Faingnaert in the eyes, he whispered, "And then I saw you. Salvation. I saw you and knew I was gonna live to spend all that gold."

"Gold?" asked Dell, the curiosity in his voice more civilian than military.

"Yes—gold," answered Thorner. "Baxter's nugget—over ten thousand tons of *gold!*"

All eyes fixed on the asteroid miner. Still sitting on the floor, he pulled off his left glove with a struggle.

"I'm the richest man in the universe, boys . . ."

And then, as the reality of what the bald man before them was saying hit the six soldiers, the woman they had forgotten leaped into the room. Curly threw himself flat on the floor as she fired over his head. Truman's first two shots tore through the heads of two of the escorts, killing them instantly. Her third and fourth shots tore through the neck and chest of the third man in the guard team. As the fourth leveled his shotgun at the major, Thorner managed to get his other glove off, freeing the derringer he had concealed in it earlier on his ship. The last of the guards died before he could pull the trigger on his weapon.

Faingnaert almost managed to get his weapon clear from its holster before Truman put her sidearm to his head. "Don't do it, Captain," she cautioned him. "A smart man could live through this."

Thorner pushed himself up off the floor, smiling and giggling, not quite ready to believe he had survived the preceding melee. Shoving Lieutenant Dell aside, he headed for the air lock controls, laughing.

"No, there's no gold, boys," he said as he locked the internal entrance to the docking area. "That was what we call a clever ruse. But I didn't lie. I *am* the richest man in the universe."

The asteroid miner gave Truman a playful punch on the shoulder, then added, "That's because I have friends. Friends that hit what they shoot at."

And then, Thorner began running the barrier plates back to their original positions so he could admit the rest of their party, even as alert sirens began to shriek throughout the satellite.

HAWKES, WATERS, GOTH, and Scully waited in the air lock for the chamber's atmosphere to reach sustaining levels. After a quick planning session and vote, the team had decided to send in two people with the only weapons they had. Thorner and Truman had volunteered instantly, bluntly rejecting all opposition. Since the major had the proper training, the asteroid miner had let her take Scully's sidearm. Thorner determined to tough things out with his wits, but welcomed the wrist derringer Goth offered.

Everyone but Scully was surprised to find that the union leader felt it necessary to go about armed, but no one commented. The two-shot weapon seemed like it would be far more useful than the various blades and blunt clubs Thorner had aboard the *Stooge*.

I wish those plates would start moving, thought Hawkes. Keeping an eye on both the atmosphere gauge and the door, he shifted his weight from one foot to the other, desperate to see what waited on the other side of the lock. Off to his left, Waters indexed his helmet mike.

"You know, Benton, just because someone's opening the lock, it doesn't necessarily have to be them. The satellite's crew could be suckering us in."

"Oh my, you think so?" responded Hawkes sarcastically. "Hadn't thought of that. Gee, what'll we do?"

The prime minister regretted the verbal attack the second he made it, but it was too late to do anything about it except to try to explain.

"Sorry, Sam," he said. "I thought of the same thing. And being just as tired and scared as everyone else, not liking the feeling of having a wall shoved against my back that I just can't seem to get around . . . well, sorry."

Waters jerked his thumb in the direction of the door. As the third roll plate began to move back, he answered, "Whatever happens, Ben—we did it for Mars."

And at that point, the four men finally saw what had transpired in the docking area of Solar Collector Station 8. As they moved into the bay through the deep wail of sirens, the first thing they saw were the four bodies lying at awkward angles just inside the door, soaking in large pools of blood. Two more men were being held near the back wall of the bay. They sat cross-legged, facing the rear with their hands behind their heads, the major covering them with a shotgun. Curly they found at the air lock controls, a small heap of weapons piled on the console next to him.

Picking up a shotgun, he tossed it to Scully, saying, "Here, old-timer, a new toy, something for those cold nights."

The asteroid miner tossed one to Hawkes, then offered the sidearm he had taken from Captain Faingnaert to Goth and Waters, as well as the one Scully had given Truman earlier. The president protested that he was not very good with guns, but Thorner urged one on him nonetheless, reminding him that they still had a lot to accomplish. Returning the union leader's now empty derringer, he said, "Small, convenient—I like it."

"Did the job?" asked Goth.

As Goth stuffed the empty weapon and its wrist strap in the carrier pouch of his environment suit Thorner told him, "Oh yeah, like a big dog."

At the same time, Truman took a moment to tell the others what had happened. After she finished her briefing, Hawkes told the boiler satellite's commander to stand.

"Diplomacy is usually my game, but your ship's sirens make me feel we don't have time for that."

"What do you want?" asked Faingnaert. The captain's face was an easy read for the career diplomat. More worried about his future with the military and his life than he was about his men or his mission, Hawkes could tell that Faingnaert was ready to deal. The prime minister wasted no time in capitalizing on the fact.

"For starters, why don't we pull the plug on those sirens?"

The captain indicated that he would have to have access to the control panel on the other side of the bay. Hawkes walked him over at gunpoint. With only a moment's hesitation, Faingnaert contacted his second on the main bridge and told him to stand down for the time being. When the officer asked for details on what had occurred, Hawkes took over Faingnaert's position at the comm and gave him some.

"This satellite has been commandeered for its acts of aggression against the planet Mars. This is the leader of the fleet boarding party. I've been authorized to extend the chance to surrender to everyone on board. If this is carried out peacefully, it will be necessary to hold you all for some period of time, but eventually you will be returned to the Earth League if you so desire." The prime minister gave his words a few seconds to sink in, then continued.

"If this offer is not accepted, however, you will be destroyed along with this satellite. There is a Class M war wagon some three hundred miles off and closing. If we do not have control of this station by the time it reaches its mark, it will obliterate all of us."

Hawkes paused once more, counting off the seconds in his head. Then he added curtly, "You have three minutes to either join your captain in honorable surrender, or accept annihilation."

After that, the prime minister broke the connection, marking the time on his chronometer. As he focused his attention on Faingnaert, he shifted his face and stance to reflect a more open and friendly manner. Locking eyes with the captain, he asked, "So, tell me, were our boys right?"

"About what?"

"Our long-range scanners told us you were going to send a much bigger burst our way. Worse than any of the others by far—correct?" Faingnaert nodded. When Hawkes pushed for a reason, the captain gave him one.

"The League wanted your shielded dome ruined. Not so much the dome, but whatever's inside it."

The prime minister looked to Waters and Scully. The security chief told him, "He means the old number ten dome—Greentop. That's the one Vincent Pebelion is turning into a park."

"*Was* turning into a park," Waters hissed. "*Was* turning into a park until the *solar flare-ups* started." The president stared coldly at Faingnaert as he continued. "It was the only dome we had worth protecting. We didn't want Vinn's work to be all for nothing, so we did everything we could to keep it safe."

Hawkes nodded thoughtfully, trying to understand what would make Greentop so important a target. Since the domes were not yet open to the general public, it would not have been reasonable of the League to expect such an action to deliver much in the way of demoralization among the population. After a few more seconds, however, he thought he had the answer.

"Greentop is where the Red Planet, Inc., stockholders' meetings are held, isn't it, Sam?" When Waters confirmed Hawkes's memory, the prime minister nodded again, contentedly.

"Politics. If the quarterly meeting can't be held where it was announced it would be held, we lose face. Obviously we're not running Mars very well, tsk, tsk. Justification for looking into martial law."

"The Earth League would take away the only green we have so they can feel justified in doing what everyone knows they're going to do anyway?" Goth sputtered. "That's pretty snowed over, even for the League."

"You remember the slogan 'your friends in Washington' . . ." Hawkes stopped speaking as his chronometer sounded, alerting him to the fact that three minutes had passed. He reestablished contact with Faingnaert's second, and the officer confirmed that the remaining crewmen were not ready to mutiny. They would follow their captain into surrender.

"Hey—we won," said Thorner. Turning to Faingnaert, the asteroid miner asked, "Tell me, Captain—how many people do you have on this can?"

"Still living . . . thirty-eight. Why?"

Ignoring the captain, Thorner told Hawkes, "I hate to say this, but there's no place to secure anyone on the *Stooge*. Not more than three or four, anyway. Guess we didn't plan this thing out much past winning."

"I guess none of us really expected to win," offered the prime minister.

"Yeah, well, sorry to upset your expectations," answered the miner. "But regardless, what exactly are we going to do with these guys?"

Hawkes had only begun to ponder the problem when Lieutenant Dell began to stand up. "There's no war wagon out there."

"Whether there is or isn't," Truman cautioned the officer, "I'd suggest you sit back down."

Hawkes kept his shotgun trained on the captain. Faingnaert motioned meekly with his hands that he had no intention of provoking anyone. While Thorner checked the locks holding the bay door against the rest of the satellite, Scully, Goth, and Waters all moved toward the back of the bay where Dell continued to shout.

"I don't believe it!" he raged. "You foxed us completely. There's no ship—there's just you! We surrendered the collector to, to . . . nobody!" Truman took a backward step to keep her weapon out of her prisoner's range. As she did, however, Waters walked past her, unintentionally putting himself between the major and Dell.

With no regard for the consequences, the president of Mars told the man, "Calm down, son, you don't understand. We had to do what we did—we couldn't allow . . ."

Scully and Truman, both understanding what was about to happen, moved forward at the same time to try and prevent the inevitable. They were too late. Dell made his move and grabbed Waters in the hopes of using him as a shield. The officer immediately got one of his hands on the gun the president was carrying. Needing his other hand to hold on to Waters, the lieutenant found he could not take complete control of the weapon. Doing the best he could, he struggled to turn it on those advancing on him.

"Sam—get away from him!" shouted Scully, but it was too late. The two men spun around twice, and then the president's weapon went off. The few rounds tore through the room. One of them clipped Ace Goth across the lower part of his thigh. It did little damage to him, but tore a bad hole in his environment suit. Waters was not so lucky.

"Sam!" shouted Scully, racing to his old friend's side. Ignoring the now empty gun in Dell's hand, the security man smashed the butt of his shotgun into the lieutenant's face, sending him staggering backward. As Dell neared the back wall, Scully hit him across the side of the head, bouncing his face off the thick metal of the bay. The younger man crumpled, blood smearing the wall as he clutched at it, sliding blindly to the floor. Instantly Hawkes turned on Faingnaert.

"I didn't do anything," insisted the captain. "You can't blame me for that."

"Shut up," commanded Hawkes. "What kind of facilities do you have on this thing?"

"We've got a medical officer . . . He has a small station, next to the galley, but I doubt he can . . . You have to understand, we're not supposed to be here. These satellites aren't meant for long-term occupation. He doesn't have . . ."

"He's telling the truth," offered Truman, staring numbly at the great arcs of blood bursting from Waters despite Scully's best effort to stanch the flow. "These things only have the facilities to house their builders. After that, they're supposed to be self-operating. It's why we didn't expect anyone here in the first place."

Thorner took over guarding the captain as Hawkes moved toward the scene. Kneeling next to Waters, he saw instantly that the president would not survive even long enough to be taken back to the *Stooge*, let alone for the trip back to Mars. Feeling helpless and stupid, Hawkes set his shotgun down and took Waters's hand in his own.

"Sam, Sam—can you hear me?"

The president coughed violently, bloody phlegm spilling out of his mouth. Then, seeing the gun that had wounded him so horribly still in his hand, he stared at it, laughing sadly at his own incompetence.

"Told you I wasn't very good with these things."

Hawkes wanted to speak, but he had no words. What had happened had been so quick, so painfully unnecessary, that he could not find any oratory within him to cover the situation. Understanding, Waters told him, "All my fault. I shouldn't . . . have been here. Engineer . . . that's all I am. Not a politician. Not . . . not a soldier."

The president broke out in another spasm of racking coughs. His lips bubbling with blood and foam, he said weakly, "You tell Glenia . . . tell her how much I love her."

"Sam, Sam," Hawkes stammered. "If only, I didn't, I, I . . ."

"All my fault," the dying man insisted. "My fault. I just . . . just wanted to . . . bring the wind to Mars."

Waters coughed again. Then, wiping at his mouth, feeling his life racing out of his body, he asked a final boon. "It's been so long since I was on Earth. So long. Benton . . . tell me about . . . the wind."

"Up in the Absarokas where I live," Hawkes started, struggling to keep his voice under control, "the Flathead tribe, they have a word for a certain type of wind. Chinook, they call it. It means 'snow eater.' It's a warm wind that comes sometimes in the dead of winter—can clear more than a foot of packed ice and snow overnight. It stays constant for four, five days, always blowing—fifty, sometimes seventy miles an hour."

Waters groaned softly. The noise echoed in the bay as everyone held their breath. Forcing his mouth to work, Hawkes continued, telling his friend, "You can't open a vehicle without being afraid that the wind's going to take the door right off. You have to lean forward everywhere you walk. You have to . . . The air is filled with trash—your neighbor's hat always seems to be flying past your window. But it helps hurry the spring. One day you have snow all around you, then the chinook blows in and, and . . . suddenly there's new grass everywhere."

And then, without realizing what he was saying, all traces of his old hatreds finally gone, Hawkes whispered, "We're going to be that warm wind for Mars, Sam. We're going to cover her with new grass, with trees and lakes and everything that was ever promised. We're going to . . ."

Suddenly, the prime minister realized that Sam Waters was dead. He folded his friend's arms across his chest, and then for a brief instant, the dull grayness of the docking bay seemed to close in on Hawkes, the walls suffocating him.

Blinking, he brought the world coldly back into focus, wondering at the same time why he even bothered.

HAWKES AND A bandaged Ace Goth stood across the room from Glenia Waters, waiting for her reaction. They had told her everything that had happened, up to and including her husband's death. Now they waited for their words to register with her—for her to give them some clue as to what they should say or do next. After a moment, she gave them one they had not expected.

"What did you do with the satellite crew?"

Both men hesitated, not prepared for such a logical question in the face of the news they had just delivered. Sensing their problem, the woman told them softly, "You told me that Sam didn't make it back when you first came in. Then you told me the whole story leading up to it. All right—I know what happened. I understand. My Sam is dead. Now if you two could shake those pitiful looks out of your eyes, maybe I'll be able to get through this."

"We're awful sorry, Glenia," offered Goth, hanging his head as he talked. "We didn't mean for . . ."

"Of course you didn't, you big idiot," Glenia whispered. "I know that. Did you think Sam meant for it to happen? We knew it was going to, though. I was hoping for more time than this, but—"

"What do you mean, Glenia—you *knew*?"

"Ever since you first came to Mars, Benton," the woman answered, "Sam and I have known there was going to be more trouble than anyone expected. And when he was elected president— oh, God, how he didn't want that."

"Really?" asked Goth, somewhat taken aback. "I thought he was pretty zoomed by the whole thing."

"He was honored," Glenia admitted. "Any man would be. But he knew it was going to be too much for him. He said it so many times—'I wasn't born to be a politician.' My poor Samuel. He really was happiest when he was just an engineer."

Then some wisp of memory drifted through Glenia Waters's mind, and finally the first few tears began to spill from her eyes. While Hawkes and Goth stood their ground, separated from the woman by the daunting canyon of their inability to protect her husband, both men ached to do something to relieve her suffering. As if she could hear their thoughts, she told them, "I asked what you did with the rest of the boiler crew."

"We locked them in their commissary," Hawkes answered. "Because of the radiation involved, the satellite has no external monitors, meaning they had no way of knowing our story was a lie. Scully and two of Thorner's crew stayed behind to watch the satellite. We've already dispatched an ore runner with a heavily armed detail of Scully's security people to pick them up. A few of our technicians are going along for the ride—so they can take care of the satellite."

"What will they do to it?" asked Glenia, struggling to turn her attention away from her grief and toward the well-being of Mars.

"They'll set it to store the majority of the radiation it collects, rather than disperse it. We have the captain's schedule. Radiation will still be released—just in case the League is monitoring for it—but only enough to convince them the boiler is still working."

"Right," added Goth. "And even then, they're going to beam it at angles, so it'll still interfere with communications but it won't bathe the surface anymore."

"And the men that were killed, and . . . and my Sam . . . What did you do with . . ."

"The remains of the soldiers we killed were brought back," answered Hawkes. "They've already been sent down to reclamation."

"Waste not, want not," Goth said cynically.

"Sam, . . . well, we thought maybe . . . just this once . . . maybe Mars could try something a bit different."

Her eyebrows arching with protective suspicion, Glenia asked what Hawkes meant. He told her.

"I thought we might take him up to the old number ten dome, where Vinn Pebelion is making his park. Sam was the first president of Mars. He died trying to make it a better place. If we were to bury him up there—not in a coffin, but just in a fiber bag—with some seeds, maybe . . . so he could keep on doing his part to make Mars a better place . . ."

And then Glenia's tears began flowing uncontrollably, flooding forth in torrents. Splashing down from her cheeks and chin, they fell so freely they began to visibly dampen her suit. Nodding her head and smiling in her grief, she said softly, "He would have been very happy."

Not able to contain their unease anymore, the two men excused themselves. Shaking her head, Glenia refused them permission to leave. As they waited awkwardly, she explained.

"Trust me, gentlemen, I wish I could let you leave. I wouldn't, wouldn't . . . mind being alone right now. But since it appears I'm going to be alone for quite some time ahead, I think that now that you've shared your bad news with me, I had better share mine with you."

"Something happened while we were gone?" asked Hawkes.

"It isn't a big problem, but . . . the Resolute has been demanding another meeting with the president. They want war declared with Earth. They want a chance to convince the president to throw his support behind their viewpoint."

"And if they don't get it?" asked Goth.

"Work stoppages, riots, vandalism. They made it quite clear they want to talk to Sam and they'll do whatever they have to to get their chance."

"And if we tell them the truth," mused Hawkes, looking blankly toward the wall, "the League will know instantly. 'The Martian president dead? No new elections planned? We can't permit this chaos.' Why does everywhere we turn lead to the League declaring martial law on us?"

"What's it matter?" asked Goth. "You're too used to playing games with this stuff. You said yourself that the only reason they'd want to declare martial law is to have a grain of truth to justify their actions to everybody on Earth, and the Moon, and . . . just everyone. But hell, you know as well as I do that whether they get their excuse or not . . . when they're ready, they're coming. And the Resolute will get its goddamned war no matter what anybody wants."

"Until then, however," answered Hawkes, "I think it behooves us to make them work for every inch."

"I agree, Benton," said Glenia. Rising, she crossed the few feet separating her from the two men. "But the Resolute's deadline for meeting with Samuel runs out tomorrow at noon. What are we going to do about that?"

Staring into the new widow's red eyes, the prime minister of Mars had to admit he had no ideas.

● ● ● "THIS IS WHY you've been stalling us?" Roger did not look happy. Turning to the physician in charge, he said, "This is some kind of gag."

"Mr. . . . er . . ."

"Doyle," Hawkes told the doctor, keeping behind the rest of the party.

"Mr. Doyle," the physician started again, "the president was on the surface yesterday in dome number ten supervising the dismantling of the shielding, when a massive solar flare up occurred."

"Why were they dismantling the shielding?" asked Victoria Cobber. "I mean, the way the sun has been the past few months, didn't it seem—"

"He did it for you people!" blurted Glenia Waters coldly. Without turning to the Resolute members, she stared through the lead glass panel at the still form of her husband. Stretched out on a solitary table, hooked up to an impressive array of life support systems, the president's corpse gave the needed shred of dignity Hawkes's lie needed. Holding back the tears she could feel building, Glenia Waters gave it the necessary emotion.

"He felt that if he could show you that work was being done to open the parks, that maybe—*maybe*—you would give him a moment to breathe and stop trying to tear Mars apart."

"We never—"

Cobber started to speak, but Doyle cut her off, his political instincts taking command before her emotions forced her to make some concession the Resolute might regret later. At the same time, Truman stepped forward, placing her arms on the Martian first lady's shoulders. Turning Glenia from the sight of her husband, the major held her as she began to sob. At the same time, Hawkes moved between them and the two Resolute leaders.

"Well, not to be flippant, but as you can see, this is about all of the meeting one can expect to have with the president for a while."

"Mighty convenient," sneered Doyle.

"Oh, yes," agreed the prime minister. His voice harsh and cutting, he said, "That's exactly what I thought. Obviously it was fear of meeting with you two—something he had no trouble doing just the other day—that drove the president to subject himself to a near-fatal dose of radiation. That's one way to get out of a meeting, all right."

"Hey, who do you think you're talking to?" demanded Doyle. Growling from low in his throat, Hawkes told him.

"A dry-banked creep with as much compassion in him as a locust. I don't know exactly what your agenda is, but it's a spare and empty thing without respect for anyone or anything. Maybe you've forgotten who it was—"

"Stop it!" Cobber's outburst surprised everyone into silence. "Just stop it! Roger, for God's sake—what's wrong with you?"

"Nothing, love—nothing." Backing off from his argument, Doyle reminded his girlfriend, "I just don't trust this bunch. They can bribe people into saying it was Resolute members that trampled you and Hawkes, but I know it's all just their propaganda machine moving into full swing."

Doyle strutted away from Cobber, staring at the prime minister, his eyes moving from Hawkes's head to his feet.

" 'Nearly killed,' they reported. I don't know—might be, but you look pretty good to me today. And now we get your little tale of woe—'The president received a nasty dose of radiation planting trees for the children of Mars.' Break someone else's heart with your stage plays, Hawkes. We still want to know when we get to have another meeting with your bunch, or do we just go ahead and start tearing up?"

"I'm going to offer the Congress a proposal. Since Mrs. Waters is the only person permitted to visit her husband at this time, I'm going to ask if she might be permitted to take his place at all functions as his representative. She wouldn't have any power to make decisions, but she could gather information for the president, and then get his decisions."

Hawkes timed his pause, giving Doyle just long enough to formulate the beginnings of a protest, then added, "Of course, this would be a strictly temporary measure. Just to get us over the next few days as the doctors work to stabilize his condition."

The two sides debated the idea back and forth for a short while, but the prime minister knew from the look in Cobber's eyes that he had won his battle. The Resolute leaders left finally, agreeing to go along with Hawkes's proposal for a week. After seven days, Doyle threatened, if Waters was not back on his feet, the Resolute would call for new elections.

As he watched the couple leave the infirmary, Hawkes thought to himself, Seven days. More than I hoped for. And the way the League is moving, probably more than we'll need.

The prime minister of Mars watched its first lady staring once more through the somehow too small rectangle of glass at her husband's remains. She had agreed to the charade of pretending that her beloved Samuel was still alive, had helped talk the doctor into going along with it.

And Scully and Vinn Pebelion, he reminded himself—they had to be brought into our little deception. Good work, Benton, now you're asking widows to put aside their grief and playact that there's some kind of hope . . .

"All for the greater good."

"What was that?" asked Major Truman. Although she could not make out Hawkes's words, the dark tone he used to utter them disturbed her greatly.

"Just making a list of things to put on my résumé, for when I go back to Earth and challenge Mick Carri for his Senate seat in the next election."

Truman called out as the prime minister made to leave, but he told her, "Forget it. You see to the first lady's needs. I'm a big boy— I can take care of myself for a while."

Whether Hawkes actually believed his statement, the major had no way of knowing. That he would be proved wrong in only a matter of minutes, however, she could never have guessed.

25

THE MAN CAUGHT up to Hawkes only a few dozen yards away from the intensive care unit's exit. He timed the moment perfectly, forcing the intersection of their paths a handful of seconds after the prime minister passed a group of nurses heading into the unit to begin their shift. If the man had not wanted to set upon Hawkes without any witnesses being present, he would have caught up to him much sooner.

The assailant's knife tore through the left side of the prime minister's coat and dress vest, tangling in the weave mesh of the protective plated vest he was wearing underneath. Hawkes flung his elbow back with savage force, catching his attacker in the forehead. As the man stumbled away, the prime minister followed up his first blow, charging his attacker before the man had a chance to bring his blade back into play.

Going for his assailant's weapon hand, Hawkes kicked at the man's elbow. His blow missed its target, striking the attacker's forearm instead, smashing it against the wall. The knife clattered away down the hall as bones cracked in its owner's right arm. The prime minister caught hold of the man's shoulder and spun him around.

"All right, and just who the hell do we have *this* time?" demanded Hawkes. Unfortunately, once the prime minister had a clear view of his assailant, he found that the man's face had been bubbled—filled with plastic underneath the skin to render him unrecognizable.

"You'll never rule Mars, you bastard," spat the wounded assassin. Biting back tears, he hissed through grinding teeth, "The Resolute will never surrender to you!"

Then, ignoring the pain tearing through his broken forearm, the man fumbled desperately under the right-hand side of his vest. His injury slowed him greatly, however, keeping him from getting to whatever it was he wanted. Seeing no reason to allow the man to gain any kind of advantage, Hawkes closed with his attacker, grabbing the man's shattered arm at the break point. Squeezing hard, he jerked the injury several times.

"Not that I want to rule anything," snarled Hawkes, "but if I did, you certainly won't be the one who stops me."

The assassin screamed in agony as the prime minister ground the broken ends of his shattered ulna against each other. Then, much to Hawkes's surprise, his attacker somehow managed to free the hidden object he had been digging for. He was unable to hold on to it, however, and the black disc slipped from his fingers. The small Graamler bomb dropped to the floor between the two men, bouncing twice.

Hawkes did not waste any time looking to see if the device was armed. Turning quickly, the prime minister put everything he had into a wild leap, throwing himself as far away from the powerful explosive and his attacker as he could manage. He had not even hit the floor when the hallway erupted with thunder and smoke and the gagging stench of burning blood.

● ● ● "AND THAT'S IT?" demanded Hawkes, holding his glass only a few inches from his face. A slight thickness in his voice, he demanded, "That's all we could find out?"

"Benton," answered Major Truman with a touch of exasperation, "for Christ's sake, what do you want? What was left of the guy was plastered against the ceiling. It's amazing Scully's people could determine as much as they did."

Hawkes did not answer, taking another long drink instead. Sitting in the armchair in his quarters the evening after the attack, he found himself in a foul and bitter mood. Despite his assailant's attempt to pass himself off as a member of the Resolute, Scully's security people had determined from analyzing his remains that he had been off-planet for an extended period of time until just before the attack.

That meant, of course, that the assassin had almost certainly come down from one of the orbiting battlewagons, and that meant it was the Earth League that had tried to silence Mars' prime minister once more. Putting his tumbler aside for the moment, Hawkes set his elbows on the arms of his chair and then linked his fingers together before his face.

"You know," he growled, his speech growing slightly slurred, "we ought to just give them their damn war."

"What?" asked Truman. "What are you talking about? Give *who* a war?"

"The League, the Resolute," answered the prime minister. "Anyone who wants one. Why not? Why the hell not?"

Lifting his tumbler again, Hawkes drained the last of his drink. Immediately, he got up out of his chair and crossed his spartan quarters to the solitary dresser against the far wall. Putting his palms against the cold metal of its top, he stared into the mirror on the wall behind it, whispering more to his reflection than to the major.

"The League wants me dead. Half of Mars wants me dead. Why not let them kick each other's asses for a while? I'm tired of being everyone's target." Reaching for the first of the four bottles he had arranged in front of the mirror earlier, he began building himself another drink.

"Enemies—everywhere I look that's all I see anymore. No one

wants to help us. The Moon, the asteroid federations . . . anyone on Earth, maybe? Don't hold your breath."

Hawkes set down the second bottle, picking up the third with his other hand. Unscrewing its cap, he said, "Don't you understand, Liz, we're fighting a losing battle here. We've got every hand against us, and when you look up their sleeves, all their arms lead back to the League. That bastard Carri, all of them . . . when they're not trying something political or legal to get us, they just send more assassins."

"It's not that bad, Benton," Truman answered in a quiet voice. Paying her no attention, Hawkes poured a generous slug from the third bottle, continuing to talk to the mirror.

"I'd like to take a side—somebody's side, anybody's side. But who would that be? Everyone wants me dead. Hell, everyone wants *everyone* else dead. I save Cobber's life—I saved that woman's life when her fellow Martians tried to kill her—and she still only hates Earth. I save their leader's life and they still call me a slave trader."

Hawkes replaced the third bottle, grabbing up the fourth. As he did, his eyes wandered for a moment, catching sight of Truman in the mirror. He looked at her—a long, frozen moment—forgetting Mars and the League, the dead behind and the war ahead, and everything else. Including Dina Martel.

Seeing only a woman, his mind looking for escape, reeling from the pressures closing in on him, he thought of putting everything aside and simply going to her.

Put aside the drink, the back of his mind whispered, turn out the lights, take her in your arms. Forget everything. Throw it away. Do it!

But as much as he wanted—needed—the release, his brain was not yet blurred to the point where he could so easily reduce the world. Pleasure seemed so much of the moment, and clearheaded, he knew he could not waste moments on himself. And thus he found himself recapping the fourth bottle, his latest drink completed and ready for him.

Closing his eyes to the mirror image before him, Hawkes took a long pull on his drink, knocking back a third of the tumbler in one shot. Approving of the taste, he wiped his mouth on his sleeve and then turned back to Truman, letting the air of crisis surround him once more.

"The Moon sells us out, the miners won't help . . . even the Martians have turned on me. So, you tell me . . . what am I supposed to do now?"

"One suggestion I could make," the major said softly. "Maybe you shouldn't drink any more tonight."

"That doesn't answer my question, does it?" retorted Hawkes. Staggering back to his chair, he half sat, half fell into it, almost losing his drink in the process, "But that's the way of things around here, isn't it?"

"Don't you think you'd better get some sleep?"

"Sure, sure . . . change the subject. Throw this back on me, everything always gets turned back on me." The prime minister took another massive drink from his tumbler, then rambled on further. "You're no better than the rest of them. Hell, maybe you *are* one of them. Just another traitor."

"You're drunk."

"Hit a nerve, did I?" Hawkes slurred his words, waving his tumbler wildly as he accused, "Sure—why not?"

Love tossed aside, other emotions crawled forward within the prime minister's brain. Fear gnawing at him, he added, "After all, one thing you have to give the League, they *do* plan ahead. Maybe you're just another one of their deep agents. They've gotten their people into the Resolute, into the Martian government—hell, they got their people into Scully's security force. So why not into my bed?"

Major Truman stared at Hawkes as if seeing him for the first time. For a moment, her memory of the man she had idealized—idolized—disappeared. She started to speak, anger slamming at her, demanding that the slap she had just been dealt be repaid in kind, but she stopped herself. Her body trembling with rage, she felt her teeth banging against each other. Biting down hard, she turned away, unable to speak to the prime minister without malice if she looked at him directly.

"Your friend is dead," she told him in a harsh, even voice. "And you don't know what to do next. I suppose it doesn't happen too often that the great and clever Benton Hawkes is left without a clue. I'm not much of a politician, and no one's ever nominated me for a Nobel Prize, but all the same I think I should give you a bit of advice."

Walking across the room, Truman stopped at the door to the hallway. She put her hand on the release, ready to leave, her mind in terrible turmoil. Part of her wanted to forget about being understanding and to remind Hawkes how much *she* had lost, how much *she* had sacrificed for him and his cause. Part of her still wanted to strike back at him, to hurt him as he had hurt her. Ignoring them both, the major said simply, "For all our sakes, I wouldn't drink so much if I were you."

And then, before Hawkes could reply, or she could say anything further, Truman indexed the door release and moved quickly out into the hall. Although she realized the prime minister was too inebriated to come after her with any speed—if indeed he was concerned enough about anyone other than himself to come after her at all—Truman ran from his door, not slowing her pace until she had made it around the far corner. Then she stopped, putting her back to the wall.

Her mind flashed through a score of ideas in a heartbeat. She considered returning, but rejected the idea instantly. Hawkes would still be drunk, would probably be drinking more. She thought of contacting Scully or Glenia Waters—even Curly—to see if they felt they might be able to talk to him. She even thought about drinking herself.

In the end, she decided to simply return to her own room and turn in for the night. The prime minister was not a child, she told herself. He was a principal, if not the pivotal, performer in the current game being played out across the solar system. That made him one of the most important men in the universe.

It was a position that came with a great number of perks, but with a great deal of stress as well. Despite the amount of time they had spent together recently—the intimacy that had grown between then—the major had to admit that she did not know the prime minister all that well.

Then, suddenly, Truman admitted to herself that Hawkes could not have meant any of the things he had said to her. She knew she had been right about everything—that he was feeling lost and trapped and backed into a corner with no way out, and that none of those sensations were anything "the great and clever Benton Hawkes" would be used to experiencing.

Her anger gone, the major retraced her steps.

He *is* drunk, she thought, and you're not. So stop worrying about your pride, soldier, and go back and make sure he's all right.

Truman turned the corner, and then saw something that started her running. Although she had indexed the prime minister's door to close automatically behind her, it was standing open. Skidding to a halt just before the doorway, she called out as she arrived, her voice filled with panic. But she received no answer.

Benton Hawkes was gone.

EVERYBODY'S AGAINST ME. Everything's all my fault. As if I can do something—as if I could do anything."

Hawkes stopped moving through the dimly lit tunnel. He was tired and dizzy and needed to catch his breath. Putting his back against the rough stone wall, he panted as he wiped the chilling sweat away from his forehead.

"Upset because of Sam?" he asked the empty corridor. "Course I'm upset. Who wouldn't be upset? He was a good man. Died trying to do the right thing. Stupid way to die."

Hawkes sat down on the floor, oblivious of the small cloud of reddish-yellow dust that billowed out from under him. Yawning widely, he raised the bottle he had taken with him from his quarters and downed another mouthful. Back in his room, when the major left, he had immediately started mixing another drink. Throughout the evening the prime minister had been making himself one Happy Times after another, a potent creation that went down smoothly but still held quite a kick.

When he got to the second bottle and found himself out of Amaretto, however, he decided to leave his quarters. Seeing no reason to stop drinking, though, Hawkes decided to take the bottle of Jack Daniel's with him. Knocking back another slug, he sat on the floor in the dim light talking to himself, not actually conscious of where he was.

"Damnit, Sam," he muttered sadly. "You shouldn't have cared. Shouldn't have cared. If you hadn't cared, you'd be all right now. You'd be here, right here to keep me company. You'd be here," he said, patting a spot on the ground next to him, dust billowing out from under his hand. "Right here."

And then Hawkes looked around and wondered aloud, "Wherever here is."

He scratched his head absently, trying to recall what turns he had made, and why he had made them, to end up where he was.

"Hey," he suddenly shouted as loud as he could. "Where am I?"

No one answered. Looking around again, the prime minister was struck by the thought that he had been in the cold, dusty tunnel some time before. The dimmer lights were new. Someone had installed the portable, self-contained illuminators since whenever Hawkes had been in the corridor. His mind seizing on the question of where he was, he staggered back to his feet, brushing himself off and looking about for clues.

"Hey," he said as his eyes spotted a shape in the rough wall that the back of his mind recognized. "I *do* know this place. I've been here—right here. Long time ago. With Sam—Sam was with me. Got to drink to my old buddy Sam."

The prime minister tilted back his bottle once more, pouring another long jolt down his throat. Liquor spilled out one side of his mouth, dribbling on his vest. Suddenly curious, he ignored the spillage and moved off down the hallway, his feet dragging in the powdery dust. The tunnel was not one of the neat, vigorously antiseptic passageways that made up most of the Martian colony. It was an old explorer bore, one of the initial Deep Digs carved out by the Originals in the first days of humanity's experiment with life on Mars.

"Awful cold down here," muttered Hawkes. "Why's it so cold?"

The prime minister's system kept pumping heat out of his body as he continued to drink. Sweat beaded on his forehead. In the back of his mind, a tiny voice cautioned him that he was making himself sick. His anger and self-pity almost triumphed over his common sense, but after a moment of internal debate, Hawkes finally set the bottle down and walked on without it.

"Don't need that," he told himself. "Need to know why Sam and me came down here. What would we come down here for?"

Hawkes leaned against one of the old support beams. Although flimsy when compared to the construction of the Above, the ancient girder was more than adequate to hold the prime minister's weight.

"Why would we come down here?"

Hawkes asked the question with a new tone in his voice. Something within his mood was changing. Suddenly tiring of self-pity, he took a deep breath, filling his lungs to the breaking point. Exhaling, he repeated the process several times, each repetition helping him to focus his attention.

"I remember what we came down here for."

The only time Hawkes had gone down below the Pit-and-Bang— the factory levels—into the somewhat dangerous older areas known as the Deep Digs was when he and Sam Waters had been led there. They had been inspecting the site where a number of Resolute leaders had been murdered by the League. Feeling somewhat more sober suddenly, the prime minister pushed off from the support beam and made his way forward. In only a matter of moments, he came to the side chamber where the slaughter had taken place. And although his memory had guided him unerringly despite the amount he had drunk, it was in no way able to prepare him for what he found.

"What's goin' on in here?" Hawkes stepped into the once barren room, turning round and round in amazement as he drank in its transformation.

The rough stone walls had been vibrated smooth and then painted a pale blue. Pictures of all the people killed in that room by the League had been mounted here and there, placed in clusters around the blast holes made by the executioners' shotgun bursts—the only scars still remaining on the now smooth walls. It was obvious the horrid gouges had been left there intentionally.

Bits of poetry, scraps of ribbon, other bits of color, the dried and withered remains of flowers, hung near all the pictures. On Earth they would have been nothing. But on Mars . . .

"Who here has time to write poetry? Where did they get ribbons and colored paper—flowers?"

The prime minister's mind reeled trying to calculate the expense. Even if the memorial makers grew the flowers in their own homes—still, the exorbitant price of seeds, the giving over of food-growing soil to something as useless and extravagant as flowers . . .

"Flowers in the darkness," whispered Hawkes. "Never seeing the sun. Grown in caves and dying in caves. Just like the people they were left for."

And then, a connection opened in the prime minister's mind, letting him know who would have gone to such trouble to build a monument that no one would see. Looking into the eyes of the person in the picture closest to him, he said, "Your children did this—didn't they?"

Again he turned, but looking at the room with a different sensibility. As he studied the various shrines in the chamber, he realized that one couple in particular had been memorialized in a far grander state than their companions. Moving toward that area of the room, he felt a great sadness stirring within him. He could not remember the names of the couple before him—mere statistics on a report he had read a year earlier—but sorrow raged within him as he stared into their faces.

"There were riots going on the last time I was standing here too," he told them. "But they were different. It was the beginning of the revolution. Things were so much different then."

The self-pity Hawkes had purged from himself began to creep back into his voice, but before it could, a cold anger swept down and expelled it from his consciousness. The different viewpoint shattered his centering focus, redirecting it toward the faces around them.

"No," he admitted, responding to the change. "*Things* weren't different then. I was."

Looking from picture to picture, Hawkes told the assembled ghosts, "I've allowed myself to be set at odds with the movement I helped create. And why? Why was that? Oh, because I had to find . . . the middle ground. The goddamned sacred middle ground."

Suddenly, in his mind's eye, the prime minister was a soldier once more, seeing his best friend and his fiancée dying on the battlefield. In another flash he felt the terror and heat of the crash that robbed him of his father. Tears running down his cheeks, he shouted, "All my life I've hated. I've hated Mars for taking my father, hated war for taking my love—and you knew it, didn't you, Mick? You and your damn League. You knew—*knew* I'd move heaven itself to keep Mars from going to war because that's the way life's programmed me! You knew I'd fight against war because I couldn't help myself."

Turning again to the focal pictures of the shrine, Hawkes stared into the faces of the couple on the wall and swore to them, "Well, not anymore. The Resolute may be made up of children, but they're children free of illusions over who their enemies are. And maybe . . . maybe *I* can be that free now too."

Hawkes went quiet then. He did it abruptly, suddenly exhausted.

As he reached out to the wall for support, however, he heard something behind him. Tired beyond belief, he muttered to whoever was approaching, "If you're here to kill me, like every third person I meet on this damn planet, I must admit you couldn't have picked a better time."

"Maybe not today, Mr. Prime Minister."

Hawkes recognized the voice. As the image of the speaker flooded his brain, he looked again into the faces of the two people on the wall before him. Suddenly, he could remember their names.

"Gerald and Marta Cobber," he said wearily. "That's their names. I remember now."

"They were my parents," answered the redheaded woman.

"I know," said Hawkes.

Victoria Cobber walked forward, two fresh flowers in her hands. Moving toward the wall where her parents waited, she added the ordinary blooms to the others, and then simply stood for a moment in silence. Afterward, she turned to the prime minister.

"There's a lot of work still to do. I mean, for the two of us to do . . . together."

"I know that too."

Cobber turned to leave and then suddenly turned back, throwing herself at Hawkes. Hugging him close, a tear breaking free, she whispered to him, "Thank you."

The prime minister hugged the young woman back gently, then closed his eyes and smiled as he said, "Funny, I was just going to say the same thing."

SO THAT'S THE whole story," said Hawkes. "Do you think you can forgive me?"

Major Truman stared at the prime minister, trying to maintain the stern frown she had welded onto her face earlier. Both of them knew that she had already forgiven him, but of course, that was not the point. He had made a fool of himself and embarrassed both of them by doing so. Now, to put them back on solid footing, it was his duty to apologize. Luckily for Hawkes, Truman understood him better than he could have imagined.

"You're a real masterpiece," the major said. "I should make you jump through a few hoops, but I suppose one of us ought to be an adult."

"You're very kind," answered the prime minister with a touch of relief.

"Un-huh, and you're a very nasty drunk."

Letting his eyes fill with mock pain, Hawkes answered, "Well, I like to think of it along the lines of, if you're going to do something, you really should make an effort to do it right."

"Yeah," the major shot back. "It's good to have skills. Now, do you mind if we get a little work done here?"

"No," answered Hawkes, holding his head with one hand as he crossed the conference room and took a seat. "Not if it's quiet work."

"I'll try not to index any keypads too vigorously."

The prime minister nodded slightly in appreciation. On Earth, or even in Lunar City, a simple thing like a hangover could be easily cured. Mars, however, was another matter. On a world where practically every necessity had to be imported at tremendous expense, medicines for self-inflicted pain ran a distant second to all others.

Martian doctors were big on letting their patients learn such lessons the hard way.

In an attempt to survive life's latest hard lesson, Hawkes had prepared himself an old home remedy, or at least, the closest equivalent he could fashion from the ingredients available on Mars. He was just reaching for another dose of it when Truman dropped the scheduler she had been accessing. Although it was not a terribly heavy piece of equipment, the resulting clatter was enough to make the prime minister's eyes roll up into his head.

The major apologized with just enough planned insincerity in her voice to cause Hawkes to doubt the accidental nature of the incident. For a moment, he debated questioning her, then decided he really did deserve it and returned to his potion. That was when Scully entered the room, banging the indexer harshly when it was too slow for him, making far more noise than Truman's scheduler. The major allowed herself a faint smile as the prime minister groaned.

"Mornin', Mr. Prime Minister," said the security man in a loud, pleased voice. "Want to hear some good news?"

"Only if it's quiet good news."

Scully studied Hawkes for a moment, then looked over at Truman. She pointed at the prime minister and held her head, mimicking great pain. The security man went "Ohhhhh" and nodded, then sat down next to Hawkes, continuing his conversation with the prime minister in a much quieter tone.

"I'll make it short. Ever since that last meetin' we had with the Resolute—the one just before the riot in the tunnel—I've been wonderin' 'bout Vick Cobber's boyfriend."

"Roger Doyle?" asked Truman.

"Yeah, that's him. Mr. Charm. Well, before we went after the boiler, I put one of my boys on findin' out what there was to know about him. It now appears there is indeed a little bit to know."

"Such as?" prompted Hawkes.

"First off, word is he worked his way into the Resolute with a vengeance. He chummed his way to the top—whoever it was best to know, they became his best friend."

"Any idea when he set up housekeeping with little Vickie?" asked the major.

"I know this will come as a complete surprise," answered Scully with a sour drawl, "but apparently he set his tack in her wind as soon as she was elected head of the Resolute."

"The world's full of surprises," agreed Hawkes. "But so what? What makes Doyle important?"

"He's not a Martian."

"What?" demanded Truman. "Then what is he?"

"Lieutenant Roger Doyle left the employ of the League roughly a year ago. Something to do with a big speech given by the ambassador from Earth . . ."

"He's a Navy man," said the major with surprise.

"Son of a bitch!" exploded Hawkes, his hangover forgotten. "That miserable bastard . . . working his way up through the Resolute, networking his way from cell to cell until he found out who the leader was . . . Is that what your people found?"

"Pretty much," agreed Scully. "My guys did a lot of interviews—slow work, friendly—pieced it up from different conversations. Everyone they talked to seemed of the same opinion, though. Doyle didn't have any interest in Cobber until she was elected up, then he went for her like a bull after clover."

"He's the one," growled Hawkes. "I can feel it in my bones. The bastard's working for the League. He's our problem in the Resolute."

"That was my thought," agreed Scully. "The only problem is, what do we do about it?"

"We turn it to our advantage." The security man and Truman both turned toward Hawkes. In grim whispers, he told them, "One of our biggest problems has been worrying about whether or not one of our battlewagon captains is a traitor. If one is, he's the one that's been coordinating everything for the League. Sending messages to Earth, keeping an eye on the boiler, on their spies . . . We find him and remove him, we're back in the game."

"Listen, Benton," Truman said softly. "I know you made your peace with Cobber last night, but do you really think she'll take your word against his? Especially when we don't have any proof?"

"Wouldn't be foolish enough to try," answered the prime minister. "Yes, I do think Cobber will work with us, but I'm not about to try and turn anyone as passionate about things as that young woman against the man she loves."

"So," asked Scully. "Whata we do?"

"Mr. Doyle was fairly emphatic about wanting another meeting with the leaders of Mars. I say we give him one."

● ● ● "WHAT IS THIS, Hawkes?"

Roger Doyle stormed into the conference room, pushing his way through the others there. He seemed a touch nervous confronting the prime minister and the others without Cobber. Covering his concern at being summoned by himself with bluster, he raged on at the assembly.

"What, you think you can make me turn on the Resolute—sell out my brothers and sisters? You think you can turn me against Victoria?" Pointing at another Resoluteman already seated at the table, the man stormed, "I'm warning you, Hawkes, maybe you can get to the likes of Jason here . . ."

"Mr. Doyle," answered the prime minister easily. "Please. We asked Mr. Harris here for the same reason as you. We just wanted to ask your opinion on something." Hawkes indicated the chair across the table from himself. "Please, sit down. This is important, to us *and* the Resolute."

Hawkes's calm caught the man's attention. Taking the seat offered, Doyle said, "Okay, okay—I can at least listen, I guess. What is it?"

"We wanted your opinion on the captains of the U.S.S. *Roosevelt* and *Die Berlin*."

"The battlewagons?" asked the Resoluteman with apprehension, startled by Truman's statement. "Why?"

"A friend of mine came in on a miner," said Jason. "She said she heard a rumor that one of the captains was going to turn on Mars—help the League."

Suspicion filled Doyle's face. Concentrating on Harris, he demanded, "Why would anyone give you information like that?"

"I told you, she's my friend. I gave her a painting once and she's always said she owes me one. This was her way of paying me back."

"It's a rumor we've heard before as well, that we were gonna see trouble from the Navy," said Scully. "But we never had the pin hit anyone so high up. Now, you bein' ex-Navy, and an officer, we thought maybe you might have an opinion."

Doyle sputtered for an instant, then hurried to cover his all too obvious surprise. He had not thought anyone would bother to check very closely into his background, and it showed. Both Hawkes and Scully read his discomfort, understanding what it meant.

Bingo, thought the security man. We got you now.

"One of the captains turn on Mars?" asked Doyle finally, fumbling to gain time for himself. "Fight for the League?"

Hawkes watched the Resoluteman carefully, studying his every response. Sitting back, letting the others continue the questioning, the prime minister remained silent, doing his best to fade into the background. He could see the wheels turning in Doyle's brain, looking for whatever advantage there might be for him within the situation. Of course, he was convinced he was maintaining his cover—which was just what Hawkes wanted him to believe.

You're just as dirty as I thought, Hawkes decided. And it doesn't take thirty years as a career diplomat to see through your act, mister. Maybe you were a decent enough lieutenant, but you're a rotten actor. This really isn't your game.

"I'll admit I don't like you people," said Doyle finally. "Tell the truth, I've never even been that crazy about you, Harris. But maybe this is different. Maybe here we should be working together." Getting his nerves back under control, Doyle filled his face with mock concern. "The more I think on this, the more I think you people might have something."

"What do you mean?" asked Scully, doing his best to seem both trusting and excited.

"Okay, I have to say that if I had to depend on someone, I'd trust Captain Donner from *Die Berlin* with my life. I knew him, served under him. He's a good man. Top-drawer. But, Willis . . . that whole *Roosevelt* crew . . . If this information of yours was right, it sure would explain a few things."

"I'll bet it would," said Hawkes. Not giving Doyle a chance to think, the prime minister leaned forward, extending the Resolute-man his hand.

"Thank you. You've confirmed our opinion. Captain Willis has been under our surveillance for some time now. If there was a traitor in our midst, he was our first choice. Always seemed a bit too damn squeaky clean to me. But you can't make policy based on rumors, can you?"

Doyle hesitated for a moment, then suddenly took Hawkes's hand. As he shook it, he said, "Maybe I was wrong about you."

"Yes," answered the prime minister grimly. "I've been wrong about a few things myself lately. Sorry to hear it's contagious."

Apologizing for having had to take up so much of his time, the prime minister asked one of Scully's people to make sure that the Resoluteman was taken to wherever he wanted to go without any delays. And once Doyle was safely on his way, Hawkes turned to those remaining.

"Well, is there anyone here who isn't as convinced as I am?" When no one disagreed with him, the prime minister turned to the young Resolute artist still seated at the table. "I want to thank you for helping us with this little charade."

"As he said, Mr. Hawkes, when it comes to Roger Doyle, there isn't much love lost between the two of us. I've had enough contact with the two of you to know that if I have to pick between you . . . it's not Roger I'd want watching my back."

"No," agreed the prime minister. "Me either. So, Mr. Harris, as long as we're in agreement, there's one other thing I'd like to ask you to do. Could you keep an eye on Victoria Cobber until we can find some more concrete proof to present her with . . . about her boyfriend?"

"Sure," answered the young artist. "I'd be happy to."

Harris excused himself then, leaving the conference room as quickly as he could. When Scully commented that perhaps the artist might not be subtle enough to handle such a mission, Hawkes answered his concern.

"Either he'll keep what happened here to himself, or he'll let something slip and start the wheels turning in Cobber's head. Whichever, we got what we wanted—someone Doyle knew, to feed him information we needed him to hear. Now that we don't need Mr. Harris anymore, watching over Cobber is as good a way as any to get a bit more use out of him and keep him out of our way at the same time."

"Yeah," agreed Scully. "It could get him killed too. And to think people call *me* ruthless."

"Well, it's not as if we're *all* not playing that game right now," answered the prime minister.

"Like I said before," interjected Truman in a noncommittal tone, "it's good to have skills."

"Right," answered Hawkes. "Now, if there aren't any further objections, let's organize a party and head on up to *Die Berlin*. I think it's time we explain our new early-retirement plan to Captain Donner."

PRIME MINISTER," SAID Captain Donner, his hand extended, "welcome aboard *Die Berlin*."

"Thank you, Captain," answered Hawkes. The prime minister shook Donner's hand firmly, a lifetime of controlled duplicity allowing him to easily mask the contempt he had for the traitorous officer.

Now, now, Benton, he told himself, *you don't have any actual proof yet. If you want the man to hang himself, at least give him the rope first.*

The prime minister stepped in through the air lock, Scully, and three of the security man's people behind him. Hawkes noted that Donner was wearing his dress sword, as was the prime minister himself. Pointing toward the blade hanging from the captain's belt, he asked, "Is that standard Navy issue?"

"No, sir," answered Donner with pride. "At least, not for about a hundred and seventy-five years. There've been a lot of Navy men and women in my family. And your piece, sir?"

Hawkes's hand touched the scabbard of his own blade affectionately. "No," he confided humbly, "nothing with quite so elegant a history as your own. Merely a decoration to puff up my appearance at formal affairs and inspections . . . which, say—isn't that what we're supposed to be doing right now?"

"Right you are, sir," answered the captain. "If the prime minister and his party would follow me, I think we can give you an idea of the reception we have in store for the League if they head out this way."

Hawkes moved ahead in the direction Donner indicated, then stopped as he came alongside the man. Motioning with his hand, the prime minister insisted, "No, Captain—I'd feel much more comfortable with you leading the way."

● ● ● THE PARTY TOURED *Die Berlin* for over an hour. The captain and his second, along with several other officers, ushered Hawkes and his people through the different weapons stations, familiarizing them with the various degrees of firepower available on a League battlewagon. Finally they arrived at the bridge, the last stop scheduled on the tour. Taking his command chair, Donner asked, "So, Mr. Prime Minister, are we up to snuff?"

"Oh, yes," answered Hawkes. "Mick and the boys would be proud."

"Pardon me, sir . . . I'm afraid I don't understand."

The prime minister drew conspiratorially close to Donner. Practically whispering into the captain's ear, he asked, "Everyone here on the bridge, Mr. Donner . . . are they loyal—to you, personally?"

Hawkes gave the words only a second to sink in, then added, "I don't mean to Mars, Captain. I mean, are they loyal to the League? Are they loyal to Mick and me?"

"Sir, I don't . . ." answered Donner with a stumbling whisper. "I mean, ahhh . . . Mr. Prime Minister, what exactly is it that you're asking me?"

Hawkes dropped his voice into a less pleasant range but kept it at the same volume. Playing his line out as if he were any other important man who did not appreciate being stalled, he kept his tone friendly but stern as he answered.

"I'm asking if you aren't the point man in charge of getting information back to Mick Carri and the Earth League. You and yours are the only people around here who know when the boiler satellite will be turned on and off, aren't you? You are the communications coordinator for this mission—aren't you?"

The captain's eyes flashed the truth. Instantly Hawkes could see that their guesses were correct—that Donner was their traitor. Wanting the man to show his hand, however, the prime minister stepped back from the captain's chair, then said a bit louder and a bit colder, "I don't appreciate games. If nothing else, we just plain don't have time for them—now especially."

"I'm sorry, sir," answered Donner with only a touch of hesitation. "It's just that . . ."

"What?" snapped Hawkes, his tone implying impatience aimed at someone else. "For God's sake, it's Doyle, isn't it? No one told you that Doyle and I have been working together, did they? That we planned out the assassination attempts together? Good Lord, just how much in the dark have you been kept?"

"Frank Pearson was a good man."

"Who?" asked Hawkes, immediately guessing. "Oh, the bubbled boy that got sent down from here. I'm sorry if there was a mix-up. It wasn't supposed to be someone close . . . Damn that Doyle. I swear that man—"

And then, cutting himself off, throwing a surprised look of guilt on his face, the prime minister lowered his voice again, asking, "Donner, your crew?"

"What? Oh, ah . . ." The younger man stammered, his mind racing, searching desperately for the correct answer. Hawkes held back, giving the captain room. Donner might have been a superb commander, but he was not a trained or very practiced liar. The prime minister was already certain enough of the man's guilt to relieve him of command, but he needed more than that, thus he and the others had begun their dangerous charade.

All around the room, both Hawkes's people and Donner's were sensing that something was happening. Scully and his people, of course, knew what that something was—knew how the situation might change at any moment. The captain's officers all found themselves staring at their leader, wondering exactly what was happening. After another moment's hesitation, Donner blinked. Ultimately, Hawkes's gamble had paid off. The captain was a soldier, a man trained to obey his superiors.

In his new role as a spy, Donner had been uncertain and afraid for quite some time. It was a game with rules he could not grasp completely. Now that someone had come along who seemed to be his superior in his new role, he was more than willing to abdicate responsibility. Falling into line, he told the prime minister, "These men are all loyal to me."

"I admire you, son," answered Hawkes without missing a beat. "Pretty big job, maintaining control of a situation this big with a staff this small."

"Thank you, sir," answered the obviously relieved Donner. The prime minister's cool and even attitude had convinced him. Since, to the captain, no one could lie that completely without betraying the slightest false note, Hawkes had to be telling the truth. Tumbling into the prime minister's trap, he added, "But it hasn't been all that hard."

"You're too modest, Captain," said Hawkes in a louder voice. "You and all your loyal crew are to be commended. This kind of work is never easy on fighting men. I'm certain none of you have been very much at ease leading these double lives."

Instantly a murmur of surprise went up around the bridge. The prime minister stood back and allowed Donner to explain to his people what had happened. Then, as soon as the captain had given them the basic facts, Hawkes cut in, immediately working to put the other officers at ease.

"As I was going to say, the pretending will all be over soon. We've taken care of the Resolute—Doyle and I have Cobber eating out of our hands. They won't be any problem. And now that we've gotten Waters out of the way . . ."

"The president?" blurted Donner. "But he . . . That was an accident . . . ah, wasn't it?"

"Oh yes, of course it was an accident," said the prime minister with a smile. "An accident arranged with the most careful of planning. And now it's time to arrange another accident. A much bigger one."

As Donner and his people all focused on Hawkes, he said, "Yes, gentlemen, it's time to destroy the Martian navy."

● ● ● "So, EVERYTHING CAN be handled through these controls?" asked the prime minister.

"Yes, sir," answered Donner, easing himself into the pilot's seat of lifeboat 96. Patting the console before him affectionately, he said, "They call her the Rumrunner because she's been rigged so that she can be released and returned from the ship unseen electronically by ship's systems, or visually from the bridge. We've got three charges aboard both *Die Berlin* and the *Roosevelt*—enough to at least cripple both ships completely, if not destroy them."

"Excellent work, Captain," said Hawkes. Looking around the lifeboat, he asked, "And so, everything is ready to go? Charges are set, all your people are on board?"

"Yes, sir," Donner assured the prime minister. "Everyone loyal is here. Once we're away from the ship, it's just the indexing of a few controls and . . . and it's all over."

"I hear a bit of regret in your voice, Captain," said Hawkes. Standing behind Donner, the prime minister slid his sword slowly upward out of its sheath, asking, "Not having second thoughts, are you?"

"No, sir. I was just thinking, in terms of manpower and equipment, you understand . . . about what a waste it's all going to be."

"No waste, Captain," answered Hawkes. "Because we're not going to destroy the battlewagons."

Donner turned around to see the prime minister's blade aimed at his throat. His face now revealing his contempt for the captain, Hawkes snarled, "Now get out of that chair. You're going to be too busy packing for your trip back to Earth to have the time to murder a thousand of your fellow sailors."

Donner sat transfixed, his mind trying desperately to adjust to his new situation. It had taken a tremendous jump for him to accept that he and Hawkes were suddenly on the same side. Now, he was being forced to jump back to his former beliefs even faster. His eyes running over the console, seeing only one option that might allow him to survive, the captain threw himself sideways, his hand slamming at the controls before him.

The prime minister lunged, but his blade missed as the lifeboat was released from *Die Berlin*'s grapples. Hawkes stumbled as the ship floated away from its moorings, as did everyone else aboard. He recovered quickly, but not before Donner had regained his own balance—and drawn his own sword.

"Now, Mr. Hawkes—let's settle this without any more lies on either side."

The prime minister scrambled to his feet, bringing his blade around in a defensive position. Donner waited until Hawkes had his balance, then struck with all the force he could manage. The prime minister parried the blow, stepping back at the same time, aware that he would only be able to do so twice more before his back was to the wall.

Throughout the lifeboat, Hawkes's people set upon the other officers, desperate to subdue them without too great a struggle. Immediately the two sides were pulled into a dangerous standoff. None of *Die Berlin*'s personnel was carrying weapons. Scully and his people had their small-caliber security sidearms, a standard part of their uniforms which no one had questioned as they came on board. But there were only three of them, and eight officers for them to cover.

Scully looked the situation over desperately. He knew that in truth he and his men dared not fire their weapons. He knew their prisoners were equally aware that any shot released could conceivably kill them all. Barking orders, he worked at keeping the officers off balance and out of the action, knowing at the same time that if he tried to help Hawkes he might doom them all.

"Better keep your arm up, Mr. Prime Minister," advised Donner. "Your defense is weakening."

Hawkes ignored the comment, working to keep his feet balanced. He had not practiced with his sword for a while, was not ready for combat.

Even if I was, he thought as the lifeboat lurched again, throwing everyone a step off balance, I've never dueled on a rolling deck before.

Donner went into a battering assault, coming from the left, then the right, back and forth. It was an attack that used a great deal of energy, but the captain did not care. He only had one enemy, one blade to smash aside, and victory would be his. Not worried about finesse or style, Donner kept up the withering attack, exhausting Hawkes bit by bit as his heavier blade slammed again and again against the prime minister's.

"Ha!" shouted the captain as he forced Hawkes to scramble aside to avoid a sudden thrust. The blow missed the prime minister, but tore through the side panel of his open jacket. As the two men danced around each other, Donner chided Hawkes.

"Sloppy, Mr. Prime Minister. I break step once and suddenly you're wearing a vented suit. Not good form at all."

Hawkes backed up without being forced by his opponent. Donner stepped fully into the center of the room, framed by the large forward cockpit of the lifeboat, a few stars, and the rapidly closing hull of *Die Berlin* filling the window. As the Rumrunner continued to float aimlessly where it would, the captain slashed the air with his blade, advancing on the prime minister.

"A nice try, though," he granted Hawkes as they continued to parry with each other. "You almost had us. I understand why you played things the way you did. Wanted to make sure you had us all, wanted to try and save the ships."

"You're right," admitted Hawkes. Stalling for time, he conceded, "Couldn't just board you, couldn't risk not being able to get you to talk."

"I thank you for the compliment," answered Donner. The captain closed his stance, making a smaller target of himself. The prime minister noted the shift, could tell Donner was about to make his final attack. His eyes shifting to the window behind the captain, Hawkes watched the nearing battlewagon fill the view.

Come on, damnit—hurry up!

And then, just as Donner lunged, his blade aimed for Hawkes's heart, the Rumrunner drifted into *Die Berlin*. The captain, unprepared for the collision, stumbled badly. Hawkes, braced and waiting, shifted his blade smoothly, stopping Donner's forward fall with edged steel. The captain took twenty inches through the heart, his shattered breastbone doing even more damage than the prime minister's blade.

Blood sluiced heavily through the fuller groove of Hawkes's sword, drenching the prime minister's dueling arm, splattering across his chest and face. As Donner staggered backward, pulling himself free of Hawkes's weapon, he put his hand over his ruptured chest, trying for only a single futile moment to stanch the warm flow pounding out of him. Then, realizing the truth, he put his own unblooded blade to his lips, kissed it, and held it out to Hawkes, hilt first.

"My blade, sir," he said. "My crew. My ship. Please use them better than I have."

And then he fell, cold and silent, leaking his life across the plate flooring of the Rumrunner.

G ODDAMNIT! I'M TELLING you it's true," snapped Doyle into the microphone. "Would I waste off-planet communications if it wasn't? I don't dare risk having this channel open for more than a few minutes, so listen to me—the word's all over Mars. Give it a week and it'll be to the Moon. Hawkes has secured *Die Berlin*. Both battlewagons are under Martian control now."

"This is unbelievable," answered Gladys Beckett, Michael Carri's chief of operations. Only minutes earlier she had been proofing her boss's speech for that evening, when an aide had flashed her screen to tell her of the incoming message on the emergency band. Rerouting it through a secure channel, she fought to control the panic rising within her as she asked, "And where's our Captain Donner?"

"Donner?" said Doyle, his voice laughing. "Donner's dead. You've got to—"

"Shut up," snapped Beckett. Indexing a second recorder while she talked, coding it to send a same-time copy to Carri wherever he was, she asked, "How could Hawkes have known? How did he take the ship away from Captain Donner? Even if Donner is dead, what about the officers loyal to him? Didn't they blow the ships—couldn't they at least blow *Die Berlin*?"

Doyle sat in his and Cobber's quarters, sending his message with the crisis broadcaster Donner had given him months earlier. Powerful enough to cut through even the boiler satellite's output for at least a few minutes, the ex-officer had saved it for a grave emergency. He had hidden the small tapper unit in his old Navy gear, a box of assorted mementos he knew held no interest for Cobber. Now he had it spliced into the apartment's communications panel.

Knowing he could not safely keep using it much longer, though, he shouted, "I don't know—I don't know any of that. None of it's important anyway. What's important is that Hawkes has both the goddamned ships, and all your plans are in the shredder! Do you understand?"

"Roger!" gasped Cobber. "What are you doing?"

Doyle jerked around, his face awash with honest surprise. His concentration had been so completely focused on Beckett's face, searching it for reactions, that he had not heard the outer access panel slide open. Had not heard Cobber enter. His mind whirled, trying to find an appropriate lie. He did not find one fast enough.

"That's an Earth office," said Cobber accusingly as she stared at the image of Beckett on her communications screen. "You're talking to the League!"

"For Christ's sake," came the operations chief's voice from the wall unit. "Get her! Shut her up!"

Cobber ran for the hallway, but Doyle caught up to her in only a few steps. Grabbing her arm, he whirled the young redhead around and threw her against the wall. Cobber hit hard—buttocks, head, back slamming against the drilled stone. Doyle caught her before she could fall.

"This is great," he sneered. "This is just great. Now what am I supposed to do?"

"You're supposed to tell me what this is all about," said Cobber weakly. Her arms pinned against the wall, she could only shut her eyes against the pain in her head as she added, "We're supposed to be working together. You . . . you love me."

"I never loved you, you little idiot," snapped Doyle. Frustrated and angry, the double agent told his lover, "You were just convenient. You shouldn't even be alive now."

As the woman's eyes flashed open, pain and resentment struggling for ascendancy, Doyle sneered.

"That's right. You should have been kicked to hell and back in the riots. But," he added, clamping one hand over the struggling woman's mouth, "I guess I can take care of that little detail now. Just one more thing I owe our dear prime minister."

"Maybe someday you'll get a chance to pay him back."

Doyle turned at the new voice, maintaining his fierce hold on Cobber. Behind him in the doorway stood Jason Harris, fists balled.

"You're not very bright, Roger. I've always said that. Someone with a few brains might have wondered if anyone else came in with Victoria. Now get away from her, you bastard."

Doyle shook his head slightly, a sad grin disfiguring him. His hand still gripping Cobber's face, he snapped her head back quickly, bouncing it off the wall behind. The young woman gave out a small, gurgling cry and fell to the floor. Turning on Harris, Doyle stepped forward.

"You want me away from her? You got it, Jim."

Harris raised his arms to defend himself—and Cobber—but he did so futilely. Doyle knocked his feeble defense aside with one hand, backhanding the artist violently with the other. Harris stumbled sideways from the blow, fighting wildly to regain his balance, until he finally tripped over a chair several feet away. The artist slammed against the floor, the air smashed out of him. Doyle walked over to him slowly, not worried about his opponent. Pulling back his left foot, he kicked Harris in the stomach savagely.

"Yeah, paint boy, I'm the stupid one." The foot flew again, connecting with Harris so intensely it flipped him over. The artist slammed against the floor again, nose breaking. "So why is it I'm not the one on his belly? Riddle me that, smart guy."

Cobber tried to stagger to her feet. She wanted to help Harris, call for help, attack Doyle, run away—her mind flooding with conflicting messages as she struggled simply to stand. At the same time, her lover's foot slammed into the small of Harris's back. The artist yelped in pain, spit and blood flying from his mouth, arcing across the floor.

"How about it, paint boy? You set me up, didn't you?" demanded Doyle. "You helped Hawkes and the others trick me."

Going back several steps to the chair Harris had fallen over, Doyle picked it up and then smashed it against the wall. As one of the legs broke away in his hand, he inspected its jagged end for a moment. Then he turned back to the artist.

Crossing the room, standing over Jason, who was still curled on the floor in pain, Doyle growled, "Yeah, you did me in, all right. But don't think you're going to live to gloat about it!"

"Drop it!"

Doyle spun around, his makeshift spear clutched tight. What he found was Major Truman and two security people coming through the access panel from the hall. Truman and one of the men had their sidearms at the ready. The other was carrying a scanner. Doyle understood immediately.

When he was transmitting, he had known he could not talk to the League for long. His illegal patch into the Martian communications system was certain to be detected. He had entertained no doubts that such detection would be investigated immediately, and had been prepared to be brief. But when Cobber interrupted him, he had not shut the tapper unit down. And now security had traced it . . . and found him . . . standing over Cobber and Harris . . . ready to kill—

Both Truman and the security man's shots hit Doyle squarely when he threw himself forward. Sadly, from the standpoint of potential questioning, the Navy infiltrator was dead before he hit the floor.

● ● ● "SO, LADIES AND gentlemen, that is the situation. The question is, what are we going to do about it?"

Mick Carri stared into the telesponder, waiting for the others to respond. There had been no time to congregate all those concerned in one place. The fact had disappointed the Senator. As easy as it was to assemble everyone needed via monitor access, the veteran politician had always felt more comfortable with real people to throw his words at.

Goddamn, but I miss the old days, he thought wistfully for a moment, staring at the flat, electronic faces all about him. You can't get really get eye to eye with someone with a wall of glass between you.

Carri also worried about tappers breaking in on the delicate meeting. One loose, unprotected transmission anywhere on the planet and the whole world might soon know their business. But despite the desirability of secrecy, the ruling body of the Earth League had had no choice. Its members had been gathered for the emergency conference as quickly as possible. Wherever they were found, the men and women of the League were instructed to find the securest access beacon possible and either join the meeting at the scheduled time or forfeit their vote. As Carri waited, the assembly began to make up its collective mind.

"I say, what can we do?" The British Holdings, Ltd., ambassador offered. "They were Martian ships. Mars just took them back."

"They were not Martian ships, Colin," thundered Deutscher Chocolate's Daniel McCay. "They were League ships. They were *our* ships. *Die Berlin* was not *their* ship! Do you understand that? Its registry does not read Property of Mars, or Benton Hawkes."

"All true," said Carri. Knowing exactly what McCay would say, the majority leader asked, "So what are you saying, Daniel?"

"That it's time for war—that it's time we stopped all our political maneuverings and just went ahead and sent in the troops, and *damn* the consequences."

"I agree," came the voice of the Chinese ambassador. "The time for acting out games is over. These upstarts have antagonized us for a year now—a *year*—like monkeys pulling a tiger's tail. It is time we put an end to this charade."

One by one the various members of the Earth League spoke their minds. Although many of them only had access to single or limited screens, Mick Carri could see all of his counterparts. Sitting in his office, one wall rolled back to reveal his electronic meeting room, the majority leader watched as the massive screen continually reconfigured itself to give him a clear view of each person speaking. One after another the faces before him were atomized and reassembled as they voiced their opinions. All the faces were different, but most of the opinions held little variation.

Finally, Carri offered up a few simple steps to the others for ratification.

"The *Roosevelt* and *Die Berlin* are ships of the United Earth

League's navy. Their confiscation one year ago by the renegade Martian government, as well as the murder of League citizens Roger Doyle and Captain Desmond Donner, among others, the attempt to bring about a breakdown in relations between the League and Lunar City, the theft of secret military equipment, and the sheltering of fugitives . . . For these and all other crimes which shall be enumerated formally later, I see no choice but for this assembly to declare a state of conflict between the Earth League and the colony world of Mars."

Carri stopped for a breath, then asked, "How say you all?"

In the end, only three League members declined to vote in favor of beginning the universe's first interplanetary war. Smiling with satisfaction as he cast his own ballot, Michael Carri was not one of them.

ADMINISTRATOR LIN, YOU have to do *something* to help us. Please!"

Chon Zheng Lin stared at the screen on his desk, Hawkes's face staring out at him imploringly from its center. Lin sat straight backed, his hands folded on his desk. Drumming his fingers once against the papers beneath them, he said, " 'Please' is a very powerful word, Mr. Prime Minister. True, it is often used tritely and with insincerity, but I know that is not the case here." Dropping his head a slight degree, the lunar administrator broke eye contact with Hawkes for a moment, just enough time to brace himself for the unpleasant task he had to perform.

"Perhaps you should have used it when you asked me to refrain from ever playing cards with you."

Now what, wondered the prime minister, could he have meant by that?

"I know what you want," he told Hawkes's image, "what you need. In fact, I was told to expect this call, or something like it, from the major in charge of the League naval detachment that arrived here last night."

Lin paused, the movement of the lines in his face indicating that he was searching desperately for words. Watching him, Hawkes was suddenly struck by what was happening.

Cards, he thought, catching the clue the administrator had thrown him. Poker—he's got his poker face on! He's trying to get me a message.

Instantly Hawkes understood what was happening. Sitting back in his chair, the prime minister looked away from the screen, mumbling and shaking his head.

If the League is already there, he thought, it's a sure bet they're monitoring all incoming Martian transmissions. Got to play this like I'm devastated, try to give Lin the time he needs to tell me whatever it is he wants to get across.

"So you see," said the administrator with a convincing sneer, "even if I wished to help you, how exactly would you propose I do that? There are marines throughout Lunar City, taking over nearly all her vital functions. No one will be coming in or going out of here for some time without their approval."

Well, thought Hawkes, there's one detail he wanted to get across. Have to tell Curly, let him spread the word through the miners and . . .

"Not with dozens of warships circling the Moon. Ships, I think, you had better worry about, Mr. Prime Minister." Lin let his face go cold, filling his eyes with an unexpected level of contempt. "This is the end of your little playacting revolution, Mr. Hawkes. When the League is done building its fleet, things will get back to normal around here."

Dozens—at least twenty-four—but his tone . . . He's definitely implying more than that, and he said they're not done building their fleet.

"You've been a great deal of trouble for all of us who are simply trying to keep the solar system running smoothly. You have serious delusions, Mr. Prime Minister, but I think that will all be taken care of in—"

And then, a shadow reached across the administrator's desk and the transmission ended abruptly. Hawkes slammed his fist down against the console in front of him so violently that Major Truman reacted with a start.

"What was that all about?"

"Lin," answered Hawkes. "He was trying to tell us when to expect the League fleet. Obviously somebody caught on."

"What do you mean?" asked Truman. "All I heard was him snarling at you."

"That was for the military. Trust me—we diplomats speak our own language. Find Curly, tell him to spread the word that anyone who's looking to avoid the League had better steer clear of the Moon for the time being. Get me Captain Willis too. We're going to have an enemy fleet at least thirty, thirty-five strong here anytime. We'd better get ready for them. Round up Scully too, will you? And Glenia . . ."

"I get the idea. You want me to assemble a basic action committee—everyone we need to get the defense ball rolling—and you want it ASAP. I think I can improvise the rest of the names."

"Then get to it," answered Hawkes with a smile. "And stop wasting my valuable time."

"You joke," the major answered. "But you realize, everything we know, everything that everybody everywhere knows—the history of the entire human race . . . It's all about to change. A lot of the past is about to get pretty insignificant."

"Yes," responded Hawkes, "I imagine so. But look at it this way—at least we'll have ringside seats."

The prime minister watched as Truman walked toward the exit panel. His eyes lingered on the curve of her back as she disappeared through the doorway, the smart, efficient, and yet still feminine way she moved. Shaking his head slightly, Hawkes sighed under his breath and then turned to the young man sitting toward his left at the communications console.

"Jason, did you ever get yourself involved with two women at the same time? Do you know what I mean? You think you know what you're doing, but every step you make just keeps digging the ditch you're in a little bit deeper."

The artist chuckled, assuring the prime minister, "Sorry, sir, but it's never been my misfortune to be that attractive."

"Too bad," answered Hawkes, indexing the blank screen in front of him, pulling up the spaceport's current registry records. "I could use the advice."

"Now that would be something, me giving you advice."

"Don't sell yourself short, Jason. You're a good man. I was meaning to ask too—how're you feeling? Any permanent damage?"

"From my little scuffle with Doyle?" asked the artist. Stretching his right arm above his head, he said, "Oh, there's a little pain when I make any big motions, but nothing permanent. Thanks for asking, though."

"Thanks for saving Cobber's life," answered Hawkes. Looking over the figures he had just punched up, he said absently, "That's not going to hurt our cause any."

"I wish she thought—" Jason began to answer, but then cut himself off. Noticing the abruptness, Hawkes realized both what the young man had said and what he had not. Turning away from the screen he had been studying, the prime minister motioned for Jason to move closer.

"You like her, don't you?" Hawkes did not press the point when the artist's face flushed. Instead he said, "Look, I wasn't kidding before when I said I would've taken your advice if you had any to offer."

The prime minister took a deep breath. The weight of memory tightening his chest made him release it with regret. Taking another, he told the younger man, "I was in love once, but the girl died. I couldn't save her. You're already one up on me in that department. Give Victoria some time. Give yourself some time. After all, everything always seems to turn out the way it should in the end."

"You really believe that?" asked Jason, hoping for affirmation.

"It's a hard personal philosophy to accept at times. I used to lie to myself and say it was mine. Once your little electronic art trick helped push me past my hate, I finally made it all the way there. But yes, I do believe it. If I didn't . . . well, let's just say I can think of more than one morning when I might not have gotten out of bed."

The prime minister tilted his head to the side, then raised his eyebrows in a reassuring manner, trying to let the artist know that he was serious. When he could tell that the young man had gotten the message, he said, "Now, speaking of electronic art tricks, how's your latest one working?"

"As best I can tell from this end, the answer is perfect. I've set up all the looped simulation programs you asked for. They're all sending continuous transmissions of you to the League—one member after another—working on them to get them to change their votes. As you predicted, the computer's limited response range hasn't been very seriously challenged yet, because no one's giving it—you, that is—very much time."

"As you said—perfect."

"Why?" asked Jason. "I mean, if you know they're not going to change their minds—why bother? I know this isn't my place, but doesn't it . . . um, sort of make you look weak?"

"Yes," agreed the prime minister. "That's the point."

When the artist's face clouded over with confusion, Hawkes told him, "The League is monitoring every transmission going out from Mars to the Earth, the Moon—most likely every bit of space chatter they can run down. If they think all my time is being spent pleading and begging, they might slow down a little. At the very least they'll think that I'm not spending any time planning our resistance—how could I be? All they have to do is review their logs and they'll see that I was tied up all day—every day."

"And of course, we couldn't organize a decent defense without Benton Hawkes," snapped the Resolute member with a trace of bitterness. "Could we?"

"You want the truth?" asked Hawkes. "No—no you couldn't. And I'll tell you why. Decency and courage and honor are good things, but they don't count for much when the other side has all the guns. History's graveyard is full of guys who only won the philosophical victories."

As Jason's hard look softened slightly, the prime minister told him, "I have two advantages here. Not only do I know how the League does things, but they know I know. If they think I've folded, that I've given up . . . well, it might not look good on my résumé . . . but if it buys us an extra month or week, even a day, if it makes them hold back one stinking battleship, then it'll be worth it."

"And if it doesn't?" asked the artist in a quiet voice.

"It'll still be worth it," answered Hawkes. "Of course, it'll only be one of those philosophical victories . . ."

The prime minister let his voice trail off for humorous effect. Jason chuckled, acknowledging that Hawkes had made his point. As he did, the prime minister's voice dropped into a serious range as he asked, "While we're covering our bases, what about the message I asked you to get to my ranch? It's been a while. Hasn't there been any word yet?"

"No, sir," answered Jason, suddenly serious himself. "I encoded it and send it when you asked . . . back right after you took *Die Berlin*. But, there's a lot of reasons why they wouldn't be able to answer. Like the fact the League is monitoring everything . . . and you wouldn't want them to know what you're trying."

"I know," answered Hawkes halfheartedly. "You're right."

"Just because we haven't heard anything," said the artist sincerely, "doesn't mean they didn't get the message."

The prime minister tried to respond, found he could not. The tightness returned to his chest, squeezing him. It gripped him cruelly, filling him with an irrational panic that took a terrible effort to drive back to the part of his brain responsible for holding on to his fears.

The moment Hawkes realized war was inevitable, he had given Jason a coded message to send to the Martian embassy. In brief, it told his foreman, Ed Keller, and Dina Martel to take everything they could and head for the Skyhook—to abandon his beloved ranch and head for Mars.

Rationally, he knew that it would make no sense for them to try and contact him in direct response to his message. Such an action was almost certain to be detected. He could trust a message sent from Mars—the colony had a power source adequate to maintain code integrity in the face of League analysis. His ranch's equipment could not stand up to such scrutiny.

So, he thought, every other day I link through to them, and every time, Dina is there to talk to me. I babble lies about how I'm desperately trying to repair relationships with the League, and she lies back that everything will be fine. It could mean that she's maintaining the operation to give everyone else cover time, or it could mean that they're all sitting there—believing the lies I hope I'm telling only whoever's listening in—just waiting for the jaws of the League to shut on them. And if I were to say a word, they'd snap shut that much faster.

"They could be fine," offered Jason, desperate to break the dark quiet filling the spaces between himself and the prime minister.

Taking pity on the younger man, Hawkes shoved away his despair with practiced ease, telling the artist, "Yes, I know. After all, as some idiot once said, 'everything always seems to turn out the way it should in the end.' "

Somehow, nothing either man said after that had much effect on the terrible silence that had set in around them.

31

"ALL RIGHT," SAID Hawkes, fatigue finally creeping into his voice, "that covers ground defenses and in-atmosphere defenses. Now, what are we going to do where it counts?"

"Not to let my ego show," offered Captain Willis, "but that sounds like my department." When no one disagreed, the commander of the Martian fleet continued.

"I wish I had a lot to offer, but I don't. We've been maintaining skeleton crews so we'd have every bit of power available to us when the inevitable comes. But what's also inevitable is that when that day gets here we're not going to last long at our current strength."

"Whaddya mean?" asked Scully. "Ya got the firepower to cut a moon in half, ain't ya?"

"Close to it," agreed Willis. "A small one, certainly. But that's not the point. Each of our battlewagons has eighty weapons banks—eight different power levels, ten banks to a level. The problem is that all our power is centralized. We've got two ships. And only two ships."

"So can't we use more ships—get more ships?" asked Ace Goth. "We've got ships in and out of here all the time . . . ore bangers, grapplers . . . What about one of those multimegas? They ought to be big enough."

"Big enough to do what exactly, Mr. Goth?" asked the captain.

"No disrespect, sir, but big, unarmed ships just make better targets. Ships need weapons, and plenty of them."

"I gotta give him that," added Curly Thorner with a sad sigh. "I'd like to take the *Stooge* out when the time comes. But what would I do when I got there—throw rocks at 'em?"

"Which brings us back to our problem," said Willis. "How

many steel-bellies did you say the League was sending, Mr. Prime Minister?"

"Our information is spotty," answered Hawkes, his voice growing more hoarse with every word. "But it looks to be as high as thirty-five, possibly forty ships."

"Then I don't know what to say," responded the captain sadly. "I'm sorry, people—but even if my gunners do the best job in the history of naval engagements . . . even if they were to stop fifteen ships apiece—something I assure you no warship could come close to doing—we still can't win."

"Because you only have two ships."

Everyone turned toward Cobber. There was something in her voice, a slight note of invention, that aroused immediate curiosity in the others around the table. Scully leaned forward with interest.

"Something's cookin' in that red noggin," he said, eyeing the young woman intently. "What're ya thinkin'?"

"Mr. Scully, some of the other Resolute members and I, we were discussing the capture of *Die Berlin* . . ."

"Yasss . . . and?"

"Maybe I'm wrong, but I got the impression from the story that the lifeboats like the one you and the prime minister ended up on . . . that they were rather large . . ."

"They *are* large—larger than one would think, anyway," Hawkes said. "But why, Victoria? Why's that important?"

"In the resistance, before we were all on the same side," said Cobber, "a lot of the time it was hard for us to get things we needed. We ended up improvising a lot. Anyway, it was that kind of thinking that got me wondering . . . If the captain is sure his battle-wagons can't win against the League's fleet, and they have all these lifeboats on them, and all these weapons . . . couldn't we just take the lifeboats and the weapons, and make a lot of little warships?"

The room stayed quiet for a long moment, the simplicity of the young woman's suggestion stunning the assembly. Everyone had questions and yet none wanted to be the first to speak. The group's collective shock wore off, however—quickly.

"That's goddamned brilliant!" shouted Thorner. "It's genius. It's colossal! It's stupendous!"

"But will it work?" asked Glenia Waters. "What would be involved? We're talking about dismantling these ships and putting them back together. That takes supplies."

"And people," added Scully. "Technicians, mechanics, and one hell of a lot of support personnel . . ."

"We'll need a set-down area," interrupted Goth. "And oxygen—square miles of it. Once we start stripping down ship segments, disengaging systems, there'll be compatibility problems . . ."

"No," answered Willis. "Not really, not as bad as you might think. Especially the lower levels—they were designed as break out components. Lift in, lift out. Quicker replacement time."

"Military's been building that way for almost a hundred and fifty years," agreed Truman. "The only problem would be trying to transfer disrupters, or radiant lines—commercial ships don't have that kind of power . . ."

"No—not to power eighty separate systems, maybe," barked Goth. "But you're thinking way too big. We're talking transferring one system to a ship—right? And okay, maybe a lifeboat couldn't power a disrupter—but multimegs are comped out for travel to the edge of the system. They've got the power to haul payloads the size of a moon."

"What about the supply tugs?" asked Glenia. "They're big. They're the biggest things in space."

"No real generating power, though," answered Thorner. "They're frictionless haulers. Big difference."

"But she's got a point," said Scully. "What about using them for base work? Empty ones fitted out as repair stations. Hangars. Whaddya think?"

"I think," said Hawkes, using a voice that commanded everyone's attention, "that maybe we're getting somewhere. That maybe we have a chance. But we've got to get organized and we've got to do it fast. Glenia . . ."

"Yes, Benton . . ."

"I think it's time people were told about Sam. I think it's time the people were told about everything."

"I agree," answered Mrs. Waters.

"Listen to me, people," said the prime minister, his voice harsh and pained. "We've got something here, something that even if it doesn't work, sounds like it'll give us a better chance than we thought we had. But it's not going to be easy."

Hawkes covered his mouth as the dryness in his throat caught up to him at last. He strangled his cough through force of will before it could take control of him. Accepting a cup of water from the major, he tossed it back and then wiped his mouth on his sleeve, jumping immediately back to his speech.

"We've got to get people working—fast," he insisted. "Outside of essentials like medical teams and environmental controls, we're going to have to shut down factories, pull people off the food vats, everything . . . and they're going to have to work night and day . . . for nothing."

"Not for nothing, Mr. Prime Minister," said Cobber. "In fact, for the first time in most of our lives, the people of Mars are going to have something to work toward that's truly important. Something a lot more important than money."

"Yes," said Hawkes with a smile, his weary eyes lighting with a positive glow for the first time in days. "I see your point."

"Don't worry about 'the people,'" added the young Resolute leader. "I'll deliver them."

"And what she can't, I will," pledged Goth.

The meeting grew in noise and intensity, every other minute bringing forth a new problem, the next second another possible solution. After another few hours, most of those assembled sounded even hoarser than the prime minister. None of them cared. They had found a way to see light piercing the approaching darkness. For the moment, that seemed good enough.

Most all of them left at the same time—everyone weighted down with new duties and responsibilities. Oddly enough, everyone but Hawkes. Sitting in the assembly room with Major Truman and Curly Thorner after the meeting, the prime minister swallowed another throat pellet, letting it dissolve while the miner slapped the edge of the table between them.

"This is out-damn-standing," he said happily. "I mean it. Yesterday this place was lookin' as fragile as a size eight ice and dust ball. Now, now . . . oh man, what can I say? You hold a mean meeting, Bennie."

"Thanks," croaked Hawkes. Tired and sore, inspired as the rest but fatigued from days of constant focus, he told the asteroid miner, "At least I get to take a break now."

"Yeah, that's kinda funny," noted Thorner. "You've been runnin' yer butt at ten times top speed while everyone else's been sittin' around. Now that everyone else is up to their sockets, you got nothin' to do."

"Ought to be a pleasant change," said Truman as she stretched her arms out above her head, pushing away the stiffness building there.

"Well . . ." The prime minister smiled. "Not nothing, Curly. But close enough, yes, to make a fairly pleasant change."

The trio sat quietly for a moment, simply enjoying the stillness of the room after the noise of the extended meeting. After a short while, however, Thorner broke the quiet.

"I sure wish I could get some of the boys together. I mean, Liz, what you were sayin' before about more firepower . . . you were right. This kind of thing, every ship could help. But all the guys I know that would jump at something like this—Madass Maurizio, the Cucumber brothers, Trevor Von . . . Most everybody's out trying to crack in on a piece of the big Io strike. By the time we could get to 'em, talk to 'em, get 'em here . . ."

"Don't sweat it, Curly," answered Hawkes. "We'll make it or we won't." Stifling a yawn, the prime minister gathered his reminder boards and other paraphernalia, ready for a shower and his bed and little else.

As the major followed suit, packing her small side bag, Thorner jokingly offered, "Of course, I know a few pirates . . ."

Ignoring the humor in the miner's voice, Hawkes shook his head to drive away the draining weariness tearing at him and said, "Well, fine by me. Any pirate of yours is a freedom fighter of mine."

"Oh, sorry," answered Thorner. "That was just sort of a joke."

"Too bad," answered Hawkes. "I met a few space pirates on my first trip to Mars. We could do worse. In fact," said the prime minister, holding his hand up in an exaggerated pose to make a joke of his own, "you know any of them that want to basically commit suicide for the lavish reward of . . . what? becoming citizens of Mars? . . . you tell them to give me a call."

"Hey," said Thorner, heading for the hallway, "I'll see what I can do. But you'd better throw in ice cream."

The miner then executed a wobbly pirouette and leaped out through the access panel, disappearing from view. Truman giggled at the sight.

"And what was that all about?" asked Hawkes.

"I don't know," admitted the major. "The meeting did go on for a while. I guess having to act normal for so long just got to him."

As the pair passed through the access panel, following Thorner into the hallway, the prime minister joked, "Think he'll find us any pirates?"

"Ummmm," answered Truman with a laugh. "No, I don't think so."

"Well, I guess that means we're on our own."

The major looked at Hawkes for a moment as they walked along, then whispered, "Nothing new in that . . . is there?"

"No," said Hawkes evenly, his voice resigned but calm. "Nothing new at all."

WHAT DID YOU say?" asked Major Truman, staring at the screen before her, praying she had not heard the words she knew had come through the comm. Understanding her shock, Captain Willis repeated his transmission, expanding on the details.

"You heard me right, Major—we've got a full fleet bearing on us. They tried a blind run, single-filing in behind the shadow of Phobos. Sentry post there just relayed their scan to us. They're coming in with an armor charge—four battlewagons on the front line, twelve heavy cruisers doing a shield sphere for four fleet-supply barges and twenty-eight destroyer wings uniting the spread perimeter."

Sixteen, twenty, Truman counted, forty-eight—forty-eight . . . It's too many, it's just too many. We can't handle that many—we never thought, didn't know—

And then, the major snapped her fears into line, ignoring the impossibility of the situation. Her hand indexing the alert line that had been prepared weeks earlier, she divided her work with Jason Harris, who had drawn the same duty hour, the two of them quickly alerting the entire colony with a few block announcements that the Earth League had arrived. As individuals came on-line one by one, the artist indexed them specific details while Truman turned back toward Willis, asking for standard confirmation.

"Captain, are you certain on your figures? Forty-eight total?"

"You got it," confirmed Willis. "We thought we saw another ship coming onto our screens for a moment, but we never registered a visual on it. Never really got a definition signal on it, either. Probably just a ghost blip doubled up on us because of their straight-line approach."

The captain turned to give an order to an officer behind him, then said, "Besides, Truman, what's the matter? Forty-eight battlebirds not enough for you?"

It's too many—it's just too many!

"Forty-eight will do just fine, Commander," answered the major, her voice far stronger than her confidence. "If that's all you can find, we'll just have to make do."

"Where are you now, Captain?" came Hawkes's voice.

As the prime minister's face folded out onto both Willis's and Truman's screens, the captain answered, "I'm aboard the *Stooge* with Captain Thorner, sir."

"Aye, aye, Admiral," came the asteroid miner's voice. "We're ready for 'em. We'll cook 'em in oil."

"Clamp it, Curly," snapped Hawkes. "This is not the time." Turning his attention back to Willis, the prime minister asked, "This has come faster than we expected and no one appreciates that more than me. Are your remotes ready?"

Then, before the captain could answer, Hawkes cut him off, shouting, "Hold it! Liz—how long can we count on secure communications?"

"How far out are they, Willis?"

"Rough on five hundred thousand standard. We can chatter for at least the next two hours. After that they'll be able to hear anything we say."

"All right," said Hawkes. "They can hear us in two hours. When can they hit us?"

"Probably about twenty minutes after that," answered the Martian commander. "No more than thirty, thirty-five."

Not a lot of time, thought the prime minister. Turning away from the urge to waste precious seconds on regret or panic, Hawkes returned to his previous question.

"All right, not as good as a week, but you work with what you have. About those remotes—did the crews finish? Do you have control?"

"Yes, sir," answered Willis smartly. "We can move both the *Roosevelt* and *Die Berlin* from here. And before you can ask, sir, everything else we planned—it's as ready as it can be."

"Well," answered the prime minister, "I don't suppose a man can ask for much more."

Taking a deep breath, Hawkes did the best he could to dispel the fatigue tearing at him. The entire colony had gotten behind the effort to defend itself over the past three weeks. Putting his best face on, the prime minister added, "Every sacrifice we could ask of Mars' sons and daughters up until this moment has been made and made without complaint. We're as ready as we can be."

Glenia Waters's face folded onto the screen, followed quickly by Norman Scully's. Victoria Cobber's face appeared next, as well as Ace Goth's and a dozen others. Knowing that by now most of the colony was patched into the ongoing conversation, the prime minister did the only thing that was left to do.

"Now, in the next few hours, we'll find out if what we've been able to accomplish will be enough. We won't have to worry as to whether or not it was worth it, though—for, as we all know, no matter what happens, no matter what the outcome today . . . it will have been worth it."

Hawkes swallowed, choking back a moment of emotion, then added, "As Samuel Adams said, 'The truth is, all might be free if they valued freedom, and defended it as they ought.' In all my life, I've never seen a people with a taste for freedom as I have here on Mars. I've no doubt that it will be defended as bitterly and nobly here today as it ever has been. They may take our lives, ladies and gentlemen, but they cannot have our freedom."

And then, not so much over the communications grid but through the halls and corridors, resounding through all the depths of the colony, a pounding cheer began to swell. Hands clapping, feet stomping, voices crying out in hope and resistance, it bound together and moved from level to level, person to person, like an electrical charge, building in force as it filled every corner of Red Planet, Inc.

Moved by the sudden, spontaneous enthusiasm of the Martian people, Hawkes told Willis, "You heard the citizens, Captain. Go win them this war."

"I'll do my best, sir." Willis gave the prime minister a smart salute and turned to his attack. Quickly snapping off a string of orders to the Navy men with him on the *Stooge*, the captain got the *Roosevelt* and *Die Berlin* under way. In seconds their engines were fired, their courses plotted, and their few remaining weapons primed.

As the two battlewagons began moving, splitting in almost opposite directions to begin their pincer run at the approaching fleet, Truman tabbed a direct line to Willis.

"What is it, Major?" asked the captain. "There can't be much we forgot. And if there is, there can't be much we can do about it."

"I just wanted to wish you luck," answered the major. "And to say I wish I was going to be up there with you."

"Thanks, Truman," answered Willis under his breath. "But, no offense, I'll be getting enough people killed today. No need to deprive Mars of any more Navy heartbreakers than we have to."

Truman knew what the captain meant, knew he did not calculate his chances of survival as being very high. Ignoring her first instinct to extend him sympathy, knowing that the warrior on the screen before her did not need any weak thoughts, she asked instead, "Can you think of anything that could help? Any last thing we haven't thought of?"

"Yeah," answered Willis jokingly. "You know, we never gave any thought at all to boarding their ships and destroying their ship-to-ship communications."

"How would that help?" asked Harris innocently.

"If they can't talk to each other, son," explained the captain gently, "they can't coordinate their efforts."

Willis did not mind the question. With the battle more than two hours off and all his orders given, he was grateful for the distraction. He was far more grateful for what came next.

"What he means is," added Truman, "that with ships as big as the ones they're bringing in, they can't fight like our lifeboats. They can't fire their weapons in line-of-sight attack. They're too big. They need—"

The major stopped. Staring blankly at the screen, her eyes unblinking, she sat silent, almost stunned as a radical idea began to form in her brain. Yelling at both Harris and Willis to be quiet as she began running computations on the console in front of her, the major called up several star charts in rapid succession, running timing estimates and directional paths with berserk speed.

Then suddenly, she leaped up from her seat and ran for the exit, only to wheel around after two steps. Returning to the comm panel, she told Willis, "Listen to me, it's still the battlewagons, tugs, and barges first—right? The lifeboats are the last line—right?"

"Of course," answered the captain with a touch of confusion. As Thorner leaned over toward the screen Willis was using to find out what all the commotion was about, the captain added, "It's our only ace in the hole. They're not much, but they're still the only thing we have the fleet might not expect."

"Hold them back until fourteen-thirty hours," ordered Truman. Indexing a countdown on her wristpiece, she asked, "Have you got that?"

"Fourteen-thirty," repeated Willis. "I've got it. It might be hard . . . Hell, it might be impossible. What are you—"

"Damnit!" shouted the major, heading for the exit once more, "you just *make* it happen, mister!"

And then she was gone. The captain stared at Harris's face. The artist stared back at the commander, neither man knowing what to say. Finally, Thorner tapped the captain on the shoulder. As Willis turned, the asteroid miner told him, "The lady said stall them until fourteen thirty? I'd do what she said." Then, putting his feet up on his console, Thorner smiled widely, reaching into his pocket for the precious single cigar he had been saving for the last few months. Biting off its end, he chewed it for a moment, then spit it with enough force to make it stick to the bridge wall.

In the background, he could hear Harris's voice, demanding an explanation. In the bridge seat across from him, Captain Willis simply stared at the asteroid miner, wondering what it was the big man could have thought of which he had not. Ignoring them both, Thorner lit what he was suddenly certain would not be the last cigar of his life and repeated, "Yep, I'd do exactly what she said." Smiling, the miner inhaled deeply, then exhaled a huge, raw cloud of smoke, chuckling as he added, "Exactly."

33

EAGUE LEAD ALPHA powering weapons," announced a lieutenant hunched over the outermost reading scanner aboard the *Stooge*. "Contact in five minutes."

"Rear cruiser line also powering," announced the officer next to him. "Forward batteries charged, ports opening."

"Lead Bravo powering, Delta powering . . ."

"Cruiser line breaking ranks—deploying standard eight-level spread formation . . ."

"You ready, Captain Thorner?" asked Willis, one eye on the jury rig of controls stretching out before him, the other on the asteroid miner.

"Only one way to do it, Captain," answered Thorner. Suddenly serious, the big man said, "So punch it in. We got us some history to make."

With a touch, Willis sent *Die Berlin* forward, moving the *Roosevelt* along in its wake. For three weeks the commander of the Martian navy had debated the various opening gambits available to him. For the past ten days he had known exactly what he would do. Now, without hesitation, he started his two battlewagons forward. Staring out through the forward observation window, Willis watched his first command glide through the dark reaches on its suicide run.

His mouth a straight line, hoping the appearance of the standard pincer opening would mask his real intent, the young captain whispered, "Goodbye, old girl."

And then, finally, the war was engaged.

● ● ● "MICK, FOR GOD'S sake—there's still time to stop this!"

Hawkes stared at the smugly smiling face on the view screen before him. Sitting in the majority leader's office, other Earth League members in view grouped around him, Mick Carri assumed a congenial, expansive manner.

"Of course there is, Benton," he agreed quietly. "There's never been a need for things to come down to war. You could've stopped this all along. You can stop it now—easily. All you have to do . . . Well, you know what you have to do."

"Mick, call your armada off," said Hawkes, his face even and calm. "You have to be able to see what's going to happen next. Ask your own commanders, if you think I'm lying. We don't have the ships to repulse your fleet, so we'll do the only thing we can. We'll use the tugs and barges that we normally use to transfer goods to Earth. If those get destroyed, there won't be any raw materials coming to you. There won't be any food—there won't be any because you'll have destroyed it!"

"Chance we'll have to take," answered Carri. Spreading his hands apart in a gesture of apparent helplessness, the senator told Hawkes, "And you don't have to run down the litany for me. We know how many millions will die. Riots, starvation, pestilence—all the models have been worked out. You want the figures, Mr. Prime Minister? Let me get them for you."

Hawkes tried to keep Carri engaged, but the majority leader muted the prime minister's cries as he had his operations chief call up the data he wanted. Reestablishing the sound to their communications, Carri looked over the screen before him, reading figures off one after another.

"If you pursue this, Benton," he told Hawkes's image, "worldwide death figures hit half a billion in the first two weeks. Then, hmmm, seems it'll only take about another ten days to top a billion.

Another eight days after that to reach another half-billion—that's when they figure the plagues will start really kicking in."

The prime minister closed his eyes for a moment, deadened by the reality he had known was headed for him for over a year. Even as Carri's voice was joined by others, all demanding the immediate surrender of Mars, all Hawkes could see was the horribly looming future.

Multiple billions dead. *Billions!* Starving slowly, killing each other for scraps, farms crushed, leaves stripped from trees, mountains of bodies, rats and disease and oceans of blood . . . all courtesy of football hero Michael Carri.

"I won't surrender Mars to you," Hawkes finally answered. "No matter how much death you try to lay at my feet. And I'll tell you why. All this planet wanted was its freedom. Nothing would have changed. Nothing would have cost Earth any more, none of you would have lost your power, except the power to do to Mars what you're about to do to Earth."

Carri's face remained unperturbed. Throughout the roomful of League representatives there were no outbreaks, no shift in emotions—just a vague, amused curiosity over what Hawkes would say next.

"We won't give our lives over to you to do with as you please," said Hawkes. "If you're determined to slaughter half the living beings in the solar system, Mick, I know there's no stopping you. But remember where the fault is, remember that the only reason it had to happen was because you couldn't accept the fact that there were people in this universe who still had the spine to say no to you!"

"There you go again, Benton," chided Carri. "Always reducing complex issues to the personal. But don't worry. No one here holds it against you. We know you just couldn't help yourself."

At that point a steward came into view. Putting his hand up to the camera to cut off any response Hawkes might have wanted to make, the senator turned his attention to the servant. Giving the man a short series of orders, Carri then turned back to the prime minister.

"Sorry, Benton, but I gave orders earlier for refreshments to be served whenever our fleets were ready to engage. You'll excuse us—we wouldn't want to tie up the big screen now."

Hawkes sat numbly, watching without comment as a small squad of waiters and bartenders began moving among the League representatives. As their laughter grew, the prime minister finally broke the connection to Earth. He had done all he could along those lines, which in the end had proved to be very little.

Very little indeed.

● ● ● TRUMAN SCANNED THE darkness ahead of her, searching for her objective. Although the scanner strapped to the outside of her space suit's arm let her know she was smoothly on course, she still could not make out anything but a few random bits of space debris, and a few stars in the distant background.

I've been pushing this miserable rig at top speed for over two hours, she thought. You'd think I'd see something by now. Where the hell is that thing?

The major steeled her nerves, refusing to give in to panic. Her thousandth glance at the timepiece built into her gauntlet showed 14.10—more than enough time to execute her plan.

Yeah, if I can get there, if I can get in, if I don't get my suit torn open by some piece of space junk . . .

Truman cut off her negative thought flow, reminding herself that she *had* to get there, *had* to get inside. When she ran out on Harris, abandoning her post, she had wished there were time to explain herself, but had known there was not. Even a single minute was too precious, the loss of any of its seconds possibly spelling the difference between victory and defeat.

Heading straight for the upper construction levels, Truman had grabbed a security man on the way, ordering him to take her to the nearest outer exit by way of her quarters. There she had grabbed the X-AC-7 flight rig that had first taken her to Hawkes's ranch. Within ten minutes, she and the security man were in an air lock and he was helping her into a construction suit.

"What's my tank level?" she had asked.

"You've got a good five hours," he told her, checking the readout twice just to be certain. Helping her belt down the stolen flight rig to her suit, the security man asked, "But tell me, five hours to do what?"

As the major checked her hand controls, making sure she had forgotten nothing that she might need, she answered the question as she continued to work.

"Now you listen to me and get this straight in one take. I'm heading out to the boiler satellite. There isn't a single ship left on the surface of the planet, so this is the only way I have to get there."

"Not very safe."

"Yeah—war's like that. Now, you get the word to Hawkes and to Willis—at fourteen-thirty hours I'm going to release the radiation we set to store at the boiler. With luck, it'll kill the League fleet's communications. Make them sitting ducks for us."

"If you make it, Major. You're talking free-flying in space. One bit of astie dust hits you at the wrong angle . . . Why can't we just send a ship?"

"I told you," she shouted as she hefted her helmet over her head.

"There aren't any ships we can spare. And if the theories on this thing are right, I'll be traveling faster than anything we could send, anyway."

Truman had locked her helmet into place at that moment and then motioned for the security man to exit the lock. As the pressures reversed and she waited for her chance to test her reckless plan, the major clicked on her throat mike, switching on the air lock's communications board at the same time. Hearing the opening hiss of the lock to the outside, she started for the door.

"Don't worry about it," she'd told the security man. "Just get that message to Hawkes and Willis. And if I don't make it . . . remind them that that's why medals were invented."

Big talk, she told herself now as she continued to rocket forward through the darkness. Big talk and big ideas. Hope some of it pans out.

Truman could feel a part of herself wildly enjoying the freedom of her mad ride. A glance at the X-AC's built-in speedometer showed her that she was traveling at ten times the speeds the rig's builders had expected it to reach inside an atmosphere. The part of her that had joined the Navy for such thrills reveled in the fact that she was traveling faster than any person had ever before in the history of flight. Another part of her was keeping her eyes peeled straight ahead, watching for that single random cinder that might tear upon one of the exposed joints on her suit and end her record-breaking travels. Several small chunks of space-borne matter had already raked along her, but so far the heavy-duty construction suit had weathered it all.

And then, the major cut her rear propulsion completely as she saw the first glinting hint of the boiler satellite ahead of her. She knew she would have to make a bypassing circle of the boiler—

time-wasting but necessary—before she could even think of switching on her side thrusters. Calculating her approach, she took a deep breath and checked the time.

14.13—I'm going to make it. This is going to work.

Staying focused on her objective, the major missed the first of the horrendous mega-explosions in the far distance behind her. Not, of course, that she could have done anything about it.

● ● ● THE DEPTHS OF space went hot white as *Die Berlin* exploded. The battlewagon had been hit by a concentration of League fire as it turned hard to port, apparently to deliver a broadside salvo into the enemy fleet. The League ships, of course, had no way of knowing that the battlewagon was unmanned, that it had been stripped of all its armament, and that by firing on it they were playing directly into Willis's strategy.

Die Berlin's loss having been planned, the *Roosevelt*'s guns had been trained on the League ships directly beyond *Die Berlin*, targeted to fire straight through the space the dying ship was occupying. Even as *Die Berlin* went up, the *Roosevelt*'s planet-killers were fired—blasting directly through the still-exploding *Berlin*.

Willis's first volley slammed into the forward decks of the battlewagon *Santana*, ripping it open all the way back to its bow thrusters. The following volley blasted into the League's cruiser line. Two of the billion-tonners were destroyed instantly, two more crippled beyond immediate repair.

"Nice shootin', Admiral," said Thorner with a wink. Chewing on the stubby remains of his cigar, he asked, "And next?"

"Next," answered Willis, his hands dancing over his jury-rigged controls, "we keep doing what they don't expect."

Racing the *Roosevelt*'s forward running speed, he sent the mighty battlewagon straight through the still-exploding wreckage of *Die Berlin*. Knowing how little time the great ship had remaining, the captain loosed all her remaining weapons at once. As the battlewagon's last ammunition was spent, he and the rest of Mars watched as three destroyer wings and another of the heavy cruisers were annihilated along with the League battlewagon, the *Honorable*.

And then, the invading fleet recovered from the surprise of Willis's tactics. A dozen different members of the fleet caught the *Roosevelt* in their sights, firing instantly. Fifty decks of the speeding ship were obliterated, torn apart and scattered throughout the surrounding space in the blink of an eye. But, although crippled, the bulk of the battlewagon sped on, exactly as Willis had hoped.

"Go on, baby," he shouted, watching the blazing wreckage of the great ship streak across the void. "You can make it—they can't escape! You can do it, you can make it!"

Several of the destroyer wings managed to clear the path of the battlewagon. As its small amount of interior oxygen burned off, the flames that had engulfed it a moment earlier all winked out at the same moment, turning the charred remains of the ship into a black spear—one aimed directly at the *Gleason*, one of the enemy fleet's last two battlewagons.

The ship wheeled desperately, trying to escape the oncoming wreck. The battlewagon's captain had been caught off guard—for another commander to launch his ship through his own dying comrades had been so unthinkable . . . and more, a fully weighted battlewagon should not have been able to maneuver so quickly.

But *Die Berlin* had been carrying no crew, and the *Roosevelt*, like its companion, had been stripped of most of its arms, many of its interior systems. It had been a hollow spear, thrown with cold precision. Finally, the *Gleason* stopped the *Roosevelt*'s death leap, dying in the process.

● ● ● "MY GOD," SHOUTED Hawkes, hope crawling through him, "I don't believe it. I don't goddamn believe it. What's the count—the final count? What?"

"Nine," shouted a woman in contact with the *Stooge*. "Nine dead, two more looking as if they're out of commission."

"Mother's son," shouted Scully. "He's knocked out almost a quarter of the League fleet!"

A cheer went up throughout the command post. No one in the room could restrain themselves. Captain Willis had played the percentages as ruthlessly as possible, and done better than even he had hoped. But then, just as a second wave of cheers went up around the room, a security screen came on in front of Scully.

"Chief!" screamed a bloody face, peering wildly up out of the console. "We've been opened! Leaguers—commandos. They landed a ship, broke through number eight dome . . . Pouring in . . . can't stop them—"

And then the sound of an explosion filled the room, and the screen before Norman Scully went ominously black.

34

HE DARK CLATTER of thick boots rang along the main promenade of the Above, Red Planet's own intricate system of directional markers and designative stripes guiding the invaders as they overran the colony. One by one, following the orders ringing through the speakers in their helmets, the commando units broke off from the incoming battalion, each heading off toward its own predetermined target.

The men did not stop for anything. There was no need. The Earth League had built the Martian colony. What few things the original maps could not tell the invaders had been updated by the League's spies over the past year. Thus they were free to move without hesitation, each one of them familiar with the layout of the colony in all its specifics.

Only five minutes after the assault team's destroyer wing crashed through the lightly reinforced walls of Dome 8, communications began to falter throughout all of Red Planet. The move was part of any standard attack, of course, one designed to both confound an enemy's commanders and throw its population into blind panic. Using the tactic off-world for the first time did not diminish any of its effectiveness.

"What the hell is going on here?" demanded Hawkes as the last console in the command center shut down.

"They've cut us off somewhere along the line," offered Scully. Checking the load in his sidearm, he added, "That message we got before said they cracked their way in at the number eight dome. That drops in less than a mile from the main communications hub. Chatter's probably been cut throughout the colony."

"And if they've dug in there," offered another of the security men, "we won't get them out easy." Hawkes looked at the man for a moment with exasperation.

"The colony is a system of tunnels bored out of solid rock," he finally answered. "Almost every facility here has only one major entrance. It'll be hard to get Leaguers out of *any* place where they can dig in."

"But then what will we do?" asked Mrs. Waters. Turning from the prime minister back to Scully, she asked, "How will we run the battle if we can't talk to anyone . . . to each other?"

"Don't worry, Glenia, they can't interfere with our ship-to-ship communication," offered Hawkes with assurance. "Captain Willis will just have to handle things without us looking over his shoulder. Since he hasn't needed us so far, I wouldn't start worrying about him now."

"Yeah, an' if we don't hurry up and get our asses in gear and handle things down here," barked Scully over the confusion, "worryin' about how Willis is doin' ain't gonna be much of a concern. Get me?"

"Scully's right," shouted Hawkes. Turning to the older man, he said, "We've got to arm ourselves and fast. What's the best way to do that?"

"The marines' supplies," said Ace Goth. As heads turned, he reminded everyone, "When we brought the sailors down from the battlewagons last year, we transferred tons of their equipment down with them. My people did the moving—it's all still warehoused in Area C."

"Then that's where we've got to get to," answered Hawkes. "Those marines are all upstairs trying to keep this planet together for us. The least we can do is try and make sure they have a planet to come back to."

As everyone started for the door, Scully ordered two of his people to stay with Mrs. Waters while the rest of them moved out. Before he could finish, however, the first lady of Mars said, "Forget it, Norman. I'm not sitting here while a bunch of thugs spit on us."

Scully made to protest, but Mrs. Waters told him, "My husband's dead, Norman. Dead protecting Mars. What do I have left if I can't live up to the same ideals he did?"

● ● ● THE TUGS AND barges showed up on the League fleet's deep radar long before visual contact was made. Once they had been positively identified, however, the enemy commander sat back in his directional chair aboard the battlewagon H.M.S. *Smythdon,* pleased with the latest turn of events.

Captain Anton Greenberg had been in command of the Earth League fleet for three minutes—ever since the battlewagon *Honorable* had perished at the hands of the *Roosevelt,* taking the fleet's original commander with it. Much more of a follower than a leader, Greenberg was quite happy to interpret the approaching barges as a friendly gesture. When he ordered the fleet to cancel red alert status, his second-in-command questioned him gently.

"Stand down, sir—are you quite certain of that order?"

"Of course, Mr. Harper. Those are food barges, man. That's what we came here for—to tame these Martian upstarts and get the flow of essentials moving again. They had two ships. *Had* two ships. And even now, our commandos are teaching them the error of their ways on the ground."

Greenberg swept his hand across the scene of the advancing barges. With a condescending smile, he said, "We came for the food, and now they are bringing it to us. The word for this is capit-ulation. Gentlemen, this battle is over. I'd say it's time we retire to the officers' lounge and let the lower classes secure those barges."

The captain stepped up closer to the bridge's sweeping observation port. Studying the approaching barges, he thought of the commendations and fame that bringing them back to Earth would mean for him. In his mind he began composing the battle reports, almost chuckling out loud at how easily they would write themselves. Especially the fact that the fleet's original commander had lost three battlewagons taking the Martians' two.

And so many other ships. Poor work, poor judgments. Luckily command fell next to me. And from that moment on, not another League life was lost.

Greenberg's future had never looked better. Striking his hands one against the other, he shouted, "Enough, gentlemen—let us retire. The first round is on me!"

And at that moment, the main gunnery units that had been moved to the lead barge opened fire, ripping the *Smythdon*'s forward decks apart, their second salvo destroying the battlewagon completely.

● ● ● "LET ME IN, damnit!"

Truman stopped slamming against the boiler satellite's door. She had entered the proper identification codes. And in truth, the security staffers posted to the boiler by her and Scully had responded instantly. The only problem was the incredible slowness of the rolling access plates. Three of them to wait for, each one taking minutes . . .

A glance at her chronometer told the major it was 14.19—

Minutes she did not have.

Finally the last of the lock's panels began to part. The moment Truman could squeeze into the lock she made her way inside, scraping paint and metal from the X-AC as she clawed her way into the air lock. Making it to the comm panel at the other end of the lock, she raised the man on duty inside.

"You've got to release the radiation," she screamed into her helmet mike. The duty man moved away from the speaker physically, startled by the volume of the major's voice. When he asked for details, she told him, "The radiation, whatever's been stored since we shut this place down. It's got to be released—all of it. Now!"

"I'll get my superior, Major . . ." answered the man, only to be rebuked by Truman at an even louder decibel level.

"There's no time, goddammit! Now listen to me. We've got to disrupt the League's communications. It won't matter to our people. They're taking out small, one-pilot runabouts. They don't have to talk with one another. But the League ships, they're too big—too spread out. Deck to deck, they can only talk to each other electronically. If we can cripple that, we can beat them!"

Pulling her left arm free inside the sleeve of her environmental suit, Truman wiped away the fog forming within her helmet. Pushing the fog aside as best she could—her wrist and neck straining against each other inside her helmet connection—the major tried to calm herself, so as to reduce the fog she was creating if for no other reason. Then, when she could make eye contact with the duty man over the monitor once more, she pleaded, "All we have to do is release the radiation. We don't even have to change any settings," she insisted. "The same distribution codes they had set when we stopped them—those would be just what we need now. We just have to push the damn button and the damn war is *over!*"

"No," a voice crackled inside Truman's helmet. "It's not that easy." The major recognized the voice of the satellite's new commander. Understanding the urgency of the situation, he wasted no time in reminding her, "When we first took the boiler, you may remember, the satellite's original crew had been stalled in their own launch because they were effecting repairs."

"And they were never completed, were they?"

"No, the repairs were completed—too dangerous to leave the circulators frozen. But the manual dish locks were never released. It was like having an extra safety clamp on all this power."

"What do we have to do?" demanded Truman. Understanding what the security officer was telling her, the major began a reversal of the entrance codes. As the air lock's access doors slowly ground in the other direction—entrance closing once more, exit reopening—she said, "I'm on my way back out. Just tell me what has to be done."

The commander quickly explained the mechanics of the problem—a simple matter of a few master links that had to be reset by hand. Nothing big. Just something no one had thought advisable to do since everyone knew the boiler would never be fired again.

Truman absorbed the few simple instructions easily. She would have no problem with the task at hand. All she needed was time.

14.23—not going to make it. There's no way to make it.

Time she did not have.

● ● ● WILLIS'S SECOND WAVE did not fare as well as his first. Greenberg's disastrous interpretation of events aside, once the H.M.S. *Smythdon* had been destroyed, the individual ships left in the Earth League's fleet took the battle to the newest threat with a vengeance.

Early in the battle, the tugs had broken away from the unmanned barges, taking the battle directly to the League. The barges, under Willis's direction, scored several kills directly after the destruction of the *Smythdon*. A destroyer wing had perished almost immediately. Then another of the heavy cruisers. After that, however, every new victory was purchased at an ever-increasing cost.

Two of the barges were obliterated without hesitation after that. For only a moment did the thought of destroying what they had come for stay any of the individual commanders' hands. With the rubbling of the first barge, however, all the rest became fair game. One of the tugs perished next. Then another. Then another barge.

A lucky shot, one missing its original target, flashed deep into space, taking out one of the League's own great, lumbering supply barges. That explosion was so violent that it enveloped a support destroyer off its port side. But then the slaughter continued. Willis worked with what he had as best he could, but his luck had run out. His moment had passed.

No longer hesitant, no longer distracted, the League ships butchered the remaining barges and tugs. One more of the great heavy cruisers was crippled—removed from the action but not destroyed—and another wing ship was taken down. But that was all. After three minutes of engagement—one hundred and eighty-seven seconds after the death of the *Smythdon*—Willis's second wave was finished. All he had left were the lifeboats.

"What do we have out there staring back at us, Curly?"

"Not the prettiest picture in the world," answered the asteroid miner. "They still got at least twenty wings and five heavy cruisers.

And three supply barges to outfit them from. One of the barges has already started grappling with cruisers you managed to cripple. Got two of them berthed already. God only knows how long until they effect repairs."

14.26, thought Willis. Can a few minutes make that much difference?

Thorner had explained to the captain what he had guessed about Truman's mission. Hawkes had relayed the major's message long before surface-to-space communications had been disrupted. So far the Martian naval commander had hoped for the best and kept the lifeboats out of detection range. If they could move in without the fleet being aware of them, if they could attack under the cloak of complete surprise . . .

"Fourteen twenty-six," noted Thorner. "Not to be pushy, yer incharge worshipfulness, sir . . . but those guys are lookin' for meat, and it's not gonna take 'em long to nose us up outta the mix. You got any orders in mind?"

Willis stared at the console chronometer before him. The coolly glowing blue number did not change.

14.26 . . .

If he were to send the lifeboats in while the fleet was still milling about, still looking for targets—

14.26 . . .

Yes, they'd be picked up, but they'd still have the element of surprise, they'd still have a chance—

14.26 . . .

Every second wasted, twenty-nine different commanders with intact fighting vessels were conferring, planning, getting ready to wipe space clean of all Martian traces in preparation for destroying the colony itself.

14.26 . . .

Trust in the major, trust to surprise—each was a gamble. Which one was the right one?

Broadcasting to the lifeboats, knowing the transmission would be picked up by the fleet but having no other choice, Willis kept his eye glued to the console as he ordered, "Final wave—attack in . . ." The blue shimmered 14.27. "Three minutes."

And then Willis broke off the communication, hoping the *Stooge* had not been located by the few seconds of transmission, hoping that risking everything on Truman's assurances would not doom himself, his ship, his fleet, and all of Mars.

● ● ● 14.28 . . .

The numbers mocked Truman. She strained with the throw valve, still unable to move it, as she had been for the last minute. It was the only step left, the last thing holding back the flood of waiting radiation. Her chest heaving from her exertions, the major stopped struggling for the moment, contacting the boiler commander once more.

"Are you ready to discharge?" she asked. Even though no radiation had been released for weeks, that absorbed by the metal of the satellite was enough to make their communication almost impossible. Once the security man inside the boiler was able to understand her question and confirmed that everything was set, she told him, "Then release on schedule at fourteen-thirty."

"Roger," he replied. "You will be clear by that point— correct, Major?"

"That's my job," snapped Truman. "You have yours. You cover your own butt, mister. I'll worry about mine!"

"But Major . . ." The commander's voice crackled in the ear-piece of her helmet. Working her way out of the X-AC-7, Truman cut him off.

"You just do your damn job!"

14.29 . . .

Working desperately, the major strapped the flight rig to the jammed control. Then, switching the X-AC on, she stood directly under it, straining with all her might as the rig added its strength to hers. The woman pulled desperately, sweat running down her arms, teeth grinding, eyes squeezed shut hard against the horrible resistance.

14.29 . . .

Come on, come on, give—damn you—*give!*

Then, suddenly, Truman felt the slightest surrender in the valve. Redoubling her efforts, feet against the base unit, the major pushed with all her strength, felt her muscles tearing, and then—

14.30 . . .

The frozen clog inside the metal of the valve snapped. The X-AC spiraled away into the dark of space. The radiant-storage wings unfolded.

Major Truman opened her eyes.

Across the void, twinkling hints of the lifeboats moved out from the protective cover of Phobos' shadow.

The left side of the boiler satellite shone suddenly as all its stores were emptied in a massive burst. Release and depletion took only a split second. Twice the time it took for the major's environmental suit to be seared away. For her flesh to be boiled from her bones. For every last trace of her to be atomized.

Every trace . . . except for the still-spiraling flight wing, already long lost in the surrounding darkness.

35

THAT'S THE LAST of them!" shouted Goth from his position high above the others. While his union people manipulated the overhead arms that could move the stored weapons forward, Hawkes and the others continued opening the containers, passing out weapons to those who thought they could use one.

A constant flow of refugees poured into Area C. Martians flowed to the storage area, abandoning their stations and their homes to the relentless League commandos. As one of the union workers broke the electronic code sealing the last weapons crate, she said, "This is it? This is not going to be enough."

"Well, since we don't have any choice in the matter," snarled Hawkes, himself depressed over the container's contents, "it's going to have to be."

The storage crate had held only three more rifles and seventeen containers of ammunition. Ignoring the siren call of hopelessness, however, the prime minister shoved aside his personal feelings and reached inside the container. Pulling forth one of the metal ammo boxes, he passed it to the person beside him while reaching for the next.

Keep working, he told himself, keep busy. Every move you make sets an example, so set one that's worth it.

At the same time, Victoria Cobber clambered atop one of the already emptied containers. Cupping her hands around her mouth, she shouted, "Listen to me—we can't give in to fear. If we do, that's the end of us. We have to be ready to strike back. We *have* to! We have to use what we have, we have to resist . . . no matter what comes."

"She's right," bellowed Hawkes. Looking out over the mob of faces before him, noting their awkward, unfamiliar grips on the weapons in their hands, he continued, telling them all, "Don't think for a moment she isn't. You can't turn away from this—you never could. The League is out to crush us. They don't want to teach us a lesson, they want us all dead so they can start over with a new group . . . but with real slaves. No illusions this time. They wanted this war. They wanted an excuse to let five or six billion people die, just to be rid of them!"

"But if they're here to exterminate us," came a frightened voice from the crowd, "what can we do?"

"You can fight!" Cobber screamed back at the voice. "Or you can die! And that's it. That's what it's come down to. They're the only choices left!"

All around the vast open area, people shouted out noises of agreement. Not pausing despite the ever-increasing level of their cheers, the young woman went on exhorting the crowd.

"If you think this is your home, if you want it to *stay* your home, then you'd better get ready to do something about it. Because the League doesn't think it's your home. They don't think you deserve a home. They don't think you even deserve to live!"

Turning around atop her makeshift platform, letting everyone in the area see her face, Cobber told the assembly, "Our grandparents came here trusting the League and they were cheated and robbed, every last one of them. Our parents tried to change the system from within and they were lied to and sent away empty and starving."

"And what about now?" cried out someone. "What about us?"

"Us?" said Cobber, her voice a thin, growling line. "We don't have anything left for them to steal, and we don't believe their lies, so us . . . us they just want to kill."

"Not if we kill them first!" came a voice from the crowd.

"Then what are we waiting for?" Running for the exit, waving a shotgun above his head, the head of reclamation screamed over his shoulder, "The League's sent us a hell of a load of fertilizer. Let's go harvest it!"

Scores of the assembled followed the man with the shotgun out into the hallway, whether they had secured a weapon yet or not. Most of them died a handful of seconds later as the invaders finally made their way to Area C.

● ● ● "WHAT DO YOU mean, the consoles have gone dead?" demanded the captain of the destroyer wing *Environment*. "All of them?"

"I don't know, sir," answered the bridge officer in confusion. "Yes, sir. I don't know what's happened, but they are all dead, Captain Gortell."

The woman stared at her scrambled screens as she futilely tabbed controls, indexing and reindexing the same orders repeatedly. Nothing helped. Suddenly the small support ship, a vessel no greater in size than several old-world aircraft carriers welded side by side, had been rendered blind and helpless. With no way to communicate with the ships around it, the captain could not guess at his next move. He ordered the wing's engines cut immediately, before the ship accidentally plowed into some other member of the fleet.

No scans available, he thought. Can't navigate, can't look for the enemy, can't defend ourselves. Don't dare risk a shot. Can't fire blind. But can't sit here helpless, either. Have to get word to one of the barges—get some tech-and-repair people in here.

"Lieutenant," snapped the captain, "get someone down to the fighter launch. Send a ship over to one of the supply barges. Tell them our si . . . tu . . . a . . . tion . . ."

"Sir?" the lieutenant questioned the captain's trailing speech for a moment, looking at him without seeing what he had noticed. Then her eyes shifted, focusing as his had on the activity beyond the *Environment*'s forward observation port.

For some reason, the rest of the fleet seemed to have been stopped as they had. All the League vessels not yet destroyed were cutting their engines or already adrift. Dreadful realization hitting Gortell, he wheeled around, stabbing his hand at an ensign whose duties had been eliminated by the ship's sudden electrical shutdown.

"Messler, get down to the air bays. Tell them to launch every support fighter we have—now! I want a protective orbit around this ship two minutes ago. Move it, mister!"

Ensign Messler managed three steps before everyone aboard the *Environment* was thrown from their feet by the first volley of lifeboat fire to reach the wing.

● ● ● "FALL BACK," SHOUTED Hawkes. "Lose yourselves in the storage area. Use it for cover, but drop back now!"

People struggled to get back behind the massive Area C safety doors. Martian forces, unskilled but numerous, kept up a protective blanket of fire from the interior upper balconies of Area C that allowed their retreating allies to regain the relative safety of the warehouse area. Then, even as the great pressure doors began to slide closed on their well-maintained tracks, the prime minister conferred with Scully.

"Norm, are we trapped in here? Did they shut the doors?"

"Nope," answered the older man, holding up a control remote Hawkes had noted on his belt a thousand times before. "I did. I rigged this box up about fifteen years back—figured havin' entry to any part of the colony was security's right. Never figured to be usin' it in reverse."

Studying the massive pressure doors, Scully nodded with satisfaction, saying, "It'll take 'em a while to get through that, anyway."

"True enough," agreed the prime minister, "but what can we do stuck in here?"

"We ain't exactly trapped," answered the security man. "What I mean is, we can get out, but where do we go? You notice those guys didn't put up a whole big fight to keep everyone from gettin' back in here."

"You think we're being herded?" asked Hawkes.

"Yep, sure do. But there's no way to know for sure. Them Leaguers took control of communications. We can't access the monitors, can't talk to anyone anywhere else in the colony, so we don't know what they're up to. I mean, maybe if we could just contact some of the other levels . . ."

"We can." The two men turned to find Victoria Cobber behind them. Even as the noise level generated by the hysterics all around them thundered louder and louder, the young woman shouted, "They only cut colony communications, not the Resolute's."

Pulling a compact, obviously handmade headset from her vest, Cobber handed it to Scully, telling him, "This is how we stayed in contact with each other without the government knowing what we were up to. Unless our friends out there know what to look for, they shouldn't be able to listen in or interfere."

"Maybe yes, maybe no," answered the older man. "They had access to all of your information same as they did ours. They might be listening in to these too."

"Risk it," ordered Hawkes. "We don't figure out what they're up to soon, not much else is going to matter."

Scully nodded, agreeing with the prime minister's assessment. After only a moment's instruction in using the headset, the security man understood its operation and began to track down information from outside Area C on what was happening throughout the colony. Setting up his portable holographic map of all of Red Planet's internal levels—a simple service device issued in the belt packs given to all his security people—he began to piece together the invaders' strategy little by little as he spoke to people on level after level. In less than ten minutes, he had no doubts as to what the League commandos were attempting. What he discovered did not encourage him.

"Long and short," he told Hawkes, "they're herdin' everybody in this direction. If I've got it right, they hit number eight not only because of how close it was to the comm center, but for its central location too. Comin' in there, they was able to spread out to the edges quick—now they're pushin' us all in toward the center. From all sides, and the top and bottom as well."

"Why, though?" asked the prime minister, looking around at the still-spreading panic all about them. "Are they simply trying to round everyone up, or are . . ."

Hawkes stopped speaking for a moment, then turned back to Scully. Pointing toward the display map glowing on the table, he asked, "Where are we now?"

When the security man showed him, the prime minister asked him to point out where all the other major population groups were at the moment, and which way they were being moved. As Scully highlighted the map, the area into which the Martian population was being pushed became obvious.

"Area eighty-six. They want us in the old end of the Pit-and-Bang," said Cobber. "But why? What's the point?"

"That's the old factory sector, the level that was going to be stripped out, correct?" asked Hawkes. When the young woman confirmed his guess, he said, "They're going to push everyone in there for extermination."

"What?"

"I've seen it before, in a dozen different countries," responded the prime minister. "Get people you don't want away from anything you do, then you just kill them. It's possible your Area eighty-six has already been set with explosives, maybe chemical or biological agents . . . possibly built in at the time of construction as a hedge against future disruption."

Cobber's face went hard and cold, the hate she had felt for so long rushing back to fill her completely. Scully stood beside her, pushing anger and disbelief from his mind, cursing them as time-wasters he could not afford.

"We've got to pull people in this direction," said Hawkes automatically, pointing at the glowing display. "This is the farthest point from eighty-six where we still have control over a defensive wall. If we can get the colony to rally here—"

"Then we'll all just die here," interrupted Scully. "A warehouse isn't as ideal a killing ground as a place that was goin' ta be torn down, but it's close enough."

"But, Norm," shouted the prime minister. "We have to do something."

"We will."

Turning from Hawkes, the older man shouted, "Goth—them

287

marines leave behind any explosives? Heavy bang—deep-bore stuff?"

"All you can eat," answered Goth.

"Get a couple of hungry guys together then," snarled the security man. "It's time to get dinner on the table."

"What've you got in mind, Norm?" asked Hawkes. "What can we do?"

"Vickie," said the older man, handing her back her headset, "you listen to me. I want you to get in touch with your people. Tell them to get everyone—an' I *mean* everyone movin'.""

Scully looked over the glowing map on the crate between them, studying it for a long moment. His eyes noting something that made up his mind for him, he nodded his head grimly and then pointed.

"This way. Get everyone in the colony to pass through here."

Cobber nodded, not understanding, but trusting the old man and ready to do what she could. Hawkes studied the map.

"Yeah, I know what it looks like," Scully told the prime minister. "Blind panic. Everyone crowdin' to the central plaza of the space-port. Rats running into a cul-de-sac. If these sonsabitches' plan is really to kill every one of us, they'll want us to go in there headfirst, with them followin'. They'll bulk up behind the crowd and just push it along . . . nice and easy and happy."

"Reasonable," said Hawkes. "So what's going to make them un-happy?"

"A little history lesson," answered Scully, smiling. As Goth and three younger men came up to the group, all of them struggling with heavy loads of explosives, the security man said, "My guess is these bastards been trackin' us with our own maps. They know *what* we built, but I'll bet my soul none of them know *how* we built it."

Shouldering one of the explosives packs, Scully said, "You get everyone in the causeway leadin' to the spaceport. Get 'em there in forty-five minutes. Forty-five *exact*." He marked the time on his wristpiece.

" 'Cause I'll be sealin' the pressure door to the inside of the colony then, and believe me, you're damn well gonna want to be on the other side!"

Both Cobber and Hawkes asked Scully to explain why. But neither of their voices could be heard—over either the deafening roar of the bombs pushing in the pressure doors of Area C, or the sounds of the invaders' weapons as they poured inside, killing anyone they could.

FOR THE FIRST twenty minutes of their attack, the lifeboats did exceptionally well. The largest weapons removed from the *Roosevelt* and *Die Berlin* had been mounted on the barges and the tugs. The lifeboats could not power such equipment, and thus had been given only the lighter cannons and disrupters. To the overwhelming delight of Captains Willis and Thorner, and their crews aboard the *Stooge*, in case after case it was proving to be enough.

"The fleet's supply barges have all retreated," marveled Willis. "They've moved completely out of their standard battlefield positions."

"Never met anybody who *wanted* to die," responded Thorner, watching the battle with half an eye, but paying more attention to his control console.

So far, even though all three of the fleet's remaining supply barges had managed to lumber far out beyond the recognizable circumference of the war zone, the warships they were meant to supply were faring far worse. Despite their smaller armaments, the lifeboats had managed to take out one of the heavy cruisers and five of the destroyer wings by going in close and concentrating their fire.

It was a highly effective strategy, one that kept working as long as the larger ships stayed blind and unprotected. Unfortunately for the Martian fleet, they did not stay that way long enough. One after another, the League's war vessels released their accompanying deep-space fighters. Although fewer in number than the modified lifeboats, they were far faster, more maneuverable, and better armed for one-on-one combat.

Willis had started the third wave of his defense of Mars with one hundred and thirty-seven lifeboats and a blanketing cover of radiation which blinded his foes. Acting on their own, the lifeboats had been able to bring down four fleet vessels without incurring any losses among their own. Then the fighters had begun to emerge.

Twenty-eight of the lifeboats were destroyed before they managed to claim another of the destroyer wings. From then on, the battle had become the lifeboats fighting for survival against the circling fighters. A dozen more of the Martian defenders were blasted from space before another of the destroyer wings was claimed.

"So, whaddya think, Willis?" asked Thorner as his eyes once more searched the distant reaches. "We gonna pull this off?"

"Your guess is as good as mine, Curly," answered the Martian fleet's commander. "We've lost a lot of good people already, and we're not having a lot of luck against their fighters."

Staring out into the black reaches, tossing another mental prayer to the pilots he had sent into the current battle, Willis added, "I guess it's all going to depend on how long our communications blackout lasts."

And then, the universe's cruel gods delivered bitter coincidence to the Martian fleet. Three lifeboats running in tandem drove straight forward toward a brace of fighters protecting the rear of the heavy cruiser *Declaration*. Miraculously, all three of the lifeboats were able to thread their way through the patterned fire laid down by the fighters, each delivering its payload to the *Declaration*'s engineering deck. The cruiser was torn asunder in one monstrous explosion at the exact second that the radiation cloud released earlier finally passed completely through the area.

By the end of the very short time it took the *Declaration* to finish burning, communications were restored throughout the war zone.

● ● ● SCULLY HUNG PRECARIOUSLY, far below the main area of the colony in the complete dark of one of the oldest Deep Digs. His elbow hooked around the none too sturdy support rail of a ladder the Originals had sunk into the wall decades earlier as a temporary travelway, he cupped his hands around his mouth and called to the younger men on the ledge above.

"You got that one set yet?"

"Yes, sir," a voice cried back to him through the darkness. "It's in there. All the way to the back. Now what?"

"You get back to the Above. You shunt up through the wall tubes like I showed ya—don't get stupid and risk the tunnels. Just get outta this area, outta the whole system in . . ." The older man touched the glowpad on his wristpiece. "The next ten minutes. And take those other two chuckleheads with you. You got me?"

"Yes, sir, Mr. Scully." Already the young man's voice seemed farther away. "I'll get them both back."

"Or die trying," added Goth softly, feeling the old ladder vibrate beneath his body.

Staring down at the vague outline of the union man below him, Scully said, "You're not soundin' very chipper there, Ace. You ain't gonna fold on me, are ya? I could get this finished alone."

"Not in ten minutes you couldn't, you grouchy old bastard," answered Goth. Making his way down the old-fashioned, hand-over-hand pipe ladder, the bag of explosives hanging off his shoulders threatening to pull him off backward, the union leader continued on carefully through the darkness.

"And that's how much time we have left—nine minutes—to get to the bottom of this thing, find the point to slap some caps, get the right doors shut down, and then get back up and out of here. And you won't be . . ."

Goth's words cut off as his foot missed the next rung of the ladder. Searching for it desperately in the darkness, his legs swinging wild, arms straining, he felt his knees tear as they smashed against the rough wall of the Dig.

"Jesus Christ!" shouted Scully. "She's pullin' out of the wall!"

"There's nothing below me, Norm—the ladder's gone! Get back up, go, go—"

But there was no time for escape. The old metal collapsing in his hands, the union leader fell, screaming, in the darkness. Then, the ladder broke away from the top, falling after Goth, taking Scully with it.

● ● ● "SEVENTEEN," MUTTERED WILLIS fatalistically. "All of that, so many good men and women . . . dead. All of it, and the bastards still have seventeen ships."

Thorner scanned the emptiness beyond the *Stooge*'s observation port. The deep black was filled with the floating wreckage of scores of ships. Many of the wrecks were still giving off white and yellow glints, their self-contained proximity lights continuing to glow after death.

"If I might ask," growled Willis, staring at the distracted asteroid miner, "just what in hell are you looking for?"

"Some friends," answered Thorner, still staring out into the darkness. "I know they would've tried. They gotta be on their way . . . they just gotta."

"What are you talking about?" asked the fleetless captain without much enthusiasm. After a long moment of silence passed between the two men, Willis suddenly sat up in his chair and caught the asteroid miner's arm.

"Damnit, mister—what're you talking about? Is there someone coming? Do we still have a chance? *Do we?!*"

Beyond the observation port, the fleet ships began moving into a prelanding formation. The final invasion of the Red Planet colony was only minutes away.

"I don't know, I don't know," answered Thorner. "I thought I'd talked a couple of guys I know into tryin' somethin'. But, if they're not here where we need 'em—even if they're out there tryin', I guess it don't make any difference now."

The miner turned slowly to the antique black-and-white picture of old Earth hanging behind him on the cabin wall. Staring at the three sad and confused men in the oversized photograph, he muttered to them in a voice laced with self-pity.

"And you guys think *you* had a bad day."

And then, suddenly, Thorner threw himself forward, calling up his navigational charts. As his fingers flew across the console, plotting the course he knew would be the one his friends would have to take, he shouted to Willis.

"Captain, you a bettin' man?"

"I've been known to risk a paycheck now and then."

"Then get your money up, 'cause we're bettin' the farm now!"

Without pause, Thorner threw the *Stooge* into a sharp run, taking it flashing through the center of the still clustering League fleet. Arcing out the other side, he doubled back through the tightest grouping of destroyer wings, hoping their close formation would keep them from firing. It did.

"Curly!" snapped Willis. "What are we doing?"

"Fox and hounds, Navy boy," shouted the asteroid miner. "Fox and hounds!"

The *Stooge* sheared through the cluster of ships and then ran for deep space. Thorner's rear monitors showed that ten of the fleet's surviving ships had wheeled for pursuit by the time the *Stooge* had straightened its escape angle. By the time the Yamato-class miner cleared the war zone, all of the League ships were following it.

"Nice doggies," said Thorner. Lighting the last of his tiny cigar stub, he blew out a thick cloud of smoke, laughing. "Let's play a game."

And then the *Stooge* blasted for deep space, just as the fleet found the fleeing ship's range and threw its first volley outward at it and its insolent crew.

PEOPLE POURED FROM all across the Red Planet colony into the cul-de-sac of the spaceport's central plaza. Some of them did it following Benton Hawkes, trusting to his judgment because doing so had proved correct in the past. Many more did it following Victoria Cobber, believing in the young girl from the general labor pool where they could trust in no others, including their famed prime minister. The rest merely followed the crowd, helpless terror destroying their ability to make their own decisions.

Tens of thousands, then hundreds of thousands, they packed into the halls and lounges, the offices, flight decks, and docking bays, the cafeterias, closets, bathrooms, the service tunnels and the launch pads—filling any space they could find that still had oxygen. Climbing over each other, sitting atop each other's shoulders, hanging from the ceilings, crawling down into the flooring.

And still they came, dragging children, boxes and bags, baskets of food, wedding albums, bottled drinks, toolboxes, whatever had been at hand when the running began. Panic rose and fell, continually sucking the calm from new victims, moving from body to body like electrical current. Every so often it would run up against a mind grounded by logic that would stand against it, breaking its power and sending it off in some other direction. For the most part, however, the colonists were saved by the fact that everyone was jamming in too close together. It had simply become too crowded for truly mindless panic.

At the entrance to the spaceport, stationed at the very edge of the massive pressure doors Norman Scully had sworn to close in less than five minutes, Hawkes and Cobber and Glenia Waters kept barking orders.

Keep moving, don't panic, help each other, if you have a weapon stay here at the entrance . . .

Two hundred and fifty-eight shareholders of Red Planet, Inc., stock stood by at the entrance, rifles and shotguns and needlers in hand. Some had managed to get hold of only a simple sidearm. Most had no spare ammunition—only what their weapons contained. They stood ready to fight, however—men and women who had never before even held a weapon, armed now with perhaps ten, twelve, fifteen lead pellets apiece. A part of each of them knew they had no skill, and that their guns were small and trifling—insignificant in the face of the force following them.

Keep moving, don't panic, help each other, if you have a weapon, stay here at the entrance . . .

"They're right behind us!" screamed one man, running, gasping hard, a child in each arm. "Killed my wife. One area back . . . coming fast—"

"Benton," shouted Mrs. Waters, staring down the long wide approachway, "I don't see any more of our people."

"Can we shut the doors now?" asked Cobber.

"How?" asked Hawkes. Staring at his wristpiece, watching the seconds run by, he answered, "Scully had the only controls I know of. Do either of you know . . ."

Both the first lady and the Resolute leader shook their heads. In all the history of Red Planet, there had never been an emergency that called for the closing of the colony's pressure doors. Throughout the decades, the doors had only been closed for the purpose of maintenance inspections—inspections conducted by the head of security.

Staring at the time ticking away, his hand tightening around the needler he had been given in Area C, Hawkes said, "Then we trust Scully. And we hold the line here."

In the distance, the sound of heavy boots tramping out an ordered cadence rang forward toward the spaceport. Two hundred and fifty-eight pairs of hands checked their weapons in response—turning off safety catches, cocking them, pumping shells into place. Behind the two hundred and fifty-eight, thousands more pairs of hands joined the battle as well, closing in prayer.

And then, gunfire rang out in both directions, and the blood began spilling once more.

● ● ● "I FOUND IT!"

Ace Goth crawled painfully back to where he had left Scully. Playing his light over the explosives he had finished rigging a few minutes earlier, the security man nodded his head slightly, his breathing shallow and ragged.

"Good," he muttered. "Good. All ready here."

Goth winced as he dragged himself along—head hurting, eyes, hands, elbows and knees and everything bleeding pain as he tore himself against the jagged flooring. His left leg had been shattered in the earlier fall, the rocks at the bottom snapping it in over a dozen places. The control remote in his teeth, he pulled himself over the yards of rough stone, sweat pouring down his bloodied forehead, filling his stinging eyes.

Years ago, the Originals known as the magmateers had bored the old Deep Digs with explosives and the frightening power of Mars' molten core. Now, Goth and Scully had entered Dyber's Shaft, the last access point to the planet's still-fiery center—dug out and primed by the Originals but never opened. That was what the two men planned to do now.

Scully, whose first job on Mars had been setting off charges in the burning depths—the last living magmateer—had been thinking about using the lava against possible invaders for over a year. As an exercise, a mental game to occupy his time on long shifts, he had worked out which doors would have to be shut in the Above to push the molten flow in different directions. Now, the game was in its final moments, and nothing had gone as he had planned.

He had not thought to go into the tunnels, to check the old passageways, to see what time had done to the death trap that had claimed so many of his friends.

And now, he thought, me too.

The old security man grimaced again, his neck muscles bulging as the pain in his side clawed at him. Two rungs from the ladder had smashed through him, one piercing his hip, the other his abdomen. Both he and Goth had been mortally injured. They had no compunction about setting off the explosive charge that would release the lava—they were dead anyway, their bodies simply had not realized it yet.

The only problem was that in doing so, they might now kill everyone they were trying to save.

Handing the remote to Scully, Goth asked him, "So, what do you think?"

When the security man fell, the control had slipped from his belt. What damage had it suffered? Had the impact erased the commands Scully had programmed into it? Or possibly altered them? Could indexing the release order shut the wrong doors? Would it direct the lava to the spaceport, destroying the colony and leaving the invaders untouched?

"No way to tell," gasped Scully. Eyes closed against the pain, he told Goth, "Screen shut down on impact. Normal. Don't know what will happen . . . if we set 'er off."

"Maybe so," said the union man. "But if we don't, the damn bastards get everything. You're . . . you're a fighting man, Norman. If we don't do this, can our people survive? Can they hold the line? Can they win?"

Blood rising in his throat, dripping from his scalp, his cheek, over his lips, leaking from his side, his stomach, Scully shook his head sadly.

"Then I say, if we can't have Mars—no one gets it."

Scully looked on, and then watched as Goth gasped his last breath, slumping backward—gone. The security man nodded toward the corpse, thinking of Goth's last words, and their consequences—everyone he knew and cared about burned to death in the rising magma, or freedom for Mars with all of their enemies destroyed in one stroke.

His life fading, each beat of his heart weaker than the last, the old security man stared at the remote in his torn and bleeding hand. As the light from his flash played over it, his eyes were caught by a tiny line of print molded in the plastic of its lower right-hand corner. He heard the words in his head, each one clean and distinct and sweet—

Made . . . on . . . Mars.

"Damn right," he whispered, closing his eyes as he indexed the command to close the pressure doors above. Then, he reached out and slapped the cap on the charge next to him. The cavern exploded, caving in, then rocking violently as the magma trapped below it pounded upward, spewing and burning. The explosion killed him instantly.

The first and the last of the magmateers.

● ● ● TWENTY-THREE OF the great pressure doors began to close throughout the colony at the same moment, forming a siphon leading upward from the last of the Deep Digs.

A split second later, Goth and Scully's last resting place was torn asunder as the chamber that had killed them was split open and flooded by a boiling flow of yellow heat.

At the entrance to the spaceport, the two hundred and fifty-eight defenders had been reduced to eighty-three. Glenia Waters lay cold and staring, dead in the first volley. Hawkes, shot through the leg and arm, sat propped against the pressure door entrance, watching the battle in dazed pain.

Next to him, Cobber was stretched out on the floor, shielded by a wall of bodies as she continued to fire on the enemy. In the distance, the League soldiers remained comfortable and smugly secure behind their portable shields, stripping away the Martian defenders one by one.

"Hawkes!" screamed Cobber. "Move!"

The great door began to flow out of the wall, pushing the prime minister forward into the dead. The Resolute leader crawled desperately over the corpses of the fallen to grab on to Hawkes's upper arm. Straining with all her might, she pulled him out of the way of the doors. Exposing herself heedlessly . . .

Becoming the last Martian to be wounded by a League bullet as the great pressure doors sealed off the spaceport.

And then, as the invaders began preparations for administering their final solution, moving forward their explosives team, unpacking the fast-spreading plague bombs they had brought with them, the rearmost of them turned, puzzled by the growing hiss and sputter advancing behind them.

And the rapidly advancing heat.

● ● ● "THERE!" SCREAMED THORNER, pointing forward, laughing insanely. "There they are! The goddamned cavalry is here!"

Willis stared out the observation port, following the miner's finger, but all he could see was the dark and ragged outline of a random asteroid, one moving at tremendous speed. The captain swallowed hard as he watched Thorner adjust their trajectory, directing his ship into a collision course with the rapidly advancing planetoid.

All around the *Stooge*, the League shelling continued. The miner double-ran his ship wildly around searing energy beams, skipping through space, dodging the plasma blasts and the old-fashioned concussion weapons being hurled at him.

Next to him, Captain Willis gripped his chair in jarring silence. He wanted desperately to know what Thorner was up to—who was coming, where he had led the overpowering remains of the League fleet, what he thought could possibly be done against the seventeen pounding warships following them.

Thorner had flown a madman's course, as only a pilot who had spent years threading his way through asteroid fields could. But still, despite all of Thorner's remarkable piloting, both men knew the weaponeers behind them were narrowing the *Stooge*'s range with every volley.

"Trevor!" the miner screamed into the comm, not caring if the League heard, knowing it was too late for them to do anything to stop what was coming. "I'm here! I'm here!"

"And bringing angry company, I see," came a smooth dark voice that spoke of warmer places. "Curly, you get into so much trouble. You really should pay your bills."

"That's what you're here for," answered Thorner. "How's it set?"

"Equator buster—a clean line split followed by forward fragmenters. Something you can work with—yes?"

Thorner eyed various readings on the console before him. Shifting his eyes back and forth from the distance and velocity gauges to the observation port and the sight of the approaching asteroid, he asked, "Got your finger on the button?"

"Just count me down, old friend, and we'll make a skyful of boom."

"Five . . ." shouted Thorner.

The *Stooge*'s speed increased, the dead-center spot of the approaching asteroid its target.

"Four . . ."

Plasma streamed past the fleeing Yamato-class cruiser at a distance of under a kilometer.

"Three . . ."

Although the League's next shot would not miss, Thorner did not change his course.

"Two . . ."

Behind the *Stooge*, three of the pursuing fleet commanders suddenly realized what was happening, their attention moving from their prey to the trap into which they had been led.

"One! Now—*blow it!*"

Trevor Von detonated the explosives strapped to the asteroid he and the other pirates working with him had placed on the trillions of tons of ore and cinder they began moving toward Mars weeks earlier.

The planetoid split cleanly down the middle, the two halves falling away from each other just in time for the *Stooge* to slide in between them. Seeing the danger, some of the fleet ships scrambled toward the middle, hoping to follow the miner through the ever-growing gap. The rest spread to the sides, wildly spiraling outward.

Neither ploy worked.

Tabbing a second preset control, Trevor exploded the two halves, turning them into an endless barrage of multi-ton projectiles. In seconds, the mountainous fragments were tearing through the League ships, exploding them one after another.

And in the spaceport, Benton Hawkes looked up with the others as the sky flashed brightly with seventeen new, but momentary stars.

EPILOGUE

"YOU KNOW, BAD as it all is," said Thorner, smiling as he leaned back in his chair next to Hawkes's desk, "I'm surprised it ain't worse."

"How much worse would you like it, Curly?" asked the prime minister softly.

"Awww, you know what I mean," answered the miner, unruffled by Hawkes's comment. "You goin' to the party?"

"No, no—I'm not in much of a partying mood," answered the prime minister. "Besides, Victoria's arranged for Sam and Glenia to be buried in the old number ten dome. No reclamation for once— just old-fashioned bodies in the ground. Something special for two noble heroes of Mars."

"Old-fashioned like? Coffins and all?"

"No," said Hawkes, understanding the shock in Thorner's voice. "Number ten is the closest thing Mars has to a forest. They'll be buried in the ground, each of them with a bag of seeds. Their bodies will nourish new life. It'll make up just a bit for the fact that we'll never find Scully's body, or Goth's . . . Liz . . ."

The asteroid miner stared at Hawkes. The prime minister had horribly dark circles under his eyes. He had lost a great deal of blood from his wounds—blood that had gone unreplaced, plasma being just one item among the thousands of which Mars no longer had any reserves. Thorner suspected the man had not slept in the thirty-six hours since the war had ended, either. Knowing he would not be able to change Hawkes's mind about leaving his desk, the big miner rose, standing in front of his chair.

"You take care of yourself, Bennie," he said, stretching his long arms out at his sides. "Try not to work too hard."

"You leaving, Curly?" asked the prime minister with genuine curiosity.

"Yeah, gotta get back out in the dark, looking for bank. I'll drop in on the party, let everyone tell me how grateful they are for the fireworks show. But you know the old sayin'—good will don't pay the bill."

The two men considered each other for a moment. Then, fighting obvious fatigue, Hawkes raised his arm and held out his hand to Thorner. As the miner took the prime minister's hand in his own, the two looked into each other's eyes. Then, finally letting go, Hawkes said, "You're a good man, Captain Thorner. There wouldn't be a Mars now without you."

"Yeah, true," answered the miner, adding with a waggish play of his eyebrows, "But if I stayed, what would I do for an encore?"

Before Hawkes could comment, the comm on his desk flashed frantically. Thorner smiled and excused himself as the prime minister indexed the blinking panel. Jason Harris's face spread across the comm screen.

"Mr. Prime Minister, I've got a transmission I think you'll want to respond to." Before Hawkes could say anything, the young artist turned to another screen, tabbing the proper circuit as he said, "He's all yours," and a face unfolded onto the prime minister's comm.

"Dina!" he shouted in surprise. "You're safe. You're alive." And then, his eyes took in the background behind her. "You're still on Earth."

"Yes, Benton, and I don't have much time. We got your message, but there was nothing we could do. There was no way off-planet for us . . . then or now."

"But . . . what happened?"

"The League had the ranch surrounded more than a month ago. Protective custody. No one in or out. We're safe for the moment, everyone's fine." As a sudden clamor broke in on the conversation, Dina paused, grabbing the collar of Hawkes's dog, trying to quiet him as he continued to bark at the sound of his master's voice. The prime minister managed a smile.

"He looks even bigger."

"He is bigger," growled Martel affectionately. Finally calming the dog, she turned back to the screen.

"Look, we know this is being monitored, so let's not waste words. The Earth is in a sad state. Things are going to get bad here—fast. Every government is talking rationing—massive cutbacks. They've already begun executing the convicts in the federal prisons. The euthanasia squads have been working overtime too. League Press has already announced they expect half the population to starve in the next five days."

"That's wrong," said Hawkes, remembering Mick Carri's figures. "That's too fast."

"Tell me about it. They're just looking for riots, for people to kill each other and give them a reason to kill more. And of course, empire builder Benton Hawkes is their fall guy for the world's troubles."

"Well," said the prime minister sadly, "as long as they spell my name right."

The two people stared at each other for a long moment, not knowing what they dared say. Finally, deciding it did not matter what Mick Carri and his League knew about Mars, Hawkes told Martel, "Things are very different here. A lot of good people died. You remember the Waterses—Sam and Glenia. Norm Scully, Ace Goth . . . Major Truman . . . We've got a new navy, if you could call it that, and we're beginning to pick up the pieces."

"There's been no official word, of course," answered the young woman on the screen. "But everyone knows the League is in a lather over you wiping their fleet. No one believed you had a chance."

"Well, for a while, neither did anyone here. But we captured three League supply barges and we're working on restoring a number of fleet vessels that were only disabled during the fighting. For what it's worth, we can probably defend ourselves now better than we could when this all started."

Martel nodded, then said softly, "I've noticed that when you refer to Mars you keep saying 'we.'"

"Yes," admitted the prime minister, "I probably do. And, while whoever's listening in is mulling that over, let me tell you that I know as well as you do that the League is keeping you all alive to use as bargaining chips against us. Well, let me admit right up front that you all make good ones."

"Benton, maybe . . ."

"No, Dina," said Hawkes, tired of diplomacy. Tired of games. Exhausted and unable to care anymore about anything beyond the truth.

"It doesn't matter. I wish I knew what was going to happen next—but I don't. So, here are the facts. The food vats are all still intact. Half our factories are filled with cooling rock right now, but we can still feed the Earth. We'll blow this place to hell if anyone tries to take it from us again . . . but, well . . . I don't know . . . let's just say we'll look at any reasonable offer put on the table, and leave it at that."

The man and the woman stared into each other's eyes. There was so much each wanted to say, but knew they could not. Both of them realized that billions were about to die. That even if a thousand supply barges were to leave Mars immediately, billions would die before the first mouthful arrived on Earth.

They both knew that the war was not over. That at best it had entered a period of stalemate—that the guns had been silenced for the moment and soon their barrels would be cool, but still aimed at each other, the fingers on the triggers more ready than ever to blast away at the enemy.

Hawkes's hand reached out, his fingers brushing the hard glass image of Martel's face. Watching the countdown she had programmed earlier fall into the last few seconds, the woman said, "Goodbye, Benton."

"I'll see you soon," answered the prime minister.

As their time ran out, Martel said, "It's a hell of a world, isn't it?"

Staring at static as the transmission ended, Hawkes whispered, "Which one?"

And then, the prime minister of Mars moved his hand, indexing the comm control that would blank his screen. Sitting in his chair, unmoving, staring at nothing, he wondered when he would finally be able to sleep. And if, once he was, he should bother to wake up. Then, pushing such thoughts from his mind, Benton Hawkes bent back to the work he knew he must do.

While all around him, the hallways and tunnels filled with mourners on their way to the party.